The Unbearable Lightness of Being In Aberystwyth

BY THE SAME AUTHOR

Aberystwyth Mon Amour
Last Tango in Aberystwyth

The Unbearable Lightness Of Being In Aberystwyth

Malcolm Pryce

BLOOMSBURY

'Do-Re-Mi' Words by Oscar Hammerstein II and Music by Richard Rodgers © 1959, Williamson Music International, USA. Reproduced by permission of EMI Music Publishing, London WC2H 0QY.

The epigraph is from 'The Emperor of Ice Cream' from *The Collected Poems of Wallace Stevens* by Wallace Stevens, published by Faber and Faber Ltd.

Lines fom 'Little Gidding' are from *The Four Quartets* in *Collected Poems 1909–1962* by T.S. Eliot, published by Faber and Faber Ltd.

Lines from 'A Peasant' by R.S. Thomas are from *Collected Poems 1945–1990*, published by J.M. Dent, a division of the Orion Publishing Group.

First published 2005

Bloomsbury Publishing Plc, 38 Soho Square,
London W1D 3HB

A CIP catalogue record for this book
is available from the British Library

ISBN 0 7475 7712 9

3 4 5 6 7 8 9 10

Typeset in Fournier by Palimpsest Book Production Ltd, Polmont, Stirlingshire

Printed in Great Britain by Clays Ltd, St Ives plc

To all those who were there during the
Jasper House years

I would like to thank my editor Mike and
agent Rachel for all their help and friendship.

Let the lamp affix its beam
The only emperor is the emperor of ice cream.

Wallace Stevens

On the day Dai Brainbocs arrived in Shrewsbury prison, Frankie Mephisto sent for him and explained the situation. He told him they didn't like bookworms and eggheads in prison and that without protection the frail schoolboy genius would be dead within months. And Frankie was the only man who could provide the necessary protection. That's when he made the offer. He told Brainbocs he had one dream left in life, and that was to visit Aberystwyth before he died and hear Myfanwy sing at the Bandstand. But, as everyone knew, Myfanwy was dying and would never sing again. You must make her well, he said. You will be put in a cell at the top of the tower overlooking the railway station. You will not be disturbed. But neither, in accordance with a paradigm established by Rumpelstiltskin, will you be allowed to leave the cell until you have found a cure. Whatever books or scientific equipment you require will be made available.

Brainbocs accepted the proposal. He said the offer of scientific equipment would not at that stage be necessary. It was his opinion that in the matter of probing the ineffable mysteries of life, disease and death there existed no finer scientific measuring scope than a gentleman at stool. And so he ordered a new chamber pot – size seven – and went to his tower.

Chapter 1

'HEY MISTER, wanna buy my sister?'

I stopped and turned. The kid was about twelve or thirteen years old and standing next to a discarded lobster pot, a tray of postcards slung from his neck. There were no shoes on his feet and his patched-up trousers stopped four inches below his knee in a comic zigzag hem. The sort of zigzag that never arises from wear and tear and must have been put there by his mum to elicit pity from the bank holiday tourists. Fat chance of that. He could have been standing there on fire and they wouldn't have cared.

'I'll give you a special price. Wanna buy? She's pretty.'

'How do you get the boot polish off your cheeks when you go home at night?'

'Who says it's boot polish?'

'It sure isn't the sort of grime you get from honest toil. Or are they shooting a Dickens movie in Aberystwyth today?'

'Never mock a man for being poor, mister. What are you looking for anyway? Maybe I can supply it.'

'What makes you think I'm looking for something?'

'In my experience there are only two reasons a man comes down the harbour wearing a face like yours. To throw himself in or because he's looking for something he shouldn't be looking for.'

'I could do with a few clients.'

'Me too. The time is out of joint, Jack. Here, take my card.'

It said, 'Dewi Poxcrop. Facilitator. Reasonable rates. Discretion assured.'

I put a fifty-pence piece on top of the card tray and moved away. He placed his grimy hand on the cuff of my coat.

'Are you sure I can't interest you in my sister?'

'Sorry, son,' I said as I pulled free, 'there's nothing lonelier than the bought smile of a harlot.'

He stood still for a while and stared at me as I trudged down the avenue of lobster pots drying in the sun. And then he shouted just as I reached the main road, 'Wash your mouth out, Mac, that's my sister you're talking about.'

During my years as Aberystwyth's only private eye the client's chair had seen just about every type of backside there was. Fat ones and bony ones; proud ones and pious; some clenched tightly in fear and others trembling with anger; some hot with indignation and some cold with hate. But only one had a tail.

She was a small monkey, and very old, with fur turning white around the muzzle and deep sad dark eyes, like two wishing wells that hadn't seen a penny in years. She wore an airmail-blue waistcoat and a collarless grandpa shirt with dark rims of grime around the collar and cuffs – the sort of ill-kempt appearance that you get when you have been sleeping rough for a few days, and these are the first days. Inside the collar, loosely knotted into the fur of her throat, was an Ardwyn school tie. She jumped nervously as I walked in the room and flinched a few more times at the banging sounds coming from the kitchenette. I was no zoologist, but she looked like one scared old monkey to me.

I said good morning but she didn't answer, just watched me closely and followed me round the room with her eyes. I took off my hat and coat and placed them with more than the usual amount of care on the hat stand. Entertaining monkeys was a new one on me but in one respect, at least, I was pretty sure they didn't differ greatly from the other women of Aberystwyth and so I walked into the kitchen to put the kettle on. My partner, Calamity Jane, was already there, packing my belongings with an exuberance that accounted for the bangs I'd heard as I arrived. The noises made me flinch in sympathy with the ape who I sensed was still being spooked in the room next door.

I tousled Calamity's hair in a good morning sort of greeting and said with as little surprise as I could muster, 'We've got a monkey sitting on the client's chair.'

'Yeah, I saw that.' She carried on packing. Normally, you are supposed to wrap the crockery in newspaper but Calamity was putting it straight into a box.

'It's quite unusual, isn't it?' I said.

'Uh-huh.'

'You don't have to be so cool about it,' I said.

When the kettle boiled I put teapot, cups, sugar and milk on to a tray and walked back into the office.

When she saw me walking in with the tray, the monkey curled the fingers of her right hand as if holding an invisible mug and then moved it up and down in front of her mouth. I nodded in encouragement. I wouldn't go so far as to say she smiled – she was a capuchin monkey and they generally keep their cards close to their chest – but a look of heightened interest was evident. She changed position and made a squeaking sound because she was sitting on top of a pile of bubblewrap that had been left on the chair. The few other sticks of furniture I possessed were due to be wrapped in newspaper but the client's chair, as source of all our income, was a totem that demanded a special reverence. We didn't have any Gainsboroughs but we had the client's chair. Although you could say that since we were moving because it had failed to perform the duties of a client's chair it was a moot point whether it deserved to be propitiated like that.

I poured the tea. The phone rang and I sat down in the chair facing our visitor. Lying on the desk in front of me was the application form for the private detective's provisional licence from the Bureau in Swansea. Calamity would soon be eighteen and was keen to get her badge: a big bright metal buzzer that she could stick in her wallet and flick out under the noses of the Aberystwyth villains. If that didn't frighten them she could always go and buy one of those plastic pin-on sheriff stars from Woolworths. They were equally effective.

I pushed the papers aside, drew the phone over and picked up the receiver.

The voice on the other end had that Chicago-Welsh hybrid that the small-time hoodlums had perfected in this town: 'What did the monkey say?'

'What monkey?'

'Don't get cute. What did she say?'

'That information is protected by client privilege.'

'That's good, that's very good, just tell that to Frankie and see where it gets you. When Eli arrives tell him Frankie Mephisto says don't forget about the book, the one Frankie Mephisto read from cover to cover and threw away because it was bollocks.'

'Who's Frankie Mephisto? Or am I being cute again?'

He hung up.

When I put the phone down, Calamity was in the room and she and the monkey were regarding me with a look of inquiry.

'Just someone from the library,' I said.

A loud, semi-musical clanging noise came from downstairs. The sort of sound you might get on a fairground ride if someone jammed on the brakes, or if you dropped a piano down a flight of stairs. Or, alternatively, the sort of sound you might get if you leant an old barrel organ up against the wall outside a private detective's office. It was followed by the slamming of a door and footsteps that echoed up the wooden stairwell. The door to the office was ajar and soon there was a man standing in it with a suitcase in his hand. I guessed he had to be Eli but he said his name was Gabriel Bassett, and since that didn't sound anything like Eli I didn't tell him what Frankie Mephisto said about the book. I wasn't sure why since it was obviously a book of some significance and Frankie Mephisto didn't sound like the sort who read many books.

Gabriel Bassett looked over to the monkey and then raised his hand in a little wave and the monkey responded by mimicking it. Then he spoke to me. 'This is Cleopatra, she's always early.' He let his gaze wander around the small office, appraising the packing cases, and said, 'Looks like we came too late.'

'We're going to Stryd-y-Popty, across from the library. It's not far,' said Calamity.

'You're not closing down then?'

'Nope.'

No, I thought. But if things got much worse we might have to. The new office wasn't all that much smaller than this one, it was just in a less desirable neighbourhood. In the past few years Canticle Street had become increasingly gentrified since the Orthopaedic Bootery started specialising in Italian designs and the Rock Café started adding fluoride to some of the lines. There were no living quarters in the new place, just an inner and an outer office and small kitchenette for the tea and a fridge for the rum. For the time being I had taken a caravan out at Ynyslas which I had mixed feelings about. It would be a beautiful place at times but there was something about the all-pervasiveness of the taste of homogenised milk that depressed the heart. Still, the money we saved would be able to make a dent in the cost of keeping Myfanwy at the nursing home and that was an overhead that no private detective's salary was ever meant to meet. Even one of the fancy ones from Swansea.

Gabriel Bassett looked down at his suitcase and then looked round the room for a suitable place to park it. I pointed to the hat stand.

'You leaving town or just arriving?' I said.

'Neither. I always carry my suitcase around.' He put it down by the hat stand, took a cup of tea and sat on a crate. He said he had a case for us to solve and we both gave him a look of polite inquiry but instead of continuing he sat on the crate making tongue movements against the wall of his cheek as if he was trying to dislodge a piece of gristle. I hadn't seen this approach before and if it was meant to heighten tension it was good.

'Is there anything more you think we should know about it?' I asked.

He reached into his pocket and pulled out a bundle of notes held together by an elastic band. It was the biggest bundle of notes I'd ever seen, but that probably didn't make it all that big. He put it down on the table and it rolled back and forth under its own weight like a rocking chair.

'I need it solved by a fortnight today. That gives you fifteen days if you count today. But since I'll come round about noon it probably only means fourteen and a half. The roll on the table is five hundred in fives, twenties and fifties. Consider it a down payment. There's another five hundred if you solve it. If you don't, there isn't.'

Calamity flicked open a notebook and picked up a pen. 'What's the job?'

'Investigate a burglary. At Nanteos Mansion, end of May. A necklace was taken – it was in all the papers.'

'We didn't see it.'

'Of course you didn't. It was May 1849.'

I opened my mouth to say something but couldn't think of anything. The monkey interjected. She did that by raising her hand and when Bassett looked at her she brought the left hand towards the right and there followed a little dance of fingers tapping palms and wrapping themselves round other fingers.

He turned to me. 'She wants to know if you've seen Mr Bojangles.'

I paused for a second. 'That looked like sign language.'

'Yes. Have you seen him?'

'Mr Bojangles?'

'It's her son, disappeared fifteen years ago. I'm sorry, I would have got to it but she always jumps the gun. Always jumps the damn gun she does.'

'Tell her we haven't seen him.'

'What does he look like?' said Calamity.

'What do you think he looks like?' snapped Bassett. 'He looks like her, only smaller.' He turned to Cleopatra and did some more signs. She gave a sort of deflated nod as if to say, 'Well it was just a long shot.'

'It's pretty unusual for a monkey to use sign language,' I said unnecessarily.

'She used to work at the university, the department of linguistics. You know those research projects they do into primate language, see if they can get monkeys to talk and things? She used to be in one. I got her cheap after they stopped the funding.'

I picked up the bundle of notes and weighed it in my hand. It was about as heavy as a cricket ball. 'Tell us about the necklace.'

'Oval, flat-cut garnets set in gold with close-backed foil collets, concealed clasp and pear-shaped garnet drop. It belonged to Cranogwen Phrys-Griffiths from Nanteos. She was the squire's daughter. Coming of age present. You know Nanteos mansion out by Capel Seion?'

'I've driven past it a few times.'

'Tell me what you know about it.'

'Georgian country house, covered in ivy, nice-looking. There's a ghost and a fragment of a wooden medieval drinking bowl called the Nanteos Cup – some people say it's the Holy Grail.'

'Do you believe that?'

I shrugged. 'I keep an open mind.'

'The ghost is real. It's Cranogwen. She died in a fire, May 1849. They hanged the stable boy for it. It was a miscarriage of justice.'

'You saying they got the wrong guy?'

'The ghost says it was the stable boy. I say she's a lying bitch. They found the kid halfway up the ivy. He said he saw smoke and was on his way up to rescue her. The peelers said he ravished her and knocked the bedside lamp over in the struggle.'

'Maybe that's how it happened,' I said.

'Whose side are you on?'

'Nobody's yet.'

'It's true the stable boy was sweet on Cranogwen, but he never laid a finger on her. It was all circumstantial. They found the necklace later in his stable, and a bridle under the girl's bed. But what does that prove? And then this ghostly handwriting appeared on the wall above the bed saying, "*comes stabuli*". It's Latin, means "keeper of the stable". That clinched it: the kid had to swing. And not even seventeen.'

'So where do we come in?'

'I need to clear his name.'

'By a fortnight today,' said Calamity with the matter-of-fact air of one crossing the t's and dotting the i's.

'Yes.'

'It's a bit unorthodox,' I said.

'So is five hundred in cash up front.'

He had a good point there.

I saw them both out to the street. Gabriel Bassett loaded the suitcase on to the barrel organ, Cleopatra jumped up on top of that and they made ready to wheel away. I said to Basset, 'Does the name Frankie Mephisto mean anything to you?'

And without a flicker of reaction he said, 'No, not a thing.'

I walked over to the car and fetched the Michelin guide to Welsh country houses from the glove compartment. I looked up Nanteos Mansion. The ghost appeared periodically in the Cranogwen Suite, accompanied by moans and the smell of burning. There was also the ghost-writing, *comes stabuli* – keeper of the stable. Since they hanged him you had to wonder why she bothered. Maybe she was just mean. I could never quite make up my mind about ghosts. Most of the time I didn't believe in them but I found them harder not to believe in when alone late at night in rambling old houses with ivy on the wall where the wind banged doors shut in empty rooms. Maybe, maybe not. Of one thing I was certain: if you own a country house and want to run it as a hotel then a ghost is about as essential as a kitchen. As for the Grail, it was the genuine article. No doubt about it. Just like the fragments of the True Cross you used to be able to buy in the Middle Ages, and the clay God had used to fashion Adam from, and that little bag of bones from the donkey that Jesus rode on Palm Sunday. All 100 per cent genuine.

There was no way I could take a case like this, but also no way I could turn down the money. I solved my dilemma by giving it to Calamity as her first solo case. She could use it to support her application for her detective's badge. I dropped her off in the gravel forecourt of Nanteos and then drove to the nursing home to pick up Myfanwy and see which of her faces she would be wearing for our drive to Ynyslas. Usually it was the wooden one in which the features were carved and immobile, and in her eyes an uncomprehending stare. But on occasion whoever it was or used to be – or perhaps really just the shadow of whoever it was – would reappear in her eyes for a while, like a ghost in an upstairs window. On days like that Myfanwy could still smile and in the waters of her eyes something stirred from time to time, recognition or remembrance – like a fish flashing through a forest pool.

The nurse who helped get her into the front seat finished adjusting the seat belt and then took out a little scent bottle and put a dab on Myfanwy's wrists. It was the stuff they sold in the gift shop out at the Waifery, made from the bluebells in Danycoed Wood. She could have saved herself the effort. By that time I already knew: no ghost was going to appear at the upstairs window today.

The absence of conversation hung heavily in the car as we drove and I turned on the radio. They were running a report of an escaped fugitive being sought by the police in the Aberystwyth area. He was a veteran of the old war in Patagonia and the public were warned not to approach him. That made me laugh. When was the last time anyone approached a Patagonian vet except to chase him off the land?

We drove on to the wide flat sands of Ynyslas and pulled up alongside a party of day-trippers. They were sitting in an old black Morris Minor, the doors wide open and the interior exuding a smell of hot engine, pipe smoke and children's vomit. It looked like they had just arrived and were still drinking the first cup of tea, the one that always tastes of the inside of a flask. Mum and Gran were sorting out the picnic. Dad was stretching his legs after the drive. Two kids were already squabbling. And Granddad sat in the front passenger seat wearing the beatific smile of one whose demands on life are so modest that a day driving for three hours in the company of his grandchildren to stare at the water for a while and drink tea was a source of joy. And one that would never lose its savour. The old man looked across as we arrived and raised his hand in greeting, just a simple movement of the hand, like the Queen, because he hailed from a world where not to have done so would have been impolite. And I returned the greeting because I didn't want him to know that world had passed. And because he reminded me of my dad, Eeyore, sitting there amid the clamour as calm as a castle moat on a moonlit night. Another half an hour and he would probably loosen his tie.

Myfanwy stared vacantly ahead across the estuary and beyond to the hills of Aberdovey. Away to the left were the dunes across which she had run once with such happiness and which now no longer possessed the power to enter the world into which she was slowly withdrawing. Somewhere from behind us, towards the entrance, came the tinkling xylophonic sound of an ice-cream van and I walked off to fetch two ices.

When I returned with two cornets smothered with ripple the family of day-trippers was now struggling to raise that three-sided wind-breaker of stripy canvas that people from the Midlands find such comfort in. I reclined Myfanwy's seat and mine and lay back to stare through the windshield at the grey cloud-filled sky. It was knobbled with the texture and colour of kneaded dough. Clouds too heavy and too low in the sky, inducing a heaviness like a hand pressing down on one's forehead, the lugubrious weight muffling all sound. The wind came in a soft roar with too much heat as if emerging from the baker's oven, and blew across the open door of the car as if over a giant mollusc. The warm hot air and the distant cries of children, combined with the diffuse brightness of the light, tugged down on my eyelids and even as I licked my ice cream I could feel the lids lowering as if the weight of the day were too heavy to sustain.

When I awoke it must have been about three hours later. The sun was setting, still hidden by cloud but betrayed by the lengthening shadows. Granddad and family had packed up and left. My ice cream lay in my lap, melted and sticky. I had a thumping headache. A hint of bluebells hung on the air like a dying echo. And Myfanwy was gone.

Chapter 2

It was way past their bedtime but Sister Cunégonde insisted on letting us have some waifs for the search. I stood and waited in a corridor. Feeble forty-watt light bulbs hung from the ceiling and were rendered insignificant by the moon outside. A row of doors led off with brass handles that rattled loosely in their sockets, like the hip joints of the mistresses who sat in the offices behind. Each door bore a name and a rank to indicate the degree of fear that should reside in the heart of whichever girl was sent to wait outside. At the end of the corridor, the assembly hall lay in darkness pierced by slabs of waxen moonlight. At the other end was another hall with a gallery where girls now ran to fetch gabardine macs and torches from bedside cabinets.

The girls started to gather in the hall, dark shapes like crows on a telegraph line, whispering and bobbing in excitement until one of the sisters said the next one to talk would be sent back to bed. So then silence fell like a guillotine blade but lasted only a few brief seconds before irresistible whispering broke the surface again. Two girls were sent back to their dormitory. Then they formed into pairs and followed Sister Cunégonde out into the night with their torches, like a phalanx of cinema usherettes lifting the siege of a walled city.

We passed through a door marked 'Staff Only' into a garden never normally visited by pupils, past shrubs that they could only appreciate through the window, and on through a door set in a high wall topped with vicious jags of broken glass. Beyond the wall, towards the edge of the estuary, lay the fifteenth-century ruins of the convent that the Sisters of Deiniol had once occupied. It threw shadows in the night like the broken teeth of a goblin. The chapel of rest was still in use and the candles inside threw a pale gleam that trembled like a reflection on the waters of a brook.

From the car, Myfanwy could have turned right and walked in this direction and perhaps got lost in the salt marsh; or turned left towards the dunes. Or gone straight ahead into the waters of the Dovey estuary. After an hour of searching, one of the girls found a locket on the dunes engraved with the word 'Myfanwy'.

I returned to the caravan and brewed tea. Then I sat in the darkness and drank, waiting for dawn. All men, if they are honest, are scared of the dark. The arrival of light, even a glimmer under the edge of a door, lifts the spirit in a way that can't be described, because it dates back to a time before language. Hope returns, night terrors evaporate. You smile at the childishness of it all, the demons who haunted your sleep. It was just a dream. But that morning I had a new companion. Dread. The light under the door was a passing car.

I drove to town and parked by the harbour and walked down towards the elbow where the Prom bent sharply and found Sospan already up and preparing his kiosk for the day. Word had already reached him about Myfanwy and when I asked which was best of all the many exotic flavours and combinations in his medicinal cabinet of ices he said in such a situation there was nothing better, no balm more soothing, than simple vanilla. And so, just like on any other day, I ordered a 99 with plenty of ripple.

I offered him one but it was still too early; and, besides, he said, leaning forward out of the booth to be closer to me in my hour of need, he needed to keep a clear head to help get to the bottom of what had happened and erase this terrible stain on the honour of the ice man's profession. His sharp mind had already intuited what the forensic scientists would later confirm: the search last night and the more thorough-going one planned for this morning were pointless. It was clear that the ripple in the ices yesterday had been tampered with and whoever did it, given that I was asleep for at least three hours, had all the time in the world to drive up alongside our car, transfer Myfanwy and drive off without arousing suspicion. The clue, said Sospan, was the *gelati* man.

'You must try, Mr Knight, try and remember what he was like.'

I shook my head. I couldn't remember a thing. Whatever chemical had been added to the ripple to take Myfanwy away had also taken with it my memory.

'Little details that are insignificant to you . . . you probably don't think they are worth repeating but you never know . . .'

'What's there to say? He was just an ice man—'

Sospan hissed indignantly. 'I am surprised to hear you, of all people, utter a sentiment like that. Imagine if I had been mugged by the postman and you asked me to describe him and I said "Oh he was just a postman", imagine the harsh words you would rightly reproach me with. That's like saying it was just another Fabergé egg. On the surface, I grant you, *gelati* men may all look alike, but each van and vendor are distinctive. Each vendor has a thousand distinguishing characteristics that contribute to his own personal style. The van will reveal clues to the initiated eye as to who owns it, where he comes from and possibly his philosophy of life.'

'I honestly can't remember much, but you are welcome to come down to Ynyslas and have a look. The *gelati* van has gone but you might find something. A Stingray wrapper or something.'

Sospan flinched and gulped as if a bluebottle had flown into his mouth and he had mistakenly swallowed it. A fugitive fear flickered in his eyes.

'Oh . . . well . . . I couldn't do that, Mr Knight, I . . . er . . . I'd love to, you know, but . . . but . . .'

I turned away from his look of pain and stared at the Pier,

pretending to find something unusually fascinating in it this morning, and affecting not to notice the grave sin I had just committed. I had just tried to seduce him to an act of heresy. I had asked him to leave his box. How could I have been so tactless? No one could remember having met Sospan outside his box. All our lives he had been but a disembodied upper torso, like Mr Punch, who flapped his arms about exaggeratedly in order to compensate for the guilty secret that maybe there was nothing else of him below the wooden stage that served as his counter. The kiosk represented the limits and essence of his world like the metal body of a Dalek. Tongue and grooved together from planks of wood and gloss-painted in blue and white, it was the carapace from which, if he ever emerged, it was like a hermit crab to scurry about when no one was looking.

'You see,' said Sospan, 'every ice man has his own particular way of doing things, his own style. I wouldn't go so far as to say it is unique like a fingerprint or anything like that, but it can still help identify him. Take the ripple pattern for instance. Can you remember how he applied it?'

I grimaced in frustration. 'I don't know! That's like asking how someone puts salt on their chips.'

A chill edge entered the tone of his voice. 'That's where you are wrong if you don't mind me saying so.'

I shrugged defiantly.

'Some of the more common trademarks of an ice man's style include the pattern of the ice-whorl, the handedness of the scoop action and the depth to which he buries the Flakes. Does he stick them up proud as a Priapus or does he sink them like the eye sockets of a snowman? Where does he get his cones from? Every one has the mark of where he bought it, like a gun. But it could have been filed off. Did he have insignia on his breast pocket? All these things you could have noticed and yet you tell me he was just another ice-cream vendor. And we haven't even got to the ripple pattern.' He pulled a thick reference work out from under the counter and opened it to the contents page.

'Each pattern can be classified according to the broad characteristics and then subdivided into various phyla.' He turned the book round and pushed it towards me and ran his finger along the contents page.

'Was it spotted like measles, or blotched like Caesar's toga? Splattered in the style known as "Chicago barbershop"? Or more like "MacDuff's counterpane"? Did it perhaps resemble a starfish, or a fairy toadstool? A goblin's hat, a vampire's tooth or a schoolgirl's nipple?'

'Schoolgirl's nipple,' I said.

Sospan smiled as if that were his favourite and then said, 'I've just had a brilliant idea.'

Today was the first official day of business in the new office and my feet hesitated for a second outside the old one but I forced them on up Canticle Street to take the unfamiliar left at the top into 22/1B Stryd-y-Popty. The street where the Poptys live, whatever they were. Judging by the windows, popty was Welsh for twitching net curtain. As with the old office, I entered through a door at the side and climbed up stairs coated in a carpet thinner than gossamer. There were two flats at the top – 1a and 1b. I hadn't met the occupier of 1a but judging by the wine bottles in the bin outside it was probably a student. Or the Mayor.

Inside, I found everything set up almost as it had been in the old place. My chair, the desk, the client's chair, the picture of Noel Bartholomew on the wall. And there was one difference: along one blank windowless wall Calamity had pinned a vertical dividing line and on one side was her name and on the other was mine. There was a tea towel pinned to her side and an index card to mine. I peered to get a better look. The tea towel was a souvenir from Nanteos and bore the words *comes stabuli* in the authentic ghostly handwriting.

'It's the incident board,' said Calamity. 'It doesn't mean we don't work on each other's cases or anything, it's just to give us a handle on the bigger picture.'

I walked over to read the card on my side. It said 'Brainbocs'.

'It's the list of suspects for . . .'

'Myfanwy.'

'It's the only name I could think of. You can take it down if you like.'

'No, it's fine. It's the only name I can think of too.'

She was sitting in the main chair, drinking tea and staring at something on the desk. She poured me a tea. I walked over and stood next to her, one hand resting on her shoulder. Laid out in front of her was a Cluedo set.

'This is the stable boy,' she explained pointing to one of the counters, 'and this is Cranogwen. You have to pretend the board represents the first floor, so I've changed some of the room names.'

I pointed to a daffodil in a milk bottle that looked out of place on the desk. 'Is that the ivy he climbed up?'

'It's only symbolic.'

'Where's Professor Plum?'

'I knew you'd say that.'

'Are you sure this will help?'

'Of course! All stately home murders conform to a similar paradigm. It's archetypal, betokening a quintessentially human need to conform.'

'Who told you that?'

'I read it in the instructions.'

It didn't require a lot of sleuthing to put the name of Dai Brainbocs down as a suspect. The man – or boy, it was hard to know – who had competed with me over the years and played ping-pong for her love. Brainbocs, the frail schoolboy genius with the withered leg, who voluntarily stopped growing at the age of fourteen to channel his energy into his research. Once, more than a thousand years ago, Myfanwy sat in a caravan with me and described the scene when Brainbocs had removed his caliper to go down on one knee and propose. A lot of people in town said it was because of him that she got sick – because of his crazy attempt to win her heart with a love potion. Not something cooked up in a cauldron but in a test tube, based on rock solid scientific credentials and drawing on the latest neurophysiological and neuropsychological research. . . Oxytocin and Phenylethylamine instead of the more traditional mandragora, henbane and eye of newt . . . She seemed all right at the time, but who could really say they understood these things?

'Brainbocs is in Shrewsbury prison,' said Calamity.

'I know. I'll talk to Meirion, the crime reporter on the *Gazette*.'

'You got any other leads?'

'I thought I'd take a look at the *Journals of the Proceedings of the Myfanwy Society* – see if any names spring out, people with an unhealthy interest – you know the sort of thing.'

'Where you going to get them from?'

'The library.'

She smirked.

'Yeah, I know.'

'You got a ticket?'

'I thought I'd apply.'

'You want me to come along?'

'Not especially; what for?'

'So I can pick your hat up for you when they throw you out.'

The National Library of Wales has four million books on a variety of subjects but not much on DIY. For that you have to go to the town library. They say it's the town with the highest ratio of books to people in the world. And the smallest ratio of townspeople who are allowed to read them. The problem was, in order to become a reader you needed to be vouched for by a respectable member of society and that tended to eliminate most people in Aberystwyth. They had a lot of books there, they just didn't like to lend them out. In fact they refused to lend them out. That's what always tripped you up. People who go there are known as readers. Ask for a lender's ticket and instantly you are marked out as someone who runs his finger under the words.

You could tell you weren't invited just by looking at the outside of the building, a fabulous white stone edifice like a big wedding cake, perched halfway up Penglais Hill. It managed that rare feat of combining monumental grandeur, the sort Albert Speer used to specialise in, with architectural good taste. They didn't actually ban normal folk. That was too unsubtle and raised the spectre of elitism. Instead, they did it the subliminal way the smart hotels do – by the glitter and polish of the door and that smile on the face of the doorman that, while appearing to be a genuine smile and employing the same muscle groups of the face, is really a warning and a challenge, one that says: Go on, I dare you. And the tasteful grandeur of the National Library said in the easily apprehended Esperanto of bricks that here was a proper library. One where you don't borrow books but come and read them and if you don't know in advance what you want you might as well not turn up. And don't even think of bringing grease-proof paper to trace the pictures.

Calamity sat on the steps outside and waited for me, safe in the knowledge that I wouldn't be long.

I climbed up and pushed through the revolving door and walked up to the first counter I saw.

'Can I help you?' The woman at the desk gave me a hotel doorman smile. Behind her glasses her eyes were conducting rapid saccades, appraising my social standing or lack of it.

'I was looking for the periodicals.'

Her eyes narrowed slightly. 'Periodicals?'

It was clear that I had caught her off guard.

'Yes, periodicals.'

'Not tropical fish? You strike me as being the sort who comes in looking for books on keeping tropical fish.'

I breathed in deeply and said, 'No, not tropical fish. Periodicals.'

She thought for a second. 'Any particular ones?'

'Yes, I didn't come on a generic quest for periodicals, I had a specific set in mind: the *Journals of the Proceedings of the Myfanwy Society*. It's a quarterly publication.'

The woman made a token adjustment of her spectacles and said, 'Are you a reader?'

'When I get the time.'

'No, I meant do you have a reader's card?'

'I thought I would apply for one.'

Another attendant sidled over in case assistance might be needed. 'Is there a problem, sir?'

'This gentleman was inquiring about applying for readership privileges.'

The new man made a harsh chip-frying sound as he sucked on his teeth.

'I thought seeing how you have so many books you might be willing to let someone read them.'

'Are you by any chance from Aberystwyth, sir?' the man asked.

'Yes, I've spent most of my life here.'

'We don't generally extend readership privileges to people from the town. However, there is an excellent public lending library there—'

'Look, mister, I've read all the books in the public one. Now I want to read the books in this one. Do you have a problem with that?'

'No need to raise your voice, sir.'

'It's my voice, I'll raise it if I want to!'

The man reached under the counter and pressed a button that was supposed to be hidden from view.

'And don't bother calling the muscle. I'm doing nothing wrong, just insisting on my rights to use the library.'

'I'm afraid the rights you refer to don't in fact exist. The right of access is discretionary and is not normally extended to riff-raff.'

'Are you calling me riff-raff?'

'No, I'm just outlining our policy.'

The two attendants exchanged smirks, and one of them made a slight but noticeable snorting sound.

I took out a piece of paper and a photo. 'I'm applying whether you like it or not. This is my photo. And this is the affidavit of my referee. He's a man of substance in this town who enjoys universal respect and he is happy to vouch for my good character.'

The man picked up the piece of paper and read it. This time the smirk was broader, the snort more pronounced.

'Your referee would appear to be Mr Sospan.'

'That's right.'

'Would this be the same Mr Sospan who has a stall vending ice cream on the Promenade?'

'That's the one.'

The man snorted again.

'Do you need some decongestant?'

I could see the two uniformed security guards hurrying over.

'Ooh!' said the woman joining in the fun. 'That should cause a ripple of interest among our readers.'

'Yes,' added the man. 'I fear the grandeur of our portico has caused this gentleman to mistake us for an opera house!'

They both burst into laughter and the woman sang a bar of 'Just one Cornetto'.

I smiled. 'I never knew it was so much fun being a librarian.'

The man wiped away a tear and examined the form again.

'Your address would appear to be a caravan in Ynyslas.'

'That's right.'

'I'm afraid we don't normally issue tickets to people whose houses can be towed away.'

'And why would that be?'

'It leads to insoluble paradox. Imagine if you became liable to the library for some damage to the books. We would issue a summons but it might not reach you since you always have the opportunity to move your house somewhere else. This is of course strictly against the terms and conditions of library membership and yet you could truthfully claim that you hadn't moved, that you had been living in the same place for the past ten years. You see the difficulty?'

'What if I take the wheels off my caravan?'

'We'd still be left with the difficulty of your profession. It says here, private detective—'

'Ooh!' squealed the woman, 'A gumshoe! Watch he doesn't slug you on the beezer!'

'Yeah, Mac, check if he's carrying any iron.'

'Look you sons-of-bitches,' I shouted. 'This is my town, I went to school here, I spent my adolescence on the Prom and in the Pier; I kissed my first girl in Danycoed Wood, and had my first pint in the Castle. This is my town not yours and if you didn't want me to read your crappy books why did you open a library here?'

Two security guards grabbed me by either arm and frog-marched me to the door.

It wasn't the first time I'd been thrown out of somewhere by two tough guys. But it was the first time it had happened in a library. As I emerged into the sunlight I shouted back, 'You should have some sharpened sticks outside the door with skulls on.'

Calamity, appearing not greatly surprised to see me leave in this fashion, picked up my hat, slapped it against her thigh a couple of times to remove the dust, and then walked over. She handed it to me as I sat on the ground, and then she left her hand there to help me up. 'Plan B?' she asked.

'Plan B,' I muttered.

Chapter 3

THE WOODEN CAR groaned to a halt and I clambered out on to the steeply inclined platform and followed the straggle of tourists who were about to have the Cliff Railway revealed to them as a metaphor for life. You sit expectantly, creaking up the hill, heart filled with anticipation of what's at the top. You can't help noticing the ride itself is pretty unimpressive, and then you get out at the top and wander around for a while looking for something the purpose of which might justify the building of such an elaborate contraption. You meet other souls wandering around with that look of puzzled expectancy, the expression that conveyed the question everyone wanted answered: 'Have you found it yet?' Since no one has, whatever it is, you stop off for a cup of tea in a musty wooden shed that smells like the place the head groundsman at the golf club keeps his tools. After that, spirits slightly raised by the mahogany-coloured tea, you go to check out the camera obscura. On the way in you read with mounting excitement about the piercing clarity of the image you are about to see in which every detail for miles around will be laid before your eyes in supernatural splendour. And then you find yourself in another dark shed, on a raised wooden pathway walking round a grey glass dish in which can be faintly discerned, as if at the bottom of a very deep fish pond where the water has not been changed in years, an image that is Aberystwyth upside down. You stare for a while, as people whisper, 'It's clear, isn't it?' and then the realisation gradually dawns that the image outside, from the cliff top, is bigger, brighter, sharper and, best of all, the right way up.

* * *

Meirion was sitting at one of the picnic tables concreted into the summit and drinking from a styrofoam cup. I fetched one and joined him. He took out a stick of Llandudno rock, snipped the cellophane off the end with a cigar trimmer, and took a suck. He said how upset he had been to hear the news about Myfanwy and I said I knew it. He said no more for a while and we sat there drinking tea, staring out over Aberystwyth in the valley. Meirion was the crime reporter on the *Gazette* and had a lot of good contacts in the underworld, but so far, he said, no one had heard anything.

'To tell you the truth, they're all a bit taken aback. It doesn't look like anyone local was involved.'

'I thought Brainbocs might have something to do with it.'

'He's eating porridge in Shrewsbury.'

'Do you know how he's getting on?'

'I hear things from time to time. There was some debate at first whether to put him in the cells with the adults. He gives his age as fourteen and has done for many years now. A bit like that chap Jimmy Clitheroe. There's no birth certificate – his mother says she found him being cared for by wolves. He's in the infirmary at the moment.'

'So what's wrong with him?'

'I don't know.'

'Whatever it is he's probably faking it.'

'Wouldn't surprise me. Ask Mrs Prestatyn, she'll know. I don't suppose Myfanwy could have just wandered off?'

'The ripple was drugged, Meirion.'

Meirion frowned. 'Mmmm. The police will be looking for the *gelati* van?'

'Of course. And I don't doubt they'll find it burned out in a field somewhere.'

'Any mention of a ransom?'

'But who would they send it to?'

'I don't know. I've heard nothing so far, but it's early days.

There was a bit of activity a while back on the stolen memorabilia front. An essay from her school days was stolen from a collector. It never made the news because often these sort of things don't – the insurance guys like to keep a lid on it so they can come to a private arrangement with the thieves.'

'What exactly was stolen?'

'A spelling test she did when she was seven. Got four out of ten. Pretty rare, difficult to fence. There were a few other things.'

'I'll look into it.'

'Talk to a fence. I'm not saying it's connected, of course. But it could be a daft scheme to drive up the value – you know, get her name in the paper.'

'Or kill her. That would drive up the value.'

'I didn't mean it like that.'

Meirion placed his arm on my shoulder and guided me back to the station. At the point where the ground falls away steeply we stopped and contemplated the town. The sea was pigeon-coloured today. I said, not really knowing why, 'Do you know anything about a guy called Frankie Mephisto?'

The arm on my shoulder tightened slightly.

'You heard the rumour then?'

'No.'

'They say he's coming out this month. Should have done another five years. What makes you ask?'

'I got a phone call from someone who mentioned his name.'

'He was the mastermind behind the robbery here on the Cliff Railway in '72. Ask your dad, he worked the case.'

'Why Mephisto?'

'The Welsh Mephistopheles. It was because of that play by Marlowe, *Doctor Faustus*. Frankie had been taken to see it as a kid and it made a great impression on him. Apparently, he came to see in Faust's fate the expression of a universal human truth, namely, there is no such thing as a free lunch.' Meirion took a long suck on his Llandudno. His face remained straight but there was the hint of a twinkle in his eye. I wondered if his little joke was from some piece written for the *Gazette* now lying gathering dust in his drawer, never printed because although the newspaper liked to maintain the fiction of a crime reporter on the staff, they didn't like to impugn the image of the town by reporting any crime.

'In fact,' said Meirion, 'Frankie had taken this human truth and made it central to his own operation. You see, he had a lot of contacts in the old days, and very often people approached him for help. And he was happy to oblige but he always warned them that, one day, he would come and call on them and ask them to return the favour. In fact he was very meticulous about this, pointing out that these were more than empty words and would ask them if they were familiar with the legend of Faust. And they would say, Faust, yeah, of course, nice bloke. Or something. And Frankie would tell them one day he would return just as assuredly as Mephistopheles. Hence over time they got to calling him Frankie Mephisto.'

Meirion finished his rock and screwed up the cellophane and threw it in the bin. Then slapped his hands to wipe away the stickiness.

'He used to tell people "no" wasn't a word in his dictionary and when he needed a favour he would send his boys round with a dictionary from which it had been cut out.'

There are two types of people who visit hospitals. Those who know someone there who is sick. And those who just pretend. Mrs Prestatyn belonged to the second group: the pros. She did a sweep of Bronglais once a week. No stethoscope or clipboard, just a hat and coat and a brazen attitude. The hospital administration knows all about such people but legally it is a grey area. You generally need a patient to make a complaint, but most people are too dumbfounded. Being in hospital is a confusing and disorientating experience. It's not something you generally get much practice at and you tend to err on the side of being too trusting and defer to anyone in a uniform, even a porter. So if a smartly dressed woman whom you've never seen before breezes in, takes a look at your clipboard and says, 'I see they've put you on the doxo-demaloline. That should loosen the phlegm', what do you say? Most folk find themselves pouring forth all the details of their ailment. And in doing so they contribute to our collective understanding of the mystery of disease – or at least the understanding shared by those of us who go to bingo.

I walked up Penglais and through the car park to Bronglais and into the cafeteria. She was sitting at a table sipping a tea and peering over the rim of the olive-green hospital china at a paperback novel. It was a 'Doctor and Nurses' romance. I watched her for a while before approaching: she read with a frown of concentration and ran her finger under the words to make sure she didn't miss one. At two pound a book they were expensive. Her head had a slight bobbing motion as if nodding in rhythmic agreement with the text and every so often she would stop in mid-nod and her frown would deepen. Then she would put the tea down, take out a pen and scribble notes in the book, in her throat a soft strangled squeak of triumph. Perhaps one of the few people in the world who read this genre and wrote marginalia. The rim of the cup was imprinted with lipstick.

I pulled the chair opposite out from under the table and sat down. Mrs Prestatyn raised her eyes briefly from the page in a quick darting movement before returning to her reading. She winced slightly and scribbled something, saying with a tut-tut, 'She's put him on twenty ccs of tripanazetramol, previous nurse gave him sulphadextranaphase – he'll lose his leg if they keep that up.' She paused and added, 'Come to empty some bedpans have you?'

'I was thinking about it, why do you ask?'

'Well, you're not here for your health now are you, if you'll pardon the pun.'

'Anyone can visit a hospital.'

She snorted. 'Try telling that to the security guard.'

She carried on reading and I said nothing more for a while. If I was ill in hospital I might resent the intrusion of someone like Mrs Prestatyn. But, as editor-in-chief of that loose-knit confederacy of gossips and tittle-tattlers known as the Orthopaedia Britannica, she was an indispensable source of information for me. As such, a professional relationship existed between us that was complicated and difficult to define, like that between the copper and his nark. And it was hard to despise a woman whose obsession derived from a time, long ago, when she had served with the St John's Ambulance Brigade. Her recurring visits now were as pitiful as the dog who returns to the house of a dead man who years ago had given him a bone.

'To tell the truth,' she said, seemingly addressing the page, 'I'm surprised you've got the nerve to show your face.'

'What does that mean?'

'Muriel at the nursing home is beside herself. I told her Myfanwy wasn't safe with you.'

'What did I do?'

'Not much by the sound of it.'

'I took her for an ice cream. If it hadn't been for me she would never have got out at all, would have been stuck in that nursing home, staring at the wall all day.'

'At least we'd know where she was.'

I winced.

'Of course,' she added, taking a mint toffee from her bag, 'if it wasn't for you she might never have ended up there in the first place.'

'What's that supposed to mean?'

'If you and that Brainbocs boy hadn't been squabbling over her. Making a love potion – never heard anything so ridiculous . . .'

'He made it, not me. I was the one who saved her.'

'In my day we gave a girl roses.'

'She was fine afterwards.'

'I seem to remember she was fine before, not after.'

She put the toffee in her mouth and continued to turn the pages, but too quickly now in the manner of one not really reading the words.

'There's no reason to believe her illness had anything to do with that. These things happen sometimes, people get ill, no one knows why, if we did . . .' My words petered out, stopped by the look on her face – that particular breed of sardonic disdain that specialists adopt when amateurs venture an opinion in their field.

'I'm sure you're right,' she said, meaning no such thing.

'And anyway, I spoke to the new doctor, he said—'

'I know what he said,' she snapped. 'He said you ask for certainty but I cannot give it. We are like little children lost on the shore of a dark mysterious ocean called disease, paddling in the shallows and imagining we understand the profound mysteries that lie beyond the horizon.'

'He said that to you, too?'

'They all say it. It's the latest fashion. In the old days they just said you'd got mumps.'

I took out a handkerchief and dabbed the sweat on my neck. It was hot and stuffy in the cafeteria, or maybe it was just the knack Mrs Prestatyn had of making me squirm. From far away I could hear the dull click, thud and whirr of crockery being loaded into an automatic dish-washer. The air was hard to breathe, a fug filled with the faint smell of disinfectant, and industrial laundry soap, the stale scent of boiling cabbage and Mrs Prestatyn's minty breath. Maybe it was just too warm. Hospitals were always like that, heated to keep sick people in pyjamas from shivering, like orchids in a hothouse. Mrs Prestatyn continued to feign reading. Finally she said, without looking up, 'So now I suppose you've come to ask about Brainbocs.'

'Meirion says he got sick.'

'Royal Salop Infirmary. Top floor. Moved him off the cell block in February.' She carried on reading her book, or pretending to. After a while she said, 'You know my rates, Mr Knight. It's not January so there's no sale.'

I unfolded a five-pound note and put it on the table and she put her book down on top of it and said the single word, 'Glossolalia.'

I waited for her to amplify but she didn't even though she knew I hadn't a clue what that was, so I said finally, 'Do I get any more for my five pounds?'

She looked up. 'You've never heard of glossolalia?'

'You'd be mortified if I had.'

She grunted and said reluctantly, seemingly having already forgotten that I had paid for the information, 'Glossolalia is the term used to describe people who create their own private language. Or, if you're more of the Pentecostal persuasion, you might call it "speaking in tongues". In Brainbocs's case attended by intermittent dissociative auditory hallucinations.'

'A private language?'

'Won't talk to anyone except in his new language. It shows clear signs of coherence and well-defined grammatical structures, possibly derived in part from the Finnish-Hungarian family. Dr Molyneux is transcribing it but progress is slow.' She paused and added, 'Also draws dinosaurs on the wall – makes his own ink from rennet and bird droppings.'

I stood up to leave and Mrs Prestatyn lifted her book and shoved the five-pound note across the table. 'There, take it.'

I hesitated and she twitched. 'Go on, take it before I change my mind. Or if you don't want it there's a box for the guide dogs by the door.'

'What's wrong?'

She forced herself not to look at me, lifted the book and said from behind it, 'Just find Myfanwy and we'll say no more.'

* * *

By the water's edge, rendered colourless by the mist, were some policemen on hands and knees searching the sand. Occasionally one of them would put something into something else that looked like a sandwich bag. If I hadn't known better I would have said they were collecting shells.

Drops of rain darkened the already damp sand like new stain on old wood. They fell on Calamity's sou'wester with soft percussive thuds like someone learning to type. The outfit wasn't new but I hadn't seen it before.

I said, 'Not much chance of seeing Paddington Bear this afternoon.'

'Which way?' asked Calamity.

I pointed in the direction of the marsh and the Waifery and we started walking away from the car with the same reluctance of people who have broken down in the desert and decide to abandon the vehicle.

'If you feel like telling me why we won't be seeing him, that's fine, but I'm not going to ask.'

'Who?'

'Paddington Bear.'

'He never goes out without his coat and hat, specially on a day like this. And now someone's stolen it from him, poor guy.'

'If you must know, my mum made me wear it. Why this way anyway?'

'My instinct about these things says this way.'

'You tossed a coin more like.'

'Seventh rule of being a private eye: when faced with only two possibilities, both of which are hopeless, it doesn't make a lot of sense to agonise over the decision.'

'Rule number seven.'

'I hope you're writing these down.'

'I'm sure rule number seven was something else.'

'If you wrote them down you'd know.'

'So this is Sospan's brilliant idea.'

'Yep.'

'Are you sure you heard him right?'

'I made him repeat it three times. He said to look for a sleeping gull.'

'You could have misheard.'

'If you can think of something that sounds like that we'll start looking. But it has to be something you'd be likely to find at the seaside.'

'Seeping hull.'

'That's good but I don't think he said that.'

'But you're not sure.'

'He said sea gulls always eat ice cream that's melted on the pavement, it's part of the evolution of their foraging habits, like foxes coming to the edge of towns to scavenge from litter bins.'

'Polar bears do that too. In some parts of the world.'

'Well, there you are, you see. They also scavenge from the bin next to an ice-cream van. Sure as eggs, he said, if the *gelati* man was using drugged ripple you'd get snoozing birds everywhere.'

'Well, I don't see any. In fact I don't think I've ever seen a sea gull asleep, have you?'

'No, but then I've never looked. And they must do it, I can't believe they never go to sleep.'

'Albatrosses can stay out at sea for seven years without ever touching dry land.'

'They sleep on ships.'

The ground was spongy like a mattress, pools of water formed around our shoes wherever we stepped. We continued to walk, without heart or belief in our quest. After half an hour of aimlessly squelching about, Calamity spotted a gull. It was sitting in the gutter of the peat cutter's cottage. And after a couple of minutes squabbling during which I was forced to pull rank, I gave Calamity a 'bunk up' and she peered at the fat grey bird that gave all the signs of being asleep in the gutter. Then she poked it and it produced a beak that was vaguely s-shaped from within its feathers, made an angry sound and snapped at Calamity. She squealed and fell backwards and I took a step back to counterbalance her fall and she stood on me like a trapeze artist and we stood there wavering like Laurel and Hardy at the circus. And then the sun found a hole in the clouds and drenched the wet landscape with liquid silver. The roof of the peat cutter's cottage flashed like a heliograph, sequins littered the grass, and beyond the hills of Aberdovey the crescent of a rainbow appeared, sharply outlined against the still brooding clouds.

'Looking for eggs?' said a voice from behind me.

I tried to turn but the jittery movement above my head as Calamity struggled to maintain her balance made me stop. The owner of the voice walked round and stood in front of me and I squinted down at a girl of about fifteen or sixteen. She was wearing wellingtons and a navy blue gaberdine mac buttoned at the throat. On her head she wore the distinctive chimney hat with the yellow 'W' insignia of the Waifery. Bright blond hair fell from beneath the brim down to her shoulders smearing the wetness of her coat like a dusting of pollen on a bee's wing.

'We're looking for a sleeping gull,' I said.

'That's a funny thing to be doing in the rain.'

'Pretty funny in the dry as well.'

'Rain's worse. Although I like it really, but it's hopeless for looking for things.'

'We're doing it for a bet.'

'Oh I see. I don't think I've ever seen one asleep.'

'We were saying the same thing.'

She reached out her hand to shake, and then realising that I couldn't take the hand stopped the motion halfway. 'My name's Seren.'

I crouched slowly and allowed Calamity to jump down.

'I'm Louie and this is my partner, Calamity.'

Calamity shook her hand and said, 'Pleased to make your acquaintance, ma'am.'

A shovel tingled on the silver air like a tuning fork and we all turned at the same time towards the cottage. The peat cutter was standing in the doorway. He was wearing brown corduroy trousers tucked into wellington boots, a tweed jacket and had a tough dark face surrounded by thickly curled blue-black hair, lightened here and there with tufts of silver like a badger. He might have been forty-five or fifty-five. He spoke to Seren in Welsh and walked off, carrying a spade.

Seren invited us into the cottage and we sat at a wooden kitchen table and waited for her to brew a pot of tea. I could see the peat cutter though the window walking off across the marsh. There was a book on the table: a scholarly tome about soil geology. I flicked through the pages, it was mostly tables and formulae and diagrams representing the various shapes of the ponds in the marsh and how they came to be formed by the wind and rain and tidal action.

'Is the peat cutter interested in all this?'

'He wrote it.'

'Really?'

'Well, he did the pictures – I mean he dug them. Some bloke from the university wrote the book and sent it to him.'

'Is Mr Meredith your dad?'

'No, I'm from the Waifery. I don't have a dad, I was a foundling. But I come here quite a lot and Meredith lets me do what I like. I saw you the other night.'

'Really?'

'I was the one who found the locket. I'm sorry about your girlfriend.'

'That's nice of you.'

'You won't tell Sister Cunégonde you saw me here, will you? She'd be furious.'

'Do holy sisters get furious?'

Seren looked at me in astonishment. 'Are you kidding! They never do anything else. Specially old Cunybongy. It's because I'm a category A Waif. They're the worst, you see. I need special attention to stop me straying from the path. That's why I'm not allowed to come here. She says I don't understand how easy it is for a young girl to stray from the path and be lost. But that's silly, I could find my way around here with my eyes shut.'

'Maybe she means it in a different way.'

'Don't be daft, what other way could there be?'

Later, as we trudged back to the car and were about to get in, I heard a cry and the sound of someone running.

'Louie! I've got one!' It was Seren and she was carrying a shoebox. Inside was a sleeping gull.

There was a barrel organ leaning against the wall when we got back and upstairs in the office was a man, a suitcase and a monkey.

'Just came to see how you were getting on with the investigation,' said Gabriel Bassett.

Cleopatra was sitting on the desk; she gesticulated and Gabriel added, 'She says good afternoon.'

We smiled at her and she made an impatient 'reminder type' of gesture.

'And also,' said Gabriel sheepishly, 'she asked whether you've seen Mr Bojangles.'

'Tell her, no, but we're keeping our eyes peeled.'

'That's good, she'll like that.' He translated and she did, indeed, look pleased.

'We've been working flat out on the case,' lied Calamity. 'And we've made a lot of progress.'

'Anything you'd like to share with me?'

We both struggled not to follow his gaze which was directed at the wall bearing nothing but a pinned up tea towel with the words *comes stabuli*. It was fairly clear that we had not been flat out or making a great deal of progress. I made a mental note to move the incident board into the kitchen.

'I see you bought the tea towel,' he said.

Neither of us could think of a suitable response to that and he said, 'You do understand, don't you, it is very important to me that you solve this case by the deadline I gave. There can be no question of further payment if you don't.'

'We understand.'

He stood up and Cleopatra leaped across from the desk and climbed on to his shoulders. They walked to the door. When he picked up the case I said, 'Do you really carry that around with you all the time?'

He stopped and looked down as if checking that I meant the case and not the monkey.

'Oh yes.'

'What's in it?'

'I don't know.'

Chapter 4

THE NEXT MORNING at nine Sospan gave us the result of his forensic analysis of the gull's gizzard. Nothing. Not a drop of drugged ripple, from which he deduced that the bird had not been anaesthetised but was just taking a lie-in, possibly, although we didn't particularly need to know this, due to exertion caused by flying around during the storm in the Irish Sea recently.

'So we wasted our time.'

'I'm sorry Mr Knight, the technique usually works very well but I think you left it too late. You should have called me in sooner.'

'There's a girl's life at stake here, Sospan.'

'No one knows that better than me, you know that. I've got all Myfanwy's records just like you. Did you make a list like I told you?'

'List of what?'

'Of everything you could remember about the *gelati* man.'

'But I told you, I was drugged, I couldn't remember anything.'

Sospan tutted. 'You've drunk from the waters of the Lethe is what you've done, Mr Knight. I would recommend you went and saw Mr Evans the Hypnotist at Kousin Kevin's.'

'And what good would that do?'

'Forensic hypnotism is a very powerful weapon in the modern detective's arsenal. I'm surprised you don't know that.'

'I'm not going to see any hypnotist. The weapons in this detective's arsenal include gumption and shoe leather, not end-of-the-pier chicanery.'

'It's not chicanery. It's a tried-and-trusted technique with a formidable capacity for unlocking the gates of remembrance.' He put a leaflet on the counter top. 'I can get you a ticket if you like.'

'I think it's a good idea,' said Calamity.

'You would.'

'Well, why not?'

'Because it's hocus-pocus.'

'No it isn't.'

Sospan tapped a finger on the leaflet for emphasis. 'Mr Evans does a lot of work for the police, ask Llunos.'

'Well he's not doing a lot of work for me.'

The argument was interrupted by the arrival of a straw-scented cloud containing Eeyore. It was the first patrol of the day and none of the donkeys had riders. I think Eeyore preferred it that way. Sospan offered him an ice but he declined with a troubled look on his face.

'What's up, Dad?' I asked.

He nodded towards a donkey in the middle of the line. 'It's the Duchess, she's playing up. She isn't happy.'

I looked over to the Duchess who had wandered up to the sea-side railing and put her head over as if it were a stable door. She was staring out across the sea with a wistful air. Maybe she dimly remembered her home being in Ireland and was wondering if she might see it again before she died.

'Maybe it's just old age.'

'Of course it's old age. I know that. We've been together twelve years. That's a lot for a donkey.'

I picked a piece of straw off his lapel. 'Why don't you rest her for a while?'

'No,' he said. 'I can't. She's the matriarch of the troop. She's the one who keeps discipline, keeps the young ones in line and teaches them things.'

'Teaches them what?'

'The craft. Things like not to fart when carrying children. Things like that. It's like the alpha dog on a husky team. Without him those dogs just won't make a move. Just sit there in the snow and starve to death. People don't understand. They think you just tie them in a line and pull them along. But I tell you, you won't get very far doing that. The donkeys have to want to make the trip. That's where the matriarch comes in. She passes on the old knowledge that the herd has acquired over the years, about the ancient foraging patterns.'

'I thought you just gave them a bucket of oats.'

'I do, but they still have the "call" inside them, don't they? It's like dogs chasing sticks. Sticks are symbolic prey. Most people feed them from a tin but the dog still has the hunting instinct that needs to be satisfied. With the donkeys, the walk up the Prom is an echo of the old foraging patterns. They start off at the harbour and head towards Constitution Hill seeking better pasture. But of course they don't have very good memories so by the time they've arrived at one end they've forgotten what it was like where they started out, so they look around and think, hmmm, not much here is there? And then the matriarch says, I know, why don't we go and try down the other end of the Prom by the harbour? And off they go. Once you set the pattern in motion you can pretty much let it run itself.'

'Herd dynamics they call it,' said Sospan. 'Every Prom built over the last hundred years has a minimum length determined by the attention span of a donkey.'

'OK. So what happens if you get a really brainy one, like a donkey Mozart, who can remember further back and tells them what it's like up the other end?'

Sospan considered and Eeyore said sadly, 'They call him a prophet and cast him out. I've seen it happen.' And off he and the herd went, continuing their endless traverse, borne on the never-dimming hope of greener pastures.

'I've been thinking about the *Journals of the Proceedings of the*

Myfanwy Society,' said Calamity through ripple-stained lips. 'They'd be pretty useful for leads and things, wouldn't they?'

'They sure would, but we don't know anyone who's got a set.'

'I think I know a way of getting into the National Library. I saw it in a movie once.' I stared down at her young face, bright and as undimmed with cynicism as a dandelion. She had changed a lot in the three odd years we'd been together. At the time we first met her face had the sickly pallor of skin hidden from the sun and brought up under the flashing, artificial light of the amusement arcade. She'd been just another hustler, like Poxcrop, and probably still would be now if our paths hadn't crossed. But the thing that struck me was how quickly the toughened street-wise shell had fallen away, like a discarded chrysalis, to reveal a great kid. It made me wonder whether I was doing the right thing taking her on as a partner in the one occupation that was guaranteed to curdle the milk of youth faster than anything: a gumshoe in Aberystwyth. But equally I knew there would have been no point trying to stop her. This was what she wanted to do. She was pretty good at it, too. And there were few more pointless endeavours in life than giving advice to people who don't seek it; no task more hopeless than trying to stop a young person making mistakes that struck you as a good idea when you were the same age.

'This movie,' I said, 'it's not *The Sound of Music*, is it?'

'*The Day of the Jackal*. Where the guy shoots the prime minister of France.'

'Did he need to get into a library badly?'

'He needed a fake identity, so he went to a cemetery and found the grave of a kid who died really young and took down the name. Then he went to that place in London where you go if you want to change your name—'

'Somerset House.'

'Right. And applied for a copy of the birth certificate.'

'And they gave it to him, just like that.'

'That's the amazing thing. They do. There's just a charge for the paperwork.'

'In books maybe it happens like that, but this is real life, we don't get the same breaks as the guys in the books.'

'I thought we'd get one of our associate partners in London to go along to Somerset House for us and then we could apply for a passport in Newport. I could find a grave here in Aber. The passport could come in handy for other jobs as well.'

'We don't have any associate partners in London.'

'It's about time we did. We can't grow the organisation without a network of contacts.'

'I've managed OK up till now – associate partners sound expensive.'

'It's a business expense, you write it off against tax. We need to get a small operator in London to enter into a preferred partnership with us. Next time we need a tail job done on a party in London we call the guy up. Then one day, when he needs some business transacted in Aberystwyth, he calls us. It's reciprocal.'

'When do we ever need to tail someone in London?'

'It happens all the time. Say we're doing a surveillance here and the party leaves on the train to Euston, you want someone to follow him but you can't do it yourself because it wouldn't be cost-effective. So you arrange to have him intercepted at Euston. That's how Pinkerton's started out. The party under surveillance goes to Kansas City so you wire ahead with a description of him. Then two operatives working in relays pick him up when he gets off the train. They follow him for a week and he never even suspects. They watch his every move. At the end of the week he goes to the station and buys a ticket, to say, I don't know, Tallahassee—'

'Kansas to Tallahassee?'

'It doesn't matter where. The important thing is, one of the Pinkerton guys is standing behind him in the queue and listens to the new destination. Then he wires ahead and two more guys pick him up when he gets off. That's how they do it.'

'OK, so what happens if you find some kid's grave and expropriate his identity and he turns out to be the dead son of someone who works at the library, and we turn up with his library ticket?'

'Nothing would happen, it would just be a coincidence.'

'Just a coincidence?'

'I was going to choose a common name like, I don't know, Billy Jones, not Amvrosiyevich Shevardnadze.'

'Yeah, maybe.'

'What do you think would happen? The woman behind the desk would go, "Oh my God! It's my son! I thought he was dead and here he is borrowing a book!"'

'It seems quite a drastic way to get a library ticket.'

'Can you think of a better way?'

'Yes,' I said. 'I can.'

I took out the card Poxcrop had left with me.

When Myfanwy got sick we didn't notice at first. She escaped from us gradually, evanescently, the way sand passes between the two bulbs of an hourglass. She seemed to be receding from us into a sea of forgetfulness. You can't blame her, I suppose. There's a lot in this world worth forgetting. But what about us who were left behind? The people who loved her? It seemed such a cruel trick: to run away and leave us with something that looked like Myfanwy, but where no one was manning the switchboard. Don't give up hope, the doctors said, although it was hard to see where they got the authority to say that since they did not know what was wrong with her. Sometimes it's hard not to resent her for this: to abandon her body and leave it in the possession of people obliged by decency to take care of it. Like leaving a parcel at the lost property and never going back. And because we loved her, we accepted the strange burden. We baby-sat for her corpse in the feeble hope that she might return to it. Like we leave a swallow's nest in the rafters in the hope that one day they will come back.

Llunos stood looking out of the window of my office and said, 'I've been talking to the people at the nursing home. They say it's not looking too rosy for Myfanwy if they don't find her soon.'

'I know.'

'I don't like to say it, but we have to face facts. We might be looking at a murder inquiry.'

'I know that too. And I know you're going to tell me a murder inquiry is no place for a private operative.'

'Just so you know.'

'I'll keep my nose out of it.'

'Yeah, I bet you will.'

He reached out and picked up a paperweight that lay on top of a pile of unpacked ring-binders. It was a scene of Aberystwyth in winter; he shook and snow fell. For many years relations between the two of us had been similarly frozen; because that was the natural state of affairs between a chief of police and a private operative. A snooper generally being regarded in the eyes of the law as someone who makes his living by getting to evidence before the police and then not telling them about it. But Llunos was not too worried about evidence since he could always invent what he lacked. And with time we had come to understand we were both fighting for the same thing. The only difference was one of approach – mine was more law-abiding.

I took a bottle of rum out of the cabinet under the desk and fetched two glasses from the kitchenette. He glanced at his watch.

'Bit early.'

'Get a new watch.' I poured the drinks

'I'm just telling you, that's all,' continued Llunos. 'For the record. Then when I have to charge you for obstruction or withholding evidence you won't be able to say I didn't warn you.'

'I'll bear it in mind.'

'I know nothing I say will make a darned bit of difference.'

'It's nothing personal.'

He nodded. 'If it was me and someone took Myfanwy I'd be the same.' He drained the glass and I refilled.

'Bit smaller than the old office.' He gave the room a look of appraisal. 'What's the tea towel for?'

I paused for a second wondering how much I should tell him. He noticed; he always did.

'Calamity is applying for her badge. She has to do a project so she's writing a report on the case of the Nanteos fire.'

'She won't find much to look at.'

'You don't think so?'

'Impeccable bit of coppering work that. Best the county's ever seen.'

I laughed. 'Let's hope not. I need something to keep her quiet.'

'The guy in charge was my great-grandfather, Syracuse Obadiah Griffiths. First peeler in the county.'

I looked at Llunos as if I was seeing him for the first time. 'I wasn't aware of that.'

'It was an experiment, you see. Sir Robert Peel had introduced this idea of peelers in London but they weren't sure whether to roll them out across the country. So they tested them out in a few places. Syracuse was the first in Wales. The mansion fire was his finest case: established the model for policing in Cardiganshire for the next 150 years. He was a great man.'

'I'll drink to that.'

We raised glasses.

'I'll tell Calamity to call you if she needs any help.'

He grunted a sort of sound that might have been agreement and said, 'Reason I dropped by was to let you know: we've found the *gelati* van.'

'That was quick work.'

'Yeah, quick.'

'Then again, can't be easy to hide an ice-cream van.'

'They found it in a deep freeze. Quite appropriate really.'

'Are we talking about those big freezers at the meat-packing plant?'

'No.'

'One of the hotels then?'

'No it was an ordinary domestic deep freeze. In a scrap yard.'

'So what am I missing?'

'The van had been in a car crusher.'

I nodded. It made sense.

'Some guy walking his dog saw it being crushed last night.'

'And I suppose because it was done outside office hours there was no paperwork and no one working there knows anything about it.'

'That's pretty much how it looks. But we might still be able to find something useful in the chassis. We're waiting for the heavy uncrumpling gear to be sent up from Cardiff.'

'I suppose there's no sign of the driver.'

'On the contrary: there's every sign of him. Judging from the pink stuff oozing out, I'd say he's still at his post.'

'Went down with his ship?'

'Looks like it.'

'Thanks for telling me.'

'I also found out something else. I took the car registration numbers from the kiosk guy and traced the people who were there that day. We found a family staying in town, they gave us the film they shot that afternoon.'

He handed me a photo. It was landscape taken pointing inland towards Ynyshir. My car was in the foreground. And standing next to it, seeming to be leaning in as if talking to the passenger, was a man. It looked like one of the old soldiers from the Patagonian War.

'He's been on the run for a few weeks now,' said Llunos. 'You might have heard it mentioned on the radio. You can keep the photo.'

* * *

There were seven people sitting in the auditorium waiting for the Great Osiris's show. And one private eye sitting on stage staring into the dazzle of a spotlight. He was the sort of gumshoe who had been taught by life to be sceptical of occasions like this; he knew all about the sorry extent of people's credulity, and about the charlatans who made their living exploiting it. But his partner, Calamity, had asked what was the prospect of a little humiliation set against the chance that he might be able to retrieve a telling detail from his memory of the day Myfanwy disappeared. It was a fair point and hard to answer. Even though he knew she was saying it because she wasn't the one who had to sit in the chair.

The Great Osiris took out a fob watch and let it dangle in front of my face, commanding me in a voice that dripped syrup to keep my eyes on the watch. It was such a familiar routine I could have recited it myself. Soon you will begin to feel sleepy, veerrry sleeeeeepy . . . I tried to play ball. The watch glittered and flashed in the light like a salmon jumping a waterfall and evading the paw of a grizzly bear. Then it flashed like a lighthouse at night, and then slid across the sky like a full moon behind rags of scudding cloud. Then it slowed down – I don't know how he did it, but I had to admit it was a good trick. The air through which the watch described its arc congealed and turned to aspic. Now the watch was hardly moving, rising, rising, rising with agonising slowness and then remained poised at the acme as if the chain had turned into a solid rod of brass. Suddenly, as if a trapdoor had opened, it fell and swooped and my eyes followed the motion, swivelling from side to side. And then the watch stopped again, and turned into a setting sun; the world grew dim and night came on and the first few stars came out, muffled by the autumn fog that seeped up from the heath, and the golden pale orb of light flickered and pulsated on the end of the stick that I seemed to have acquired. An owl hooted and my breath steamed in the frosty fog. The gas lamp seemed to be safely alight and so I moved on to the next: another fifty and I could go home. Horses whinnied and I leaped aside as a carriage sped past with a silvery jingling of harness and clopping of hooves. I raised my fist but the carriage had already disappeared into the murk. Stupid nobs, I thought, think they own the turnpike. I moved on to the next streetlamp. And then the world was filled with blinding light and I was staring out at eight people who were standing up and applauding.

As we threaded our way back through the buildings of Kousin Kevin's Krazy Komedy Kamp, Calamity explained with eyes sparkling with awe what she had witnessed. 'It was unbelievable! He said he knew all about hypnotic regression so I told him to take you back to the day in Ynyslas but he sort of overdid it and you went back too far. He said it's a bit like tuning a radio – sometimes you sort of overshoot, and sometimes you undershoot. After a while you started talking in the voice of a little boy and the Great Osiris tried to make you come back, but you just carried on and on. Soon you were crying like a baby and then all of a sudden you were talking in a strange voice and the Great Osiris asked you what the date was and you said it was 1065. And he said, "Oh, so just before the Norman Conquest" and you said, "What Norman Conquest?" And then he brought you forward a bit and you said you couldn't stop to talk because there was plague in Talybont. And then he brought you forward a bit more, and guess what?'

'I turned into Francis Drake.'

'No, you were a lamplighter in 1849. And I asked you if you'd heard about the fire at the mansion and you said yes and what a terrible thing it was and I said, "Do you think the stable boy did it?" And you said, "Of course not, he was fitted up by the peelers." Calamity stopped and then added, 'Amazing eh?'

'Lamplighter,' I said quietly.

'With a long pole to light the gas.'

'I thought we were supposed to find out what happened at Ynyslas.'

'Oh,' said Calamity, slightly deflated. 'You didn't really say much about that, except you mentioned seeing an old soldier, and he had a tattoo on his forearm that said "Deeper than the love".'

Chapter 5

THERE WAS A police tent erected over the spot from which Myfanwy disappeared and beyond that, at the shore of the estuary, was Cadwaladr. He was loading things into a boat. We walked towards him with a slight reluctance since he appeared to be engaged on an unusual activity – gainful employment. Cadwaladr was one of the veterans of the war fought in 1961 to defend the Welsh colony in Patagonia. You often saw these men in their tattered greatcoats drifting from town to town, riding the boxcars, or just wandering; searching the land for an answer that no one seemed to have to the question, why Patagonia?

Since the beginning of time, men have looked across the sea and imagined a land beyond the horizon where life would be easier. As boys, we stood on the shore and looked at Aberdovey, imagining that the girls over there were sweeter. And from time to time we met men from Aberdovey in the pubs of Borth with strange looks of disappointment on their faces. But why did the settlers in the last century, with all the world to choose from, opt for the southern tip of South America? What blinded them to the golden rule of colonisation? That ancient wisdom which says, it's hard to grow crops in a land where they have penguins.

The historians are silent on the subject, but I suspect it has to do with that great unsuspected dictator of human affairs, the smart aleck. The man who stands on the dockside as you leave for the promised land and scoffs. The Great Smirker. There's always one, and he was probably already there in Africa when the apes came down from the trees and decided to walk to Europe.

Men will put up with almost anything rather than face the derision of the Smirker. And so the Welsh settlers did what all pioneers do when they arrive and find that the brochure lied. They shivered in crofts made with bricks of turf and wrote home saying how great everything was. It's another California. Salmon jump from the river into your hand. Birds lay their eggs straight into the frying pan. The rivers are lemon-curded with gold.

When the soldiers arrived in 1961 and wrote home saying it was crap, they weren't believed. Their complaints dismissed as the customary ball-aching that soldiers at the Front have always done. Of course they are not happy, what soldier sitting in a trench ever is? Of course they say the place stinks, when did a soldier ever admire the scenery?

Still to this day they are not believed. Cast out as ungrateful moaners, lacking in gratitude for the unique chance given them to die in South America. Lost souls who perished in the service of the unacknowledged dictator. Their only epitaph: they died that he might smirk.

The boat was big enough for four or five people and bore the name *Persephone*. Cadwaladr was loading tins of creosote. He stopped and looked up, nodded slightly, and reached out a hand. We shook.

'Hope we're not disturbing anything,' I said.

'Just finishing for the day. Taking them to the other side for tomorrow morning. You can come along.' He ushered us into the boat and climbed in himself to sit facing us, with his back to Aberdovey. He started rowing across the estuary.

'What's the job?' said Calamity.

'Creosoting the Dovey Railway Bridge.'

'Just you?' I asked.

'Just me. And the birds.'

He said no more for a while and there was no sound save the soft rhythmic plop of the oar dipping into the water. In the middle of the channel, Cadwaladr altered course slightly until we were moving towards the point where the railway bridge intersected the northern shore. The sun was beginning to set and filled Cadwaladr's face with a golden lustre, like the buttercups we held under our chins as children.

'I've reached the fifth pile from the Dovey end,' he explained.

We craned our necks politely but they all looked the same from this distance: treacle-coloured stumps in an arrow-straight row across the water. There was a signalman's cottage at the northern end and west of that the old lighthousekeeper's cottage, once called Ty Gwyn but now universally known as the Loothouse after the time when Frankie Mephisto's gang were holed up there counting the takings from the Great Cliff Railway Robbery.

'Big job for one man,' I said.

'That's how I like it. Takes me all year. By the time I finish one end it's time to start again. A lot of people don't like the sound of that. They disdain it, say it reminds them of that Greek fellah, the one who had to roll the stone up the hill for eternity. To me it means a job for life, nothing wrong with that.'

We said we could see his point.

'And then there's the people you get to meet,' he added. 'That's another thing I like about the job.'

'I wouldn't have thought you would meet many people doing this.'

'I don't. Not a soul. That's fine by me.'

Cadwaladr reached a point in the sound that look indistinguishable to us from every other point and decided it was time to change direction again.

'Heading for the Loothouse,' he said. 'Can't go directly because of the sandbanks.'

'When the tide goes out you can walk across,' said Calamity.

'Wrong,' said Cadwaladr. 'You can only walk halfway across. Then you stand there and sink in the quicksand.'

'I bet I wouldn't,' said Calamity with the wisdom of youth.

'Don't ever try it,' said Cadwaladr sternly. 'You sink in and it congeals round your leg like quick-drying cement. The more you struggle the deeper in you go. Then all you can do is wait for the tide to come in and finish you off. But you don't have to wait long—'

'I know,' said Calamity, 'it's faster than a galloping horse.'

'I don't think it's that fast, but it's certainly faster than you can walk, but it's also sneaky. Does a pincer movement, creeps round you in channels and fills in the bits ahead first. So by the time you notice the tide is coming in, you're done for.'

The new course he had chosen brought us up to the jetty. We climbed out and helped him stow the creosote in the shed and then sat to watch the sun set. Cadwaladr took out a pipe, filled it slowly and began to puff in contentment.

'I s'pose you heard about Myfanwy?' I said.

He nodded gravely.

'There was a veteran wandering around that day. The one they keep mentioning on the radio.'

'You don't know that,' said Cadwaladr with a testy edge to his voice.

'What do you mean?'

'You don't know it was the same one.'

'We think it is.'

'Us fellahs get blamed for everything. You're supposed to be my friend but you're just like the rest of them: if there's a crime done and a veteran is in the vicinity then folk automatically point the finger at him.'

'We're not accusing him or anything. But he talked to her, see?' I handed him the photo. 'He might be able to give us some information, might have seen something. The only problem is, if he's on the run he's not going to talk to the police, but he might be willing to talk to you.'

Cadwaladr handed the photo back having scarcely looked at it. 'I don't recognise him. He's not from round here.'

'He had a tattoo on his arm,' said Calamity. 'It said "Deeper than the love".'

'We don't know for sure if that is true,' I said.

'Yes we do.'

'It's possible the soldier had a tattoo,' I insisted. 'But it's also possible I just dreamed it.'

Calamity pulled a face at me.

Cadwaladr scraped a match along the head of a bolt sunk into the timber of the jetty and relit his pipe. 'That would be Rimbaud. He has that tattoo. Rimbaud would never hurt Myfanwy.'

'We believe you.'

'What did he do wrong?' said Calamity

'He didn't do anything wrong, it was the policeman who drew first blood.'

'No, but why are they after him?'

'They want to question him in connection with the one crime they can never forgive: minding his own business. He was just walking through Glanwern or one of those towns, probably going back to Bala to see his mam, and then some hick cop sees him and thinks, Oh aye, what's this? Minding his own business, is he? What's he mean by that, then? Sounds a bit suspicious, if you ask me. So the cop tries to run him in, but it takes more than some big-bellied flatfoot who sits on his arse all day swatting flies and signing speeding tickets to take down a man like Rimbaud. He might not look like much but inside he has the heart of a warrior. So he says, No, I don't want to go to the police station. I've done nothing wrong, and he declines the offer. Two hours later the big-belly wakes up with a sore head and radios for reinforcements. They spend a week tracking Rimbaud through the Forestry Commission land. A place where Rimbaud is in his element, of course. Probably they would have given up before long, but then Rimbaud makes it personal. He sets some man-traps, sharpened stakes, and smears them with his – I don't know how to say this in front of a child – but, you know in Patagonia we used to poison the spikes of the traps by using our own pollution. Old Big-belly got an infected wound on his foot.'

'What does the tattoo mean?' asked Calamity.

'It's a quote from Remarque, the chap who wrote *All Quiet on the Western Front*. "Deeper than the love between two lovers." Remarque saw the true essence of warfare, you see.'

We waited for him to continue but he didn't. Cadwaladr knew a lot of things but sometimes getting it out of him was like waiting for the ketchup to ooze out of a new bottle.

'Have you ever thought,' he said at last, 'what a strange thing it is for a man to go and die for his country? To give up his life like that? A young man who has just discovered girls and liquor? Why would he do such a thing? For what? A life is all we have. You'd think he wouldn't sacrifice it for anything. And yet he goes to fight in some god-forsaken place like Patagonia. Why?'

'You tell us, Cadwaladr,' I said. 'You were there.'

He nodded with a puzzled look as if this last fact was a new discovery for him. 'Yes,' he said thoughtfully. 'I was there.'

We waited again while he cogitated. Then he looked round at me and said, almost urgently, 'But tell me why you think he does it.'

'Glory,' I offered.

'Yes, that's right. He does it in exchange for something that doesn't exist.' He spat into the water. 'Glory. The biggest lie of all. A will-o'-the-wisp, fool's gold.' He shook his head. 'No, that's why he goes there. Not why he stays. Two things make him stay. Shame and love. When a soldier arrives at the Front, what does he see? Glory? Of course not. He sees charnel. He sees a man eating corned beef from a tin next to a corpse upon whose eyes a rat is feeding. And in that moment he is faced with a choice. To run, or stay and become complicit in the crime of concealment. Because these things are kept hidden from the people back home. They are too much, they are such that no human being should have to witness them. And in not speaking out against them, in staying and sharing the tin of corned beef, he becomes one of the damned and shares their shame. And the other reason he stays is love: the love he bears for his brothers in arms. That was the quote, you see: "Deeper than the love between two lovers." You remember me telling you about Waldo? Poor Waldo who killed the man in the dust of the ravine and dipped his arms in his blood while the man begged for deliverance for the sake of his daughter, Carmencita, who was but a child and should not have to face the world as an orphan? And Waldo laughed even though he knew the armistice had been signed a week? This Waldo was Rimbaud. After the war he went away for ten years. No one saw him, no one knew where he went. And then one day he reappeared in the lanes of Wales. His name was now Rimbaud, he said. And he had seen the true meaning of suffering and been purified by his vision. I tell you, every man who fought in that conflict came back with an albatross around his neck. Rimbaud returned with a flock.'

He paused and his spirit slowly returned to Ynyslas from the frost-blasted killing fields of South America. 'Even so, he would never hurt Myfanwy. I'll look out for him, but he's probably miles away by now.' He stood up and began to untie the boat. The conversation was over for today.

There was a note from Sister Cunégonde taped to the door of my caravan when I got back that night. She asked me to drop by when I had a moment and I went round next morning. The girl who opened the front door to me curtseyed before offering to take my hat.

'Good morning, sir,' she said in what struck me as register slightly louder than necessary. She lowered her voice and whispered, 'Seren asked me to ask you not to grass her up to Cunybongy about the other day,' and then louder again: 'This way, sir.'

She led me along a corridor, through the assembly hall, into another corridor and then through the door marked 'Staff Only'.

It led on to a small oval lawn surrounded by flower beds and rockeries and a privet hedge on the farther side that had an arch cut into it. The lawn was a failure: the grass refusing to grow and leaving a bald spot like a potato in a threadbare sock. The girl led me round and through the arch in the privet. We found ourselves in a vegetable garden and up ahead Sister Cunégonde was in the act of placing a wellington boot on to a spade and turning over the soil. She looked up and smiled.

'Dig and ye shall find!' she said.

'That's the motto of my profession too.'

'Thank you for taking the trouble to come.'

'No trouble, it was on my way.'

'I don't think so, not unless you were going to Machynlleth. Your office is in Canticle Street isn't it?'

'Used to be, we've moved to Stryd-y-Popty.'

'Lucky old Poptys!' said Sister Cunégonde. She was short and plump with fine white hair tucked into her wimple. Her smile was warm – the sort that went with the job. 'I'm making a lawn as a control experiment. I s'pose you noticed the sorry excuse for a lawn over there under the common room window – I don't know how many times I've reseeded it.'

'It's probably the salt in the environment.'

'That's what I said to the chap at the Farmers' Co-op in Chalybeate Street. He said the grass they sell is a special salt-resistant strain, they thrive on it. He said the problem is my soil. Well, we'll see, won't we? I'm going to try his seeds one more time. If they grow here but not over there then I'll accept the problem is my soil. What do you think?'

'I'd say it was something to do with the soil, local conditions and all that. What do the people in the village say?'

'They say it's haunted! But what do you expect? They're from Borth. It used to be a pond once.'

'Sister Cunégonde, don't take offence, but you didn't invite me over to talk about gardening, did you?'

She let out a breath of air in a gentle puff.

'I should have guessed you'd see through me. Can we go to my office?'

Sister Cunégonde rested her elbows on the desk and made a steeple of her fingers. I stared past her shoulder through the schoolroom windows – the type you open with a hooked pole.

'We have a girl here who has been sick for a while – German measles. She's back in the dorm now and she says her locket has been stolen. Her name is Myfanwy Pritchard. Do you see what I am getting at?'

'You think it's her locket we found during the search?'

'I'm very sorry to even mention it to you at a time like this. Lord knows what you must be going through.'

'It's not a problem, just tell me what's on your mind.'

'She claims Seren stole it.'

'And then planted it on the dunes?'

She looked at me and squirmed. 'Yes.'

'Why?'

'So she could pretend to find it.'

'Maybe she didn't have to pretend.'

'Any other girl and I might believe it. But not Seren. She did it to draw attention to herself. She's that sort of girl.'

'What sort is that?'

'A show-off. She doesn't get on too well with the other girls, doesn't fit in. She lives in her own little dream world. She tells everyone she's a foundling.'

'And she's not?'

'She was brought here by the social services. It's hardly the same thing is it?'

I agreed that it wasn't.

'Do you think I should tell the police? I really don't want to have a load of policemen walking around the grounds, it's bad enough having an incident like this on our doorstep, exciting the girls. I told them you were from the gas board, I hope you don't mind. Goodness knows what they would do if they knew you were a private investigator. Do you think there will be a lot of trouble?'

'Not too much,' I said. 'She'll have to go to prison of course—'

Sister Cunégonde gasped.

'With a good lawyer she should be out in ten to fifteen. They may have to close the school down as well – probably put you all in the stocks.'

Her face relaxed into a smile. 'Oh I see, you're pulling my leg. You don't think it's the end of the world, then?'

'I've come across worse cases of wickedness. Have you spoken to Seren?'

'Yes, she denies it, of course, but she's not a very good liar.'

'Leave it with me,' I said as I prepared to leave. 'I know Llunos, I'll clear it with him.'

As I stepped off the bus outside Aberystwyth railway station a paperboy moved out of the shadows and took up a position to my left. As I walked he kept step.

'I'm not looking for a paper, thanks.'

'You'd be out of luck if you were, Mac, these are props. Not for sale.'

I recognised the voice and stopped. 'Poxcrop!'

'Keep walking if you don't mind.'

I started walking again.

'Why the newspapers?'

'Man in my position can't hang around the station without any business being there.'

'You could have come to the office.'

'Nothing personal, but I wouldn't like to be seen coming out of your office. I'm taking a risk as it is.'

'You must know some scary people.'

'Don't joke about it. I got your message. What can I do for you?'

'Does the name Myfanwy Montez mean anything to you?'

'Sure, the night club singer. Disappeared from Ynyslas three days ago. You like night club singers? My sister can sing. Like a nightingale.'

'The word is someone is trying to sell some stolen memorabilia – do you know what that is?'

'Photos, signed albums, concert programmes . . . sure I've handled merchandise like that before.'

'See what you can find out about it. I also need a ticket for the library, the big one on the hill.'

'You want books? I've got plenty.'

'These are special.'

'Tell me what you need, maybe I can arrange something. Getting an actual ticket isn't easy. Best way is to go to the cemetery and find the grave of someone who—'

'Yeah I know. That's too drastic. I'm looking for the *Journals of the Proceedings of the Myfanwy Society*. Years 1970 to present day.'

'I'll need some dough.'

'How much?'

'Ten pounds should get me started.'

'You could buy a bakery with that. Try this.'

I put a fiver on top of the card tray.

'Consider that as a down payment.'

The office was filled with an intoxicating cloud of acetate fumes and Calamity sat in the middle of it, writing capital letters in marker pen on pieces of white card. Her tongue protruded from her mouth in the manner of one totally absorbed.

'What are you doing?'

She jumped slightly. 'Er . . . hi! How're you doing?'

'I'm doing fine. Thanks. Now what are you doing?'

'Nothing much.'

'Calamity.'

'Last night after I got back from Ynyslas I . . . er . . . went to see a medium.'

'You're kidding!'

'Just doing some background checks, you know.'

'Not really.'

'She gave me the names of a few underworld contacts.'

'Do you mean the criminal underworld or the one where Beelzebub lives?'

'Well, both really. Small-time hoods who were active at the time of the Nanteos fire. I'm making an ouija board. Thought we could take some witness statements.'

'That's silly.'

'I knew you'd say that.'

I walked into the kitchenette to put the kettle on and spoke as I worked.

'I don't approve of this.'

'I thought you said it was my case.'

'It is but I still have to keep an eye on you.'

'You can't stop me following my hunches, that's what the job is all about.'

'Following hunches is fine, but you can't take witness statements using a ouija board. You'll never get your badge if you do things like that.'

'Louie, sometimes an investigator finds the normal channels are blocked. In such cases she is grateful for whatever leads and scraps of information she can find.'

'Yeah but the investigator draws the line at the supernatural.'

'Just give it a go. One of the contacts is quite promising. His name's Arwel Gluebone.'

'Arwel Gluebone.'

'I thought you could help me lean on him a bit. You know: good cop, bad cop.'

I slipped down into the chair and watched as Calamity spread out the cards, turned a tumbler upside down, and then went across to close the curtains. She sat down and we put our fingers on top of the tumbler.

'Am I the good or the bad cop?' I asked.

'Bad. Shhh now.' Calamity closed her eyes and adopted a sort of spooky expression.

'Gluebone, are you there?'

The tumbler slid over to the Y.

'You moved it on purpose,' I said.

'I didn't,' protested Calamity.

'You must have done.'

'Sshhh! OK, Gluebone, I just want to go over a few things we discussed last time. You say you were taken in for questioning two days after the fire, right?'

The tumbler acquired a life of its own and slid across the table, doing a complicated arabesque from card to card. I didn't know how Calamity was doing it, but it was good. She wrote down the letters as they came. It said:

I stole candlesticks and stuck up toffs on the turnpike; I never done no kinky stuff like that.

'Why did they take you in then, Gluebone?'

I didn't do nuffin' I swear! It was the peelers. They were trying to fit me up. They needed to lock someone up quick y'see . . .

Calamity kicked me gently under the table. I looked at her.

She mouthed the words, 'Tough cop.' I pulled a face and she flashed an impatient frown at me.

I heaved a heavy sigh and said, 'OK, Gluebone, you bucket of shit, let's cut the fairy stories and start singing, shall we? You ravished her didn't you?'

I never I never!

'Thought you'd get one back on the old rich bastard in the fancy carriage, huh?!'

I tell you it wasn't like that.

'Tell us who did it then.'

I can't!

'You mean you won't!'

No I can't, it's more than my life is worth.

'I thought you were dead?'

I am! It's just a figure of speech – we still use it over here.

'Over where?'

The Shadow-Aberystwyth.

'What do you do down on the estate, anyway, feed the ducks?'

'He's a gardener's assistant,' whispered Calamity.

'I know your sort: all those lonely nights on your own in the potting shed, made you feel a bit frisky, didn't they? And there she is every night changing in full view of everyone in the bedroom window, all that fancy French lace and finery—'

She was a penny-farthing, I wouldn't touch her with a martingale.

'Tell it to the fairies, Gluebone, you did her in and tried to pin it on the stable boy—'

Says who?

'The lamplighter.'

You mean Pigmallow? That swill-pouch? Ha that's a laugh!

'He's no swill-pouch.'

I say he is.

'He's worth ten of you Gluebone . . .'

There was a pause, and then:

Oh I get it – the old soft peeler, hard peeler routine . . .

There was no more movement from the tumbler.

'Guess I must have leaned on him a bit too hard.' I smiled and Calamity frowned as if she thought I'd done it on purpose but couldn't say so. She gathered the cards together.

'We just need to work him a bit more. I reckon he's almost ready to give up the goods.'

I leant back in my chair, laced my fingers behind my head, and stared out of the window. The sound of traffic throbbed in the distance hypnotically, and slowly my eyelids slid down and I fell asleep. I awoke about ten minutes later to the sound of the phone ringing. Calamity answered. 'Knight Errant Investigations . . . Yes . . . Yes . . . Oh hi! . . . Fine and you? . . . Yeah we're fine . . . She what? . . . Oh. No . . . sorry not yet. But we're looking. Yeah, I can imagine. Tell her we're sorry. OK. Yeah and you too. Bye.' She stared at the phone for a second, lost in thought, and then looked up. 'That was Gabriel Bassett. Cleopatra was asking if we'd seen Mr Bojangles.'

'The air out at Ynyslas certainly tires you out, doesn't it?'

'You can say that again, we had a complaint from the coastguard about your snoring. They couldn't hear the helicopter.'

She took a card over to the incident board and pinned it on.

'What's that?'

'Just some stuff about one of my witnesses.'

'Which one?'

'Oh, you know, just background.'

Chapter 6

EEYORE LEANT HIS head against the wall of cheap Formica and viewed the world through that lozenge of grey the railway company call a window. Normally, trying to hold a conversation in these old diesel multiple units was like trying to talk in the engine room of a ship, but it was always eerily silent when the train slowed down as it approached Borth. We glided to a halt. One person got on, one got off. It never changed, as if they only sold one ticket per train. Eeyore peered out. 'Always looks like the town has got its shirt on back to front, doesn't it?'

I knew what he meant. Borth had length but no width. It was like a fake Dodge City constructed by a movie studio in which all the buildings were frontages and the train line was built on the wrong side.

We pulled out of Borth and continued gliding silently, hardly picking up speed, towards Ynyslas and Dovey Junction. The morning sun had just cleared the horizon above the flat watery world and threw a horizontal beam that made us squint and duck the dust particles that appeared from nowhere like swarms of gnats. The light had the colour of lemonade – not the stuff from the sweetshop, but the homemade drink, chilled and left on the sideboard in a glass pitcher and craved by children in the Famous Five books with the desperation of cocaine addicts. It filled the carriage with warm pale honey and gilded the golf course and beach and sea, and turned the marram grass on the dunes to golden stubble along the chin of the sky.

The track curved gently to the right and the carriage leaned slightly to accommodate the centrifugal forces, and we leaned, too, stiff as insects preserved in our cell of pale amber, and I thought of Myfanwy.

Whenever I look back it is always a particular afternoon that I recall. A summer's day when we ate strawberries and went swimming and lay back on hot sand and stared at the impossible blueness of the sky. Just a nice afternoon which has since acquired a freight of significance it never possessed at the time. Maybe that's what happiness is. Something beautiful we can only see from a distance, like the end of the rainbow. Silver plate added later by memory to days we have lost.

I remembered the man who had been in my office earlier that morning. He was the sort you get from time to time. Came to report a missing person – that great mainstay of the snooper's profession.

'I can't live without her,' he said.

'Really?' I said. 'How did you manage in the years before you met her?

He didn't have an answer to that, he just whined. I told him to pull himself together. And get a shave. I said, 'My partner, Calamity, will be along in a second, do you want her to see you in that state, you great big lump?' He said he didn't know what to do, and I said he could start by being a man. He asked, what good that would do. I was going to throw him out. Then Calamity arrived, looked round the empty room and said, 'Who were you talking to?'

'Just voices on the radio.'

Even in midsummer, when the sun's fire smelted the Prom, Eeyore would insist on wearing a jacket and tie to lead the donkeys. It wasn't a great suit, and usually came from the charity shop, but it was a suit. But today he had his Sunday one on, which was a little better but had less straw. Eeyore hailed from an era when to make a journey in anything more auspicious than a bus necessitated dressing for the occasion, even if, as today, that journey was off to see two men in prison. One in a tower of bars, and one in a self-constructed tower of Babel.

'Last time I went to Shrewsbury,' said Eeyore, 'the train had proper carriages. With a corridor.' He knocked the plastic wall with a knuckle. 'They sell this stuff in Woolies. You wouldn't want it in your bathroom, would you?'

'Maybe they think if they make it cheap enough no one will rob it.'

'They're right. Frankie Mephisto would never have sullied his hands on a train made out of plastic wood veneer. A real train has proper upholstery, and a guard with a flag, and the name of the company written along the side in gold letters.' He warmed to his theme. 'Same with police cars, you see. What are they now? British School of Motoring cast-offs with an American siren. No self-respecting crook is going to be chased by that. It's degrading. In the old days we had Jags with bells. With real bells you've got a proper chase. The young don't understand these things. They think a siren is easier to maintain, same as these awful trains, and maybe they are, but why does everything have to be easy? Polishing your shoes isn't easy either but I could never respect a man who didn't do it.'

The last few words trailed off as he returned a wistful gaze to the world outside. Eeyore was troubled. Since the matriarch had fallen sick, discipline in the herd had broken down. Last night Sugarpie bit Erlkönig on the flank and this morning Miss Muffet was gone.

'She'll be back, Dad, don't worry.'

'I know.'

'Couple of days, give her time to get a bit hungry, she'll come back. They always do.'

'I know son. I wasn't even thinking about her.' He continued looking out, lost in thought, across the landscape crawling by, and added, 'Just can't think where she could have got to.'

Mrs Prestatyn had visited Eeyore a week ago, and that was the reason he was here today and not searching for a wayward donkey. She'd received a letter from Frankie Mephisto in Shrewsbury prison. It wasn't the first time he'd written to her, she said. He'd been sending her letters on and off for the past few years. And she'd never told anyone. But he was due out this month and that changed things. Mrs Prestatyn's daughter had been seventeen when she disappeared. It was just after the Great Cliff Railway Robbery, of which Frankie was the mastermind. She left one morning to go fishing in the estuary, as she normally did in summer, and never came back. A few weeks later they found out that the gang had used the Loothouse to count the money and in the cellar they found the missing girl's shoe. It didn't prove anything. She could have gone there herself, for any number of reasons, but the coincidence was too great for most folk. Eeyore had worked the case. Every old cop has a case like this: the one that stays with him long after he leaves the force. It binds him to Mrs Prestatyn in a way neither of them quite understands. Like a secret shared between two lovers from long ago. Once a month he walks past her house on the Prom and waves at her in the window, airing a room that has lain empty for twenty-five years.

The letters from Frankie were always the same. He said he had been visited by the Holy Ghost. That he had changed. And he asked for Mrs Prestatyn's blessing.

'It was never proved that Frankie's mob killed Mrs Prestatyn's girl,' said Eeyore. 'We never found a body or anything. Just the shoe. Frankie always said they had nothing to do with it.'

'Do you believe him?'

'No.'

'Do you think he's likely to change his tune now?'

'Not really, but I feel as if I owe it to Mrs Prestatyn to try.'

'Surely he's not serious?'

'It's hard to say. I've seen cases like this before. It's always damned difficult because people like Frankie devote a lifetime to the art of counterfeiting honesty and sincerity. So how can you tell? And yet you can't dismiss it, because twenty-five years in prison is a long time. It changes a man. Except for the irredeemable psychopaths, they all mellow to some extent; it's not unknown for them to find the Lord. Or He finds them. If Frankie would just tell Mrs Prestatyn where her girl is buried, so her soul could find peace, that would be a Christian act about which there could be no dispute. And what would it cost him now? After all this time? Nothing as far as I can see.'

'Asking for her blessing strikes me as a tall order.'

'That's because you only see her as she is now. You don't see what a good woman she was before she lost her daughter. She used to be a lifeguard, did you know that?'

I shook my head.

'Long ago, when she was a young woman. Saved a couple of drowning holiday-makers, gave them the kiss of life. We tried to give her a commendation, once, civic honour or something. But she spurned it; scorned the very idea of receiving a prize for saving a life.' He nodded to himself. 'I admire that.'

The train slowed down at the approach to Shrewsbury station and glided between the eleventh-century Abbey and the stadium of Shrewsbury Town Football Club. Two sacred arenas where men chanted and waited for a miracle that never came.

A group of hard-looking men stood at the platform's end; men with shaven heads, and flattened noses that reminded me of the boxer at the funfair who takes on all-comers. And never loses. Crude, homemade tattoos adorned the backs of their hands. We walked up to them and Eeyore made a slight nod in recognition to the lead man and he returned the nod.

'Archie.'

'Eeyore.'

'Long time no see.'

'You're looking well.'

'You too.'

It was the highly deferential exchange of men who respect but do not particularly like each other. The head man, Archie, was shadowed by two men who were obviously the muscle of the group. They stared at us through narrowed eyes, wary of trickery.

'Frankie sends his regards,' said Archie. 'You'll forgive me for asking, but are either of you carrying?'

We shook our heads and one of the tough guys ran practised fingers through my coat checking for ironware. He was about to start on Eeyore and Archie stopped him. 'The old man's OK.'

We were blindfolded and helped into the back of a car that smelt of old leather.

'Are the blindfolds necessary?' I said. 'I thought Frankie was serving the remainder doing community service.'

'His whole life has been a service to the community, only some sections of it don't see it that way.'

After a short drive, the car stopped and we were ushered into a building in which everybody spoke in whispers and people's feet made loud squeaking sounds. There was also a rustle of newspaper. We climbed some stairs and went through a spring-loaded door that smelt of brass polish and then the blindfolds were removed. I found myself looking into the eyes of an owl. A stuffed one, in a dusty case.

Frankie Mephisto came out from behind the case and reached out a hand in greeting to Eeyore. He was smaller than I expected, thin and wiry, but slightly rounded around the belly in the way old people sometimes get when they lose their flesh but still put it on around the waist. He was wearing a pale green paisley-pattern shirt and matching tie with a sleeveless maroon v-necked sweater. The sort that comes as a set in a cellophane-wrapped ensemble from British Home Stores. His face seemed amiable enough, and had that vague familiarity that notorious criminals share with celebrities. His pate shone with the patina that foreheads get from a lifetime of hitting noses.

'Good to see you, Eeyore.'

'Frankie.'

'My boys been looking after you?'

'Can't complain.'

'Come, we'll go to my little cubbyhole and a have a cuppa.' He led us through a room of glass cases, covered in dust, a natural history section that had been closed for a decade or more. His cubbyhole was piled high with papers and books. There were seats and a desk, a kettle and a jar of instant coffee.

'You were lucky to be sent to a prison overlooking the station, given how you feel about trains,' said Eeyore in a weak attempt at pleasantries.

'Luck has nothing to do with it. It's Home Office policy. It's like a baby's dummy.'

'I thought maybe they would try and wean you off.'

'No point; it goes too deep. Ask the Jesuits.'

'The Jesuits?' I asked politely.

'It was them, wasn't it? They said, "Give me the child until he is seven and I will give you the man."'

I slid my gaze across to Eeyore who hardened his features with that expression meant to convey the instruction, 'Humour him!'

'Seventh birthday, that's when it happens. That's the day a crook discovers his vocation in life – banks or trains.' Frankie poured the boiling water into the cups and stirred the instant coffee. 'Rightly speaking, he doesn't actually choose – that's done for him by his aunt. Wouldn't you agree? She's the one who chooses the birthday card.' He turned to Eeyore for confirmation, and Eeyore nodded as if it was kitchen table wisdom.

'She's the one.' He stirred the coffees loudly with a dessert spoon. 'You remember that card – all boys get it – either a racing car on the front, or – ah sweet memory – a puffing billy! And those gold embossed letters, *Now you are Seven*. And inside, the postal order for five shillings. That's when the love is born.'

'And you never lose it.'

He laughed wistfully, 'No you never lose it. What was it Oscar Wilde said? "Each man robs the thing he loves."'

I let my gaze wander across the glass cases that were piled higgledy-piggledy outside the room.

'Why are you tormenting Mrs Prestatyn, Frankie?' asked Eeyore. 'Don't you think she's suffered enough?'

Frankie looked serious. 'We've all suffered, Eeyore. All of us. She doesn't have a monopoly on it.'

'You took away her girl.'

'So they say.'

'Everyone knows it was you, Frankie.'

'There was never any proof.'

'They found the shoe at the Loothouse.'

'So what? When's the last time you walked along the beach and didn't find an old shoe washed up? What does that prove?'

'It's buried in Llanbadarn Cemetery, a single shoe in a coffin; Mrs Prestatyn goes and puts flowers on the grave every week, waiting . . .'

'Just like Cinderella.'

'It was your mob, Frankie. The only thing we don't know is what you did with her.'

'Say it was,' said Frankie thoughtfully. 'Say it was. What of it? I was an angry man in those days, Eeyore. A man with a heart so full of fury I scarce knew myself most of the time what I was doing or why. But I'm not the man I was when I came here twenty-five years ago. I didn't write to torment her; I sought her blessing, that's all.'

'She doesn't believe you. You've made a lifetime career out of lying and deception.'

'Oh, I know that. I know she doesn't. She wrote and told me – I bet she didn't tell you this: she wrote and told me I was putting it on so when I died I could sweet-talk my way round St Peter at the Gate. But she wouldn't let me get away with it, she wrote. She said she would see me dead yet, and stand over my corpse and then she would bend down and bite my tongue out so I couldn't bamboozle my way into heaven. Bite my tongue out she said, like in that movie set in the Turkish prison.'

'You can't blame her for feeling like that.'

'Let me tell you something, Eeyore. You see all this? This building?' He flung out an arm. 'This used to be the school where Charles Darwin studied, did you know that? That guy who said we were descended from the apes.'

'I didn't know that,' said Eeyore.

'That's right, they laughed at him, but they obviously didn't know anything about apes. I've been reading all about it. It's shocking the things apes do in the wild. They kill their children and eat them; drive the elderly out and watch them starve; rape the girls; wage war on each other. Can anyone seriously doubt that we are descended from them?' He motioned towards the cabinets with the hand holding the coffee mug, 'They are our brothers to the last detail. We've even got one in there that died of a heart attack like my old man. And one that lost his eye in a fight like my mother.'

'Where's this leading, Frankie?' I asked.

Frankie gave me a frigid stare, the sort of look that recalls a time when no man would have dared talk to him like that. He broke off and stared into the middle distance where problems of the ineffable are traditionally to be found.

'I used to think that's all there was. All we were. Apes in suits. But then one day, fifteen or so years ago, something happened. Something happened to change all that.' Frankie paused a while and his eyes glistened with the beginning of tears. 'You could say on that day I walked with Jesus. I know you will sneer. You will ask what on earth would Jesus want with a slag like Frankie Mephisto. But you would be wrong to think like that. Slags like Frankie are exactly the sort of sinner Jesus came to save. On that day he walked with me, and he told me, he said, "Frankie, I came down to earth to teach you lot how to love, and you fucking ignored me!"'

He wiped a sleeve roughly across his brimming eyes, stood up, and invited us over to the window. 'That used to be the old prison over there a hundred years ago. And down there, where the car park is now, was the gallows. That's one reason why they moved Darwin's school. Because they thought it was inappropriate for the schoolboys to witness public executions in their school yard. Biggest mistake they could have made, if you ask me. Every school should have a gallows in the yard. That way the kids might learn something.'

Eeyore and I walked back towards the door.

'Just tell the poor woman where her daughter is buried,' said Eeyore.

'I can't do that, Eeyore,' said Frankie. 'I can't do that. Even if I wanted to, I couldn't. Because I don't know. I had a *consigliere* who took care of things like that.'

'And who was that?'

'You know I can't tell you.'

'Can't you at least ask him what he did with the girl?'

'I have done. He says he can't remember.'

We walked down to the river and along the footpath towards the Royal Salop Infirmary. It stood perched high on a hill overlooking the Severn, a building that had started life a century ago as the traditional home of the damned, a workhouse.

They had told us we were wasting our time. They said Brainbocs lived in his own cell now, one for which there was no key. A portable bubble that went wherever he did, enclosing him with a perimeter that stopped a foot or so from his outstretched fingertips. A bubble whose walls were made from the translucent membrane of a language no one understood. A tower of Babel with the entrance bricked up. They said he seemed happy enough in there but didn't admit visitors.

The secure wing was on the top floor and an orderly showed us to the door.

'Lives in his own private world,' he said. 'Sits and talks all day to an invisible interlocutor.'

He reached into the pocket of his white coat and drew out a set of keys and let us in. It was bright and sunny inside the room. Brainbocs sat curled up in a foetal position in the corner, rocking gently on his haunches and intoning something to himself. All around were images of dinosaurs, crudely scribbled on every wall.

'They brought him from the prison in this state. We've never seen anything like it before.'

Brainbocs looked up at us as if a few rays of light from our world had managed to penetrate the membrane.

'Why dinosaurs?'

'Who knows? Some chthonic zoomorphic associations . . . salvific anamnesia perhaps . . .'

'Maybe he just likes dinosaurs,' said Eeyore.

The orderly looked surprised and he stroked his chin. 'Mmmmm, we hadn't thought of that,' he said. 'It's conceivable, I suppose.'

'What made him go like this?' I asked.

He considered his reply. 'He was given a task when he arrived in prison. To solve a problem for Frankie Mephisto.'

'What sort of problem?'

'A metaphysical one.'

'It must have been a hard one,' said Eeyore.

The orderly agreed. 'Clearly. Chaps like him normally have a tough time of it in prison, as you know. They are much in demand as . . . er . . . as . . . bedtime companions. Frankie offered the boy his protection in return for which he had to solve the metaphysical problem. He was locked in a tower with nothing but a chamber pot on which to sit and cogitate. When they opened the door three months later this is how they found him. Fascinating case. We're hoping it will make us famous.'

The clinical detachment with which the orderly talked of the boy's suffering struck me as callous. But, to be fair, it would not have rankled with Brainbocs. He embodied perhaps better than anyone the Promethean arrogance and moral ambivalence of the scientist. Since leaving the cradle he had been obsessed with the need to peer through doors the gods have closed to us, to pick the locks, and tamper with forces better left alone. Pandora, Baron von Frankenstein, the men from the Manhattan Project . . . the roll call of Man's dishonour is long but they were mere trick cyclists in a circus compared to Brainbocs and the forces he once tried to let out of the bottle.

I unzipped my travelling bag and took out, with a faint prickling of embarrassment, a Myfanwy 'walking-talking' doll I'd picked up earlier from Siop-y-Pethe in Great Darkgate Street. Eeyore watched me, his brow curving in what might have been a look of interest or a frown. I pulled the cord and the doll started to sing in a squeaky voice.

'Myfanwy boed yr holl o'th fywyd
Dan heulwen disglair canol dydd . . .'

Brainbocs stopped rocking and listened, eyeing us sideways, like a bird.

'Aug hofiar oll o'th add ewidion.'

'That's amazing!' said the orderly. 'The doll speaks the same language!'

We turned to face him in joint surprise.

'How can it be possible? The same language?!'

'It's Welsh,' said Eeyore.

'What?'

'It's Welsh.'

'What's that?'

'They speak it over there in Wales.' He pointed through the wall, vaguely westward.

'You mean those people have their own language?'

'Yes.'

'Well bugger me! We thought he was making it up.'

Brainbocs started to sing along. And then so did Eeyore in a soft melancholy baritone.

'A rho dy law, Myfanwy dirion
I ddim ond dweud y gair Ffarwel.'

'It's the song *Myfanwy*,' I said. 'Something like, "Give me your hand, my sweet Myfanwy, But one last time, to say farewell."'

The orderly scratched his head, then picked up a sheaf of papers and threw them down in disgust on to the bedside cabinet. 'Dr Molyneux will be devastated. He's been transcribing it for the *Lancet*.'

I walked over and placed the doll gently in the hand of Brainbocs. He gazed at me with the trusting eyes of a child; then returned his gaze to the doll. I directed his hand to the draw-cord at the back and showed him how to make her sing. He tugged and released the cord. The homunculus Myfanwy crackled into life, her china blue eyes flicking open like those of Frankenstein's monster when the lightning hits the gothic spire above the lab. Brainbocs's eyes, too, shot open but in purest wonder. A sound like a baby's chuckle came from his throat and from the throat of Myfanwy a different sound emerged: tiny and tinny, as if she had fallen down a manhole and was singing from far away in the labyrinth beneath the city, the song we knew her by twittered forth. Brainbocs stroked his doll.

'At least he'll have someone to talk to now,' said Eeyore. We turned to leave. At the doorway I picked up the transcripts of Brainbocs's private language and shoved them into my bag. 'I don't suppose Dr Molyneux will be needing these now, he can take notes direct from the doll.'

We walked down a corridor where once only the damned had

trod; the echoes of our footfalls pursued by the plaintive sound of a boy and doll singing a duet.

'Myfanwy boed yr holl o'th fywyd
Dan heulwen disglair canol dydd . . .'

Chapter 7

LLUNOS WAS WAITING outside the railway station in a prowl car, and he had a photographer with him. He nodded to me and I climbed in.

'So what are we doing then?' I asked

'We're doing something we should have done a long time ago. We're closing down Aberystwyth.'

'Uh-huh,' I replied distantly. I was tired after the journey to Shrewsbury. The sky had turned the colour of geraniums, which was soothing to stare at, but they were flowers from a hothouse and thunderclouds were piling up above the rooftops. I could still hear the strains of Brainbocs singing, echoing down the corridors in the workhouse of my head.

'Five days she's been gone, and so far not a squeak from anyone. Which isn't right. Someone knows. Someone always knows. There's a new game in town. It's called Llunos plays hardball.'

'How does it differ from the old one?'

'The people of this town will look back on the old version as a golden age; they'll think they were blessed.'

I noticed a police van fall in behind us. 'You reckon hurting people will make them tell us what we want to know?'

'Usually does in my experience.'

'How does closing things down help?'

'It hurts them where it hurts most. The wallet. Everywhere you go in this town someone is making money. Some straight, some crooked. But either way the tough guys take a rake off. From tonight they don't get anything. Not until they tell me what they know. The town is closed.'

He wiped the back of his hand across a brow slimy with sweat, but achieved no relief. His shirt stuck to him; his eyebrows were sodden; it was going to be one of those nights. A night for the policeman to sit with feet on the desk in the blast of a fan. A night to listen without interest to the scuffles and shouts from the entrance hall as the flatfoots bring in the evening's trawl. A night when even the sea is too tired to move and clings to the face of the earth like petroleum jelly; and the stones of the beach release the heat of day like the lining of a kiln, or one of those authentic tandoor ovens the Indian restaurants boast of possessing (that ancient method of cooking savoured by long dead moguls and pissed people). A night to sit in the febrile air, torpid, motionless so as not to quicken the metabolism like those lizards that lick their own eyes. A night in which the only movement should come from the hammer, anvil, and stirrup in the policeman's ear as he listens to the confessions of lonely farmers from empty hills whispering on the edge of sanity on the late-night radio phone-in. A night to do nothing at all except hope for it to pass and for tomorrow's freshening breeze. A night to do nothing, least of all close down a town.

We pulled up outside Alexandra Hall.

'We'll start with the bivalves,' said Llunos as if the bottom of the evolutionary chain was the obvious place to start. We walked up to the twenty-four-hour Whelk Stall. The kid in charge was setting out the evening's selection: pools of vinegar in crinkle-sided cardboard trays in which floated the shrivelled viscera of the sea; wooden spoons; jars in which more bits of sea flesh floated like preserved organs in a ghoul's laboratory; the stench of seaweed on rocks uncovered at high tide.

'Are you sure they are bivalves?' I said.

The kid looked on warily as the phalanx of uniformed police closed in. Llunos banged his palm on the counter top and said 'Shop!'

The kid pointed to the menu pinned to the outside of the kiosk.

'Whelks,' said Llunos.

The kid pointed.

'Are they bivalves?'

The answer was a blink.

'You got a tongue in your head?'

'They get 'em from over there.' He pointed to the rocks.

Llunos stuck his fingers into the vinegar and took out something that looked like gristle. He popped it into his mouth, grimaced and spat it out. Then he picked up the tray and held it out to me.

'Take one.'

'I'd rather not.'

'I need a second opinion. Don't want to bust this kid for something he didn't do.'

The look in the kid's eyes wavered between fear and uncertainty. I took a whelk and crunched it. 'Just like usual – a vinegary gritty rubbery knot of nothing.'

'What do you think the grit is?'

'Sand in the intestine I suppose.'

'That's what I thought.' He shouted to one of the deputies. 'Throw him in the cell. Impound the kiosk.'

'What's going on?' shouted the kid. 'What did I do?'

'Stealing sand from the beach,' said Llunos and walked off.

We wandered up to the bandstand. A handful of pensioners sat in deck chairs arrayed in a semi-circle, a coach party from somewhere far away that was worse than here. They were watching a woman sing. She was in her forties – heavily made up and wearing jeans cut for her granddaughter – singing, to an audience that probably didn't need the advice, 'Don't sleep in the Subway'. The audience looked on with stony, expressionless faces; grim masks of politeness concealing resentment and shame. They knew no one was seriously expected to enjoy this singing, it was charity. This was no superannuated seaside entertainer brought low by life – a fate that might have echoed their own.

It was not someone whose name had once topped the bill and then slipped season by season, rung by rung, down the ladder until it reached the bottom line on the poster, to share billing with the birdsong man and the balloon twister. This woman had never sung professionally in her life and was here because she volunteered to a group of people who spent their lives organising teas for the donkey derby. A committee of fools who, in a different lifetime, would have administered the Poor Law and collected alms to buy bars for the workhouse windows.

We watched in disgust and sorrow for these kindly people who perhaps last visited Aberystwyth more than twenty years ago and danced at the Pier, or dodged a fist fight between a mod and a rocker. Llunos signalled to the deputies to close the metal concertina doors of the bandstand and, in an act of genuine charity, took the mike out of the singer's hand. He said, 'Show's over folks, back to your lives.'

Up near the Pier we stopped at the hot-dog barrow. Llunos rolled up his sleeves and then mimed the action of a competition weight-lifter dusting his hands in chalk. He squatted down, put his hands under the barrow, took the strain, grunted and slowly rose keeping his back straight and powering with his thighs the way the work safety posters teach you. The kid in the barrow made a 'Wh . . . wh . . . wh . . .' sound before gravity finished the work that Llunos had started and the barrow crashed on to its side.

'King of exercises: the squat,' he said.

Frying sausages and anaemic buns spilled out across the pavement. The vendor crawled out and watched from the floor as Llunos proceeded to stamp on the food like a grape-crusher. The deputies grinned in awed disbelief and Llunos shouted at them, 'Well, don't just stand and gawp, help me!' They jumped to attention and joined in the trampling. The vendor made a token verbal protest but wisely left it at that. I felt sorry for him but I knew there was no point saying anything. This was Llunos's way of finding Myfanwy and the strange thing was, it was just as likely to work as anything I had done. We closed down the hot-dog stall for selling food that failed to meet various hygiene regulations and moved on. But before we did, Llunos cursed the hot-dog vendor for the mustard on his shoe and made him clean it off.

The Punch and Judy man was charged with unlawful assembly and conspiracy to shout 'Oh no he didn't!'

From there we turned inland and walked down Eastgate Street to the Indian. It was still early, a time when the eye of the hurricane is passing over the restaurant and a deceptive, preternatural calm reigns. Through the window we saw real candles on the tables and linen that was starched and crisp and white. Three hours from now and the linen would have been replaced by builder's polythene. The only diners were couples on their first dates. They sat opposite each other and talked stiffly in undertones about trivia. You passed them, sometimes, these people sitting in the window, and long after you got home the image danced before your eyes, of two ghosts whom you dimly remembered from a time long, long ago at infant school. You hadn't seen either of them for thirty years, life had changed them beyond all recognition from the toddlers they had been, and yet you recognised them instantly. For a brief moment you were struck by the coincidence of seeing them sitting opposite each other in the window, and then you realised that, given the limited pack life had to deal, it was inevitable. Like horses on a merry-go-round, you tried them all in the end. The only way off was to marry or die.

Oscar the manager smiled and walked across.

'I hear you're serving dog here,' said Llunos.

The manager looked hurt, and whispered, 'Keep your voice down, you're giving trade secrets away.'

'I'm not joking, pal.'

'Llunos, please, you know those stories are just urban legends.

Do you think I would serve dog to the good folk of Aberystwyth? Of course not, it's just soya with dog flavour.'

I laughed and said, 'No law against that.'

'Whose side are you on?' said Llunos.

At the Pier we walked down the tunnel of wood along the side towards the Moulin. Twin black velvet curtains marked the door to the famous club. There was no doorman at this hour and not even the hat-check girl, so we walked through unchallenged. It still smelled faintly of last night's drink and cigarettes and on some tables the detritus of the previous night had still not been cleared. Silver disco balls hung from the roof, motionless like the innards of a stopped clock; nearby were the swings which in better days had been manned by satyrs. In these leaner times even Pan had to lay off staff. There are few places in the world more forlorn than a night club in daylight. We walked across the dance floor and headed towards the door marked 'Private'. Our metal-tipped shoes clacked harshly on a floor that was seasoned, like the floor in the saloon at Dodge City, with the varnish of human woe. Over the years it had borne witness to every transaction that could pass between two human hearts. The last time I had been here was the famous night Mrs Bligh-Jones danced the last tango in Aberystwyth and then went off for a rendezvous with her lover. The bullet that passed through her head can still be seen embedded in the brickwork outside Woolies.

And it was in an earlier incarnation of this club, in another part of town, that Myfanwy used to hold us in thrall to her voice; a place where lesser mortals went upon the eternal errand of mankind, to sip the wine of bewilderment and exchange their hearts. Later, some of them would turn up in my office tormented by the suspicion that their sweetheart's heart had grown cold. They squirmed on the client's chair, impaled by the need to know the truth.

So I would tell them the truth about love.

The story of two people who found each other after a

lifetime's searching. Two lovers so perfectly attuned it was uncanny. God must have fashioned them from the same clay; Destiny with a big D bought the tickets for the bus on which they met. They were made for each other. It was spooky.

And they would look at me in wonder, faces lit up with amazement, b . . . b . . . but how did you know?

I said I'd heard the same story four times already that week.

No, the truth about love is this: if they'd missed the bus they would now be saying the same things about a person they met five minutes later on the Prom; their love was an accident; their lover just a nobody, gift-wrapped by their own imagination. There was nothing uncanny about it. They should have kept the drawbridge to their hearts closed; kept the moat free from weed. That's what I did. And then one day Myfanwy swam across. It was as if we were made for each other. It was spooky.

The door at the back opened on to a narrow corridor with a faded maroon carpet. Along one side were windows looking out on to the sea and along the other a series of doors. A woman in a low-cut cocktail frock barred our way. She must have been getting on for fifty, hair bundled high and sculpted with spray, dull with the intense purple-black colour that comes from a cheap dye bottle. A mama-san straight from central casting.

'We're on business,' said Llunos.

'There's no one down there,' said the mama-san.

'No need for you to look so worried then.'

He stopped at a door with the air of one who knows exactly what he is looking for and raised his knee. He nodded to the photographer who hoisted his camera. Llunos kicked the door open and the cameraman leaped in and filled the room with a blinding flash. A man sat up in a double bed astonished. On either side of him were two girls, naked except for their stovepipe hats. They pulled the bedclothes up over their breasts and stared doe-eyed in wonder. A small boy dressed as a cherub stood in the corner playing electric harp. He wore a curly blond wig, a nappy and had gold paint on his face. It was Poxcrop.

'I can't believe it,' said Llunos in fake amazement. 'It's the Mayor!'

'What the hell do you think you're doing?' demanded the Mayor.

'Cleaning up the town. I thought you'd approve.'

'I'll have your badge for this!'

'I thought you'd say that. That's why I brought along Lord Snowdon. Anything happens to me and Mrs Mayor gets the holiday snaps.'

'This is outrageous!'

'Save it, I'm not listening.' He turned to the naked girls. 'OK, Councillors, get your wraps you're going to the station.'

I walked over to Poxcrop. He said, 'It's not like how it looks, Jack.'

'Sure. No law against playing the harp. I'm musical myself.'

Llunos came over, as the Mayor hopped from leg to leg trying to get into his trousers.

'The kid's all right,' I said. 'He's a friend of mine.'

'Funny taste in friends.'

'It's not like how it seems,' said the kid.

'No,' said Llunos. 'It never is.'

'You want juicy photos,' said Poxcrop, 'You should have called me – I got plenty.'

I laughed and pulled off his wig. Llunos grabbed him gently by the wrist and said, 'It's all right kid, you're not in trouble here. Maybe you can do me a favour, would you like that?'

Poxcrop nodded.

'You saw what happened here tonight,' said Llunos. 'I want you to tell people about it. Spread it around. Tell them Aberystwyth has closed for business by order of the Mayor and the Chief of Police. And we don't re-open until someone gives me the name of the scumbag who took Myfanwy.'

From the Pier we carried on to the harbour, to the point where the pavement ends and continues for another hundred yards in an artificial limb of wood. Lorelei, the ancient streetwalker, stood leaning against the railings, perched above the rocks of the beach. Lorelei the sailor's doom; standing and waiting; just waiting. Even here at the harbour mouth there was no breeze to bring relief from the sultry night, but unmindful of the seasons Lorelei stood huddled in a jumble-sale coat. The fabric was mottled and blotched in a pattern suggestive of a leopard – the cat seemingly put on this earth just so that night clubs would have sofas and harlots coats to wear.

Llunos sidled up to her and stood at the railings with the air of someone who had something to say but has thought better of it. She glanced at the policeman briefly, then returned her gaze to the ocean and her thoughts, whatever they consisted of: she who had seen everything there was to see inside a man's heart and had not been impressed by it. After a second or two Llunos touched her gently on the elbow and said, 'Take care.' Then turned away. For some, the news that Aberystwyth was closing down came too late.

I picked up the car and drove home to Borth, and stopped off at the Friendship for a pint. The air was now pregnant with static and you could read the message of what the night held in store in the eyes of the dogs in the pub – fear reflecting in the wetness for the terror they knew was coming but for which they had no name. I drank slowly, without pleasure, and thought of my own terror.

Those fools, the poets, compare a girl in the bloom of youth to a flower. But that's not right; flowers are too tough. A soap bubble would be better. A thing of wonder, too fragile to exist. Myfanwy didn't understand this. She was in her early twenties and considered herself immortal. But her invulnerability was a chimera, nothing more than the involuntary trick of a girl sleepwalking along the edge of a cliff, who manages it only because she doesn't open her eyes. Watching her walk down the street to buy a copy of *Just Seventeen* and return in one piece was to behold a miracle of deliverance.

She didn't understand it because she was young and it takes a long time to acquire an understanding of the basic truths of life. Such as mortality. And the ease with which flesh can be damaged beyond repair. And of the things you find locked away in the little-used rooms in that mansion called the human heart. Llunos showed me an article once in *National Geographic* about a girl in Nepal sold to a brothel at the age of seven. I looked at it and had to wonder what could be worse. And then he told me the woman who sold her was her mother, and I had to wonder what could be worse. Then he described how the girl had escaped and found her way home. And how her mother beat her and sent her back. And I had to wonder . . .

Every policeman knows the truth: there is no limit to the things that people will do to other people. And every torturer knows the way to make a man betray himself. It doesn't matter how tough he is, how many torments he can endure on his own body, he can't endure even the whisper of evil being done to his darling. The thought reduces him to a gibbering fool. Torquemada knew it. So did Vlad the Impaler.

I put the half-finished pint down on the table and said goodbye to the only decent soul in the pub. The dog. I drove slowly down to Ynyslas. The sky in the west above the bay was sparking repeatedly now, like broken neon. And each time the sea and horizon would be revealed and then fade into darkness again when the sluggardly thunder caught up and rumbled. Midway between Borth and Ynyslas the flash in the sky picked out a girl walking uncertainly down the edge of the lane. I stopped and offered a lift and she climbed in, smelling of ale and cigarette smoke. It was Seren, the girl Sister Cunégonde had accused of planting the locket.

We drove in silence for a while and then, just to say something, I said, 'Been to the pub?'

'Uh-huh.'

She was wearing a Levi's jacket over what looked like an old wedding dress from a charity shop or church bazaar. It had deep gashes in the fabric, through which the white lace of her underwear peeped, cuts that could only have been done deliberately unless the bride had been savagely murdered. It was gathered at the waist in a thick, studded leather belt that looked like the collar of Spike the cartoon dog, and the hem of the dress, also made by slashing, stopped a few inches below the belt. The rest was flesh – pretty bare tanned legs and Doc Martens boots. Her hands lay in her lap, covered up to the fingers by the denim of sleeves that were too long.

'Did you have a nice time?'

'Not bad.'

'Was Sister Cunégonde there too?'

'Ha ha. She hates me.'

'I'm sure she doesn't.'

'Shows you how much you know. She'd kill me if she could get away with it. The only thing that stops her is they'd send her to prison.'

'I expect she likes you but finds you a bit difficult sometimes.'

'Bollocks! She wants to kill me. I caught her once trying to suffocate me with a pillow when I was sleeping. I said, "What the fuck are you doing?" And she told me not to swear. Like you're not allowed to say "fuck" when someone is trying to murder you.'

'How much have you had to drink tonight?'

'Nothing much. Six gin and tonics and two Babychams, three halves of cider and a rum and coke. I know why she hates me, too. Do you want to know?'

'OK. Why?'

'Because she thinks Meredith's my dad. See! That's another thing you didn't know. She's jealous, you see.'

'Why would she think that?'

'Because everyone in the village thinks it. Because he went away, you see. Then he came back for a summer before I was born and then went away again. And, bingo, nine months later I turn up on the church steps.'

'I thought you were brought by the social services.'

'I was speaking figuratively.'

'Oh, I see.'

'Like the Bible. It sounds like rubbish but it's a special way of telling the truth.' She giggled. 'Meredith's not my dad. Anyone can see that.'

'Why would Sister Cunégonde care anyway?'

'Because she and Meredith were lovers once. When they were kids. He got her up the duff. I bet you thought I didn't know that either.'

'So she's jealous?'

'Right. That's why she's always staring at me, you see. When she thinks I'm not looking. And why she pulls a face like she's swallowed a toad. She's trying to figure out who my mum was, trying to guess which of the girls from Borth lay in the hay with her darling Meredith going, "Oh, oh, oh, no, no, Meredith, no, no, yes, yes, yes—"'

'All right, I know what it sounds like.'

'You watch, one day she'll murder me for sure, stuff a pillow on my face while I'm asleep and everyone will think it was an accident.'

We reached the Waifery and I pulled up at a safe distance so the sound of the car would not alert anyone to the return of a missing waif.

'Does she beat you?'

'No. Never. Just makes me eat bread and water.'

'Bread and water?'

'Well . . . bread and tea.'

'Anything on the bread?'

'Only ham. Or cheese. Sometimes chicken. Are you going to tell about tonight?'

'Probably not.'

'You're a private eye, aren't you?'

'Yes.'

'Will you do me a favour?'

'Depends what it is.'

'If I die and they say it was an accident, will you investigate my death?'

'Seren, you're not going to die.'

'But, if I do, will you?'

'But—'

'Please Louie! Please. All you have to do is ask what happened and see if there was anything fishy about it.'

'OK. I'll do that. Now will you do me a favour?'

'Of course. Ask anything in the whole wide world.'

'Tell me why you planted the locket on the dunes.'

'Who says I did?'

'You know damn well who. Why did you do it?'

'Are you angry?'

'No.'

'Did you love Myfanwy?'

'Yes.'

'I'm so sorry. I wish I hadn't done it.'

'But why did you?'

'I don't know.' She opened the car door and put one leg outside and said in a voice that mimicked Sister Cunégonde, 'I suppose, because I'm impossible.'

Seren climbed the gate with the ease of someone who has had plenty of practice and I sat in the car for a while watching the darkened school. Then I got out and started to wander aimlessly along the sands by the water's edge, with no particular direction in mind, just away from the caravan that I had made my home. The thunder rumbled, getting closer. The only other sound was the occasional bark of a dog. I smelt the rain before I felt it. A hot, bright, sharp summer wetness that suddenly filled the air. And then a fat drop of water on my face. And then a patter of them and soon a continuous curtain. I ran towards the shack at the bottom of the peat cutter's garden.

It was a stable, built of stone with exposed low beams of wood and a slate roof. Some of the tiles were missing and through the gaps I could see the luminescence of a rainy night sky. A horse, unseen in the darkness, whinnied and stamped and bumped about in a stall. The drum beat of thunder and the presence of a stranger filling him with a fear that was palpable to me. The reek of straw and the hot meaty smell of horse combined with the tang of warm rain hitting parched soil.

The light was on in the peat cutter's kitchen and I could see him at the table, sitting motionless, perhaps studying the soil geologist's book. Perhaps doing nothing at all except staring at the grain of the wood and searching for meaning. Gradually, the rumble of thunder grew fainter and the flashes briefer and almost as suddenly as it started the rain eased off. I was about to leave when the approach of a storm lamp weaving across the marsh stopped me. I waited. I could make out the outline of a figure in the night carrying the lamp, heading towards the cottage. The figure knocked on the door. The peat cutter got up and walked out of the rectangle of light that was the kitchen window. A few seconds later the back door opened; there was little light from inside. I could intuit rather than see him on the threshold interrogating his visitor. He seemed reluctant to let the visitor in but the visitor remonstrated and he stepped aside and the visitor stepped in. Seconds later they both appeared in the tableau of the kitchen window. They stood awkwardly on either side of the wooden table, neither of them sitting down, talking, not angrily nor cheerfully but as if agitated by some long past grievance, as if two ghosts had met by coincidence on a lonely road in the middle of the marsh. The visitor was a woman, perhaps fiftyish, about the same as the peat cutter and though they struck formal poses it seemed to be the stiff formality of people who have once known each other well. The conversation became more intense. The woman seemed to be imprecating the man and he responded repeatedly by shaking his head. And then he raised an index finger and shook that at her in accusation. And then seeing this she pointed to herself in an exaggerated pantomime as if to say, 'Me? Me?' 'Yes, you!' the man seemed to be saying and the woman threw her hands out as if that really took the biscuit. She became more impassioned and the man turned away and grabbed the sides of his head with his hands as if he didn't want to hear any more and then alerted by what must have been a noise he spun round and rushed over to the woman, who appeared now to be crying. And Meredith the peat cutter seemed to melt at the sight of this and held out his arms as if the woman was on the verge of falling to the floor. He took one final step forward and Sister Cunégonde collapsed into his arms and wept.

Chapter 8

'DO THIS,' SAID Calamity. She wrapped the fingers of her left hand round the two middle fingers of her right.

'Why?'

'Trust me. Now do this.' She tapped her palm with her index finger, pointed at her eye, waved her hand and then made a curious gesture like someone emptying a bag. 'OK? Got that?'

'This is sign language, isn't it?'

'Now do this.' She speeded up like someone doing high-speed origami.

I tried to copy the sequence and Calamity corrected me until I'd about got it right. Maybe the accent was a little strong, but the words were in the right order.

'OK, so what did I just say?'

'You just said, "Sorry but we still haven't seen him."'

'Who?'

'Mr Bojangles. That's what you just said.'

'Where did you learn to do that?'

'I have my sources.' She picked up the card she had been scribbling on and walked over to the incident board. She pinned it on and stood back with the same satisfaction of someone putting the first bauble on the Christmas tree.

'Another clue, huh?'

'Slowly but surely. Bit by bit, the full picture emerges.'

'Is that how it works?'

She looked up slightly and across as if peering askance at the neighbour's garden.

'Yours isn't looking too good.'

'I keep my incident board in my head.'

'That means you haven't got anything yet.'

'I've got loads of things.'

'Share them with your partner.'

I held out a finger and grabbed it as if ticking off items in a long list. 'One, I've got a girl from the Waifery who deliberately planted a locket to mislead the search party. Two, I've got the Mother Superior from the Waifery who is definitely not dealing in straight goods. Three, I've got Brainbocs. Four I've got a Pat vet called Rimbaud seen in the vicinity of the car after I left to buy the ice creams. And five . . . five . . . he's got a tattoo.'

Calamity nodded. 'Uh-huh. My hunch is the veteran's a red herring.'

'My hunch says he knows something.'

'Yeah, but my hunch came first.'

'But my hunch counts for more because it's based on more experience.'

'What does that prove? A hunch is a hunch.'

'Sure, but they can't both be right, so when hunch meets hunch something has to give.'

'So you're pulling rank in the hunch department?'

'When your name is on the frosted glass outside, you get to out-hunch your partner.'

'All right. That's a lot of "gots". What does it all mean?'

'No idea whatsoever.' I walked over to the wall and bent forward to read the cards. 'What about you? Housekeeper dismissed shortly after the fire. Is that suspicious?'

'I don't know yet, it's just a detail. You never know which ones will turn out to be significant.'

'That's true. Gems showed signs of fire damage. What does that mean?'

'The peeler's report said the gems were found in the stable and were the main evidence used to nail the kid. But the jeweller's evidence – not presented at the trial – said they showed signs of fire damage which means they must have been removed after the fire, not before.'

'That's very good. You know, it was Llunos's great-grandfather who was in charge of this, don't you? Cardiganshire's first peeler.'

'I know. He told me. He's writing a book about it.'

I started reading again. 'Groundsman testified that he saw the boy climbing into the room, later altered testimony to say he saw him climbing out.'

'Claims he was mistaken, but I don't see how you can make a mistake like that.'

'That's very good. Where do you get all this?'

'Here and there.'

'What does that mean?'

'Oh, you know, around and about.'

'You haven't been talking to Gluebone again have you?'

'No!'

We heard the by now familiar unmusical clang of the barrel organ beign dumped against the wall outside and the sound of foot and paw steps on the stairs.

'Hi there,' said Gabriel. 'Just dropping by because Cleopatra wanted to ask if you'd—'

I raised my hand to silence him and turned to the monkey. I did the sequence of hand signs, just as Calamity had shown me. When I finished, there was a brief, astonished pause and then Cleopatra squealed, jumped into the air, landed on the floor, did two forward somersaults and then ran in a single bound up the desk, up the wall, and – don't ask me how – along the ceiling, until she got to the light fitting from which she swung with one arm, screeching 'Woo woo woo!'

Gabriel turned to me in amazement. 'You've seen him!?'

'Seen who?'

'Mr Bojangles.'

'No, we haven't seen him.'

'But you just told her you'd seen him.'

'I said I hadn't.'

Gabriel slumped into the client's chair, rested his head in his hands and said softly, 'Oh Lord.'

It took about ten minutes to get Cleopatra down from the light. And another ten minutes to explain how sorry we were over the mistake. To try and smooth things over I asked Gabriel to tell us about Mr Bojangles, and he filled us in on the background.

'The primate language research unit used to supply a lot of monkeys to the physics department for the satellites. You remember the space programme in the Seventies?'

I nodded. 'Yeah, like most people in Wales, we were glued to the TV.'

'There'd been animals in orbit before, of course, the Russians sent dogs and the Americans sent some chimps. But this was the first time any of them were able to tell us what they saw up there. It was quite a coup. Cleopatra was the wife of one of the astronauts – a chimpanzee called Major Tom—'

Cleopatra took a letter out of her waistcoat pocket and proffered it to us.

'She still keeps his first day cover.'

The envelope had University College of Wales insignia on it and a single stamp showing a group of chimps in a space suits. There was also a Latin motto: *per ardua ad astra.*

'That's Major Tom, there, second from the right.'

'Good-looking guy.'

'During their time together they had a son, Mr Bojangles, and he . . . well . . . he . . .' Gabriel seem uncomfortable with this part of the story. 'He went away . . . to . . . er . . . to Timbuktu.'

'Timbuktu?'

'Yes . . . the . . . er . . . university. I expect you've heard of it?'

He looked at us with eyes that implored.

'Yes, of course. It's a great institution. The Harvard of the Sahara . . .'

Gabriel translated and Cleopatra swelled with pride. She took out another letter and reached it across.

'He still writes when he can get the time,' explained Gabriel. 'But his research, well . . .'

'I expect he doesn't have much spare time, being a famous scientist,' I said.

'No,' said Gabriel sadly, 'he doesn't get a lot of time to write.'

I looked at the letter. It was postmarked Llanrhystud.

When Bassett left I found a note slipped under the door from Poxcrop. It told me to meet him at the Cliff Railway base station at eleven and bring a bone. It didn't say how big or what kind, but I dutifully stopped at the Spa in Terrace Road and bought a chop. I arrived five minutes late and asked the shoeshine kid if he'd seen Poxcrop. The shoeshine kid was Poxcrop.

'You're late, Mac,' he said looking up from his shine stool, not bothering to rise.

'Don't try and kid me you've got better things to do with your time. What have you got for me?'

'Two hot tips but there's a little problem about my expenses . . .'

'I already gave you a fiver.'

'I've been undervaluing my services. I've been hearing about you, about how sweet you were on the night club singer. Seems to me—'

I grabbed Poxcrop by his collar and jerked him to his feet.

'Look here, you little runt!'

Poxcrop threw his hands up in mock surrender. 'No violence, no violence!'

The stationmaster rapped sharply on the window of his office. Heads turned. Disapproving looks were dispensed. I let Poxcrop go and he brushed himself down with a well-rehearsed air of insulted dignity.

'I abhor physical violence. I'm a businessman. Either you respect certain civilised norms or we can't do business.'

'If you want to stay in business don't ever make another remark about my relations with Myfanwy.'

'All right, you're in love, I can understand that. Plenty of guys feel the same about my sister.'

'Just tell me what you've got. If it's good I'll give you some more money.'

Poxcrop looked round and then drew me over to the shadows in the corner next to the milk-dispensing machine. If he'd wanted to flag the fact that he was about to contract some nefarious business he couldn't have done it better. To complete the effect he lowered his voice.

'I've been speaking to a fence. Not one of the usual ones. This guy is a deeper level. Maybe the deepest. The police don't know about him. If they find out, he'll know it was you who told them. If that happens he'll know it was me who told you. Then I'm dead. That's why I need the money, y'see. Insurance. For my mum in case something happens to me.'

'Tell me what the guy has got and I'll see how deserving a cause your mum is.'

'Take the train to the top and walk over to Clarach. Count the fourth caravan from the stile. Watch out for the dog in the shed, sometimes it's not chained up. That's what you need the bone for. The guy in the caravan has something. I can't tell you what it is, you have to see for yourself. He's expecting you, so just knock and say I sent you. His name's Mooncalf. And here—'

Poxcrop took out a marker pen and put a cross on my hand. It didn't leave a mark.

'What's that?'

'Ultra-violet light like they use in the discos. Just for security.'

'OK. What else? You said there were two things.'

'My sister has been offered a part in a movie. Special production for the What-the-Butler-Saw format.'

'You must be very proud.'

'She met someone on the set who'd recently auditioned for a part in a different movie. I think it might interest you.'

'Go on.'

'I think you need to sit down first.'

'I'm OK standing.'

'No, trust me, you need to sit down.'

He pulled me over to the waiting room and we went inside.

'This movie they were shooting,' he said. 'Look, Mac, get upset but don't get upset with me, I'm just the messenger, I didn't write the message.'

'Get on with it.'

'They were shooting a movie of Myfanwy's funeral.'

He paused and scrutinised my face to see how I would take the news and whether he needed to duck. He didn't. I said nothing. It was too bizarre.

'Her funeral?'

'That's what the guy told my sister.'

'Where can I find this guy?'

'Believe me, Mac, I want to tell you, really I do, but these are dangerous times and I have to think of my poor mam.'

I took out the roll Gabriel Bassett had left on my desk and peeled off a fiver. Poxcrop produced a sheet of paper from his coat pocket. It was a photocopy containing a list of numbers with the crest of the Bank of England at the top. He read the serial number of the note and searched for it on the photocopied list. 'No offence, but I've been done like this before.'

'Where do you get that?'

'Official police issue – to the Penparcau bureau de change.'

'Is there a bureau de change in Penparcau?'

'You're looking at it, Mac. You want dollars? I can get you a good rate.'

'Not today, as far as I know they still use pounds in Clarach.'

'You know where to come if you do.' And then, finally satisfied of the note's authenticity, he slipped it into his coat pocket and said, 'Ever hear of a guy called R. S. Thomas?'

'No.'

'He's a poet. Writes about rain and sheep and abandoned farmhouses. Quite popular. I don't get it myself, they told me art was the stored honey of the human soul, not gooseberry jam.

> 'Dust in-breathed was a house
> The wall, the wainscot and the mouse.

'Now that's what I call a poem, you want to know why?'

'Because it rhymes?'

'No, you're getting me all wrong. I'm agnostic on the rhyme question. What matters for me is how the poet touches your soul, not whether he can rhyme seesaw with Margery Daw. It's a poem because it embodies an eternal human truth, Mac.'

'Doesn't a poem about an abandoned farmhouse do the same? Doesn't it make you ask why they left?'

'Of course but not every human truth deserves to be embodied, that's the point I'm trying to make. Take the other fellah, the one who wrote about the anthracite horses and the dog in the wet-nosed yard. Now there you have something worth embodying! Our dog did that before he got run over. Wet-nosed yard, it touches you somewhere deep.'

'Tell me why I might be interested in this particular poet.'

'Because he wrote a poem about a chap called Iago Prytherch.

> 'Iago Prytherch his name, though, be it allowed
> Just an ordinary man of the bald Welsh hills,
> Who pens a few sheep in a gap of cloud.
> Docking mangels, chipping the green skin

From the yellow bones with a half-witted grin
Of satisfaction—'

'All right, all right! If I want the rest I'll go to Galloways. What's it mean?'

'The best bit's where he gobs in the fire.'

'Get on with it. I've missed two trains since standing here discussing poetry.'

'Point is, a lot of people like that poem. A lot of people here and a lot of people not here.'

'And who would they be?'

'People from overseas. American college kids, mainly. They come over here with their Yale sweatshirts and baseball caps and they want to meet Iago Prytherch. I don't see why myself. When I go to America I don't ask to meet Hiawatha, but there you go.'

'I think maybe you should give me some of that money back.'

'Don't be in such a rush, I'm filling you in on the background so you don't get caught out later. The point I'm trying to make is this, all these people – literary pilgrims they call them – come here and want to meet Iago Prytherch. So what do you do? I'll tell you what you do. You make their dream come true, just like for the kids who write to Father Christmas at the North Pole. You ever been to the North Pole? I tell you, there's nothing there. Not even a post office. Not even a box to post your letters in. In fact the only way you can tell you're there is by looking at your compass.'

'But a compass won't work at the North Pole.'

'That's it! That's exactly what I'm trying to tell you. It won't work. So as soon as it stops working you know you've arrived. But don't expect to find a post office. But the funny thing is, all those kids get replies to their letters. It's the same with the literary pilgrims. They get off the Devil's Bridge train at Nantyronen and who do they meet? Iago Prytherch is who. It's a home-stay, you see. The real and only official Iago Prytherch home-stay.'

'And how exactly does this information deserve five pounds?'

'Think about it. The guy's a fictional character so how can they meet him? Same way you can go to a department store at Christmas and meet Santa. They get someone to play him. And who do they get? They get the ghost-train howler.'

'And who's he?'

'You've been on the ghost train, right? The one that comes every autumn with the funfair. You've seen it?'

'Yeah I've seen it.'

'What does it arrive in?'

'A Pickfords van.'

'That's right. Track, train, castle, landscape and ghosts. All in the back of a Pickfords van. How scary can that be? It can't. In fact that's the first thing you notice. It's not scary at all. The second thing you notice is this: even though it's not scary there's always a guy sitting at the front when it comes out of the last tunnel screaming his head off. He's the howler. He's a stooge. And the guy who plays the howler is usually one of those bit part actors who hang around on the fringes of the What-the-Butler-Saw industry. And last autumn's howler usually turns into next season's Iago Prytherch in what is known as a perennial cycle of birth and renewal. One that testifies, like the barber-shop pole, to the vanity of all human striving.'

'I don't understand.'

'Read your Bible, Mac. Vanity of vanities, saith the preacher. All the rivers run into the sea; and yet the sea is not full.'

'What's that got to do with a barber shop?'

'Not the shop, the pole. Did I say shop? Have you never noticed? It turns and turns, the red spiral stripes move ever upwards, but they never get anywhere; nothing changes. That's like you and me, Mac. We never get anywhere. Like the waves on the sea always coming in but the sea stays in the same place.

Like Cadwaladr creosoting his bridge. Like the cars of the Cliff Railway perennially changing position. One up, one down. Vanity of vanities, and the phoney Iago Prytherchs pass over the face of the earth like the leaves on the trees.'

'What's any of this got to do with Myfanwy?'

'I'm trying to tell you but you keep interrupting. The guy playing the current Iago Prytherch is the guy that auditioned for a part in the movie of Myfanwy's funeral.'

I put another fiver in Poxcrop's pocket and ran for the train.

They call it the train you take when your life has gone wrong. The Aberystwyth Cliff Railway. It creeps up the hill at the speed of lichen. You get off at the top, fortify yourself from a styrofoam cup with tea the colour and strength of a horse, and walk to Clarach. If Borth is the poor man's Aberystwyth – and it isn't – then Clarach is the poor man's Borth. And that's about as poor as you can get without selling a kidney. It's not a one-horse town, not even a hoof, maybe the imprint left by a horseshoe nailed once long ago to a fence or maybe just a handful of oats.

After a short walk over the hilltop you arrive at the top of a valley that the sun never kisses; never even shakes hands with or even acknowledges with a curt nod. On the way down you pass dung-caked sheep with contempt in their eyes. Animals so destitute they spend their whole lives on an incline, front legs higher than the back in the morning, back legs higher than the front in the afternoon, eating gorse and perhaps grass on special occasions; and they give you that look. Pity or contempt? It's hard to tell but when the sheep lets out a loud *blaaa* and a fraction of a second later the whole hillside erupts in answering bleats you can't stop yourself thinking: in your heart you know it's impossible, but it sounds suspiciously like laughter.

Down below, I found a few grubby bits of land on which caravans were anchored with bricks and strung together with a cat's cradle of washing lines and TV aerials; white pebbles from the beach were laid out to signify territorial possession. The one store sold homogenised milk, the *Daily Mirror*, buckets and spades and suntan lotion in anticipation of the day when continental drift returned Clarach to the spot it had once occupied near the equator. Aeons ago it had been part of the supercontinent called Gondwanaland and the imprint of fossilised tropical ferns in the rocks of Constitution Hill testify to the good times that had been and may one day come again. But not this summer. And probably not the next.

This was Clarach. For entertainment you can lose some money at the amusement arcade situated in a breeze-block room that anywhere else on earth would be called a garage. Or you can take a car out to the main road and drive fast over the hump-backed bridge near the church. Or, if the melancholy fit is upon you, you can walk to the patch of grit smeared against the land's edge which the map describes as the beach and walk out to the end of the rocks and look to your left. If the tide is low enough, and you can go out far enough, you can see a little bit of Aberystwyth peeping out from behind the cliff. In that moment you regret all the bad things you ever said about her.

I stood and rapped my knuckles on a caravan door that was thinner than the lid on a tin of throat lozenges. I waited and listened. A tinkling sound of chain came from the shed, and a rustle of straw. A dog whimpered. The shed door was ajar and I threw the bone in and knocked again on the caravan. Footsteps came from inside, a TV was turned down, and then the door opened and a rat ran out gasping for air.

Leave a dish of clotted cream in the sun for a month and break the crust and breathe in. Then you'll know what opening that door was like. It was like the mouth of a corpse opening and emitting a puff of air that has lain for weeks in the nutrient-rich chamber of the decaying thorax. The hand that held the door open was clawed up with arthritis and clad in a fingerless mitt. The sort that is standard issue for people who fence stolen goods. The face that belonged to the mitts was half-concealed by the collar of a raincoat. I'd never met Mooncalf before but everything about him had a strange familiarity. His coat was the colour of a diseased lung used in those explicit anti-smoking posters they hang in doctors' waiting rooms. His hair was from the leaflet the school nurse hands out about nits. His face was the one they use on the posters that warn kids not to accept sweets from strangers. He fished out a torch from inside his lung-coloured coat and shone it on the mark that Poxcrop had made on my hand. Then he beckoned me into his crypt. The air was so thick and rich and foetid you could chew it. After one breath you wanted to brush your teeth. And your nose. I followed him to the table at the far end. The curtains were closed and flies buzzed unseen in the darkness. On the table was a plate on which lay a slab of cheese. The cheese seemed to be pulsating and, as my eyes grew accustomed to the murk, I realised it was crawling with maggots. The surface of the table was stuck with fur like a half-sucked boiled sweet kept in a pocket for a month. He saw the shock on my face and explained,

'I like a bit of company.'

'Yeah, that's the great thing about maggots, they're not fussy.'

'Take a seat.'

I said I preferred to remain standing. I wanted to keep the minimum amount of surface area in contact with the caravan. At the moment it was just the soles of my feet and I could always burn the shoes.

'I was just making a cuppa. Would you like one?'

He poured tea into a cup smeared with green fur and plonked a spoon into a milk carton and ladled out a heaped spoonful.

'No thanks, I've just had my lunch.'

'How much money did you bring?' he asked.

'I've got enough. What is it you are selling?'

'It costs a thousand pounds. I don't want to deal with time-wasters.'

'I asked you what've you got.'

'And I asked you how much you've got.'

I pulled out what was left of the five hundred Bassett gave me. 'There's five hundred here, I can get the rest if I like what you've got. And skip the serial number check. Now show me.'

He peered at the bundle of notes and nodded to himself. Then he walked down to the bed part of the caravan and pulled a roll of material down off the top of the wardrobe. He brought it over and placed it in my hands like a cloth merchant in an Arab bazaar.

'It's her winding sheet,' he said.

I looked at him with a face of childish horror. 'Her what!?'

'Winding sheet. Look.' He took it off me and walked back to the other end of the caravan. There was a short washing line strung between the two walls. From it hung the decaying and threadbare rags that were his underlinen, grey and sepulchral like moth pupae fastened to the wall of a tomb. He pulled the underwear from the pegs with soft snapping sounds and pegged up the sheet. He came back and turned on a lamp that emitted a faint mauve light.

'Ultra-violet,' he explained. 'See? Like the Shroud of Turin.'

In the weird, otherworldly light a pattern became visible in the cloth. The faint, negative image of a girl lying full-length with her arms crossed upon her chest like a knight carved on a stone tomb.

'She looks so peaceful, don't you think?'

'Where did you get it?' I hissed.

'It's genuine, if that's what you're wondering.'

'Where did you get it?'

'I won't say.'

'I'll beat it out of you.'

'Be my guest. I'm not afraid to die. Are you?'

'I'm serious.'

'And so am I. Do you really want to risk your life by beating me up?'

'You think you could kill me?'

'I'm sure of it. All I need to do is give you a little bite. I'm like a komodo dragon. Have you heard of them? You find them on the island of Sumatra. Their saliva is so dirty that they just have to give their prey a little nip and wait for it to die of blood poisoning. It doesn't take long.' He giggled and made a token snap with his teeth in my direction. I jumped backwards and he giggled again. I rushed to the door and ran out choking on the fresh air. And then I fell to my knees and was sick.

Two hours later, after having showered and scrubbed myself clean, I made a small pyre for my clothes on the beach near Constitution Hill. I was poking the fire with a stick when a man hailed me from the Prom and came hurrying up to me. It was Llunos.

'If I'd have known,' he said, 'I would have brought some marshmallows to toast.'

'You wouldn't if you knew where these clothes have been. Have you ever come across a man called Mooncalf?'

Llunos jumped backwards and spluttered. 'Mooncalf! You went to see Mooncalf? This is hazardous waste, mate, you shouldn't be burning that here.'

'You know him then?'

'Oh yeah, I know Mooncalf. I never miss his cheese and wine parties.'

'I'm serious.'

'Small-time fence, deals in religious artefacts – icons, relics, things like that. Most of it junk palmed off on gullible old ladies. He trades off the myth that he's somehow at a deeper level than the other fences in town, that he never gets arrested because the police don't know about him. Truth is, the reason he never gets arrested is we *do* know about him. There are only so many things a man will do for a policeman's salary. He keeps a dog chained up in the shed at the back – the whining keeps the neighbours awake. Talk about a dog's life. You must have wanted a picture of the Virgin Mary pretty badly to go and see Mooncalf.'

Llunos left me to my bonfire, telling me he'd put the Myfanwy locket on my desk and reminding me to get a permit to burn this sort of stuff next time. I poked the flames again with the stick and watched the sparks fly and wondered. Llunos usually knew about these things so if he said the guy was a fraud he no doubt was. And making a fake shroud probably isn't all that hard. But one thing bothered me. I'd only held the shroud for a second or more. And now my hands smelled of bluebells.

Chapter 9

THERE WERE SOME unusual items on the desk when I got back from my bonfire. A locket. A pig's head. A hammer. And a newspaper cutting sent by Meirion. I picked it up and read. It was a photocopy from their archives about the Nanteos fire.

Behold Othniel Parry, a simpleminded mute who cleaned the stables. One of God's children they said. He loved his horses and adored his mistress. In fifteen years he never so much as kicked the stable cat. And yet we are asked to believe that all of a sudden he took it into his head to climb into my lady's bedchamber, ravish and brutally murder her, set the room afire, and then, calm as you like, pocket her gems and climb out of the window and down the ivy. And on what marvel of detective work are we supposed to build this credulity-straining hypothesis? The bumbling ineptitude of that oaf, Syracuse Obadiah Griffiths, the worse advertisement for this newfangled idea of a peeler that it is possible for human wit to conceive. And in support of this, nothing more substantial than the medical fact attested to by her physician, Dr Weevil, that Crangowen was found not to be virgo intacta. *Certainly, if the rumours are to be believed, you will find no one who could speak with greater authority on the subject than Dr Weevil. We are not well versed with the classics down on Cambrian Street where this journal is printed so we tend to call a spade a spade. And a girl who puts herself about like our lady Cranogwen is – if we may make use of a term derived from French – known as a velocipede. And what are we to make of this curious piece of evidence, the bridle found under the mattress? Did the stable boy really leave it there, for reasons we only gawp at? Or do we prefer his version of events: that he was in the habit of lending it to the doctor who liked to indulge in a little horseplay with my lady? Sadly, none of this seems to matter one jot with the authorities and so we must prepare ourselves for a singularly unedifying prospect: that we shall hang for violating my lady's honour the only man in the district innocent of the charge.*

Calamity came in from the kitchenette with a cup of tea.

'I see the butcher called,' I said, glancing at the pig's head.

'It's what the Feds use, for blood-spatter analysis and things.'

'The Feds?'

'FBI. I was thinking about the marks on the wall above the bed. The legend says it's ghostly blood – but it's probably just damp. Just trying to eliminate it from the inquiry.'

'Where does the pig fit in?'

'You have to bludgeon him on the head with the hammer and examine the different blood-spatter patterns. The real forensic guys do it all the time. Pigs and humans have very similar bludgeon characteristics. I'm hoping to establish that the ghostly bloodstains are inconsistent with a frenzied assault.'

'And what will that prove?'

'I'm working on the theory that the ghost is a phoney, the work of agent or agents unknown, for purposes unknown.'

I picked up the locket and walked to the door. 'Are you really going to hit him with the hammer?'

'I thought you would do it.'

'I'm not hitting a pig with a hammer.'

'I'll put him in the fridge in case you change your mind.'

'I won't.'

I walked down Canticle Street to the Aberystwyth Yesterday museum that had recently moved to the old Coliseum cinema. The girl told me Mr Lewis, the curator of the Myfanwy exhibits, was on the second floor. I climbed the narrow stairs that once led to the circle, and reflected on the long-lost Saturday mornings spent here absorbing the lesson that a man's essential moral character is reflected in the colour of his cowboy hat. Today, amid the earthenware hot-water bottles in two shades of brown, and the bronze-age vistas in papier-mâché, the lessons were different but the didacticism hardly more subtle: Clip the sheepdog, who served the people of the town loyally and obediently and never bit anyone, now stuffed and put in a glass case as his reward. And Mr Lewis working on a new tableau entitled 'Myfanwy's Goodness'. He was trying to find the best position for a framed photo of her patting a guide dog. I asked him about the recent activity on the memorabilia black market and he pretended not to know anything about it. So I put the price of a few pints of beer in his top pocket and he recovered his memory. A number of items had been stolen recently from private collections. Of particular note was the essay written when she was nine entitled 'My Idea of Heaven'. He pulled down a book and opened it to a page showing a photographic copy of the essay. It was only a fragment, most of the original manuscript having been lost, but the pieces that remained had been reassembled with the same painstaking care normally reserved for scraps of Babylonian papyrus. Mr Lewis ran his finger along the lines, and translated Myfanwy's childish handwriting. '"My idea of Heaven. A house with a chocolate tree, a view from my bedroom of Borth, permission to play Kerplunk all day long . . ." All fairly conventional. But this is the interesting bit, here, see.'

I leaned closer.

'See this, just a fragment but fascinating. "Where we collected the white bones of Hector."' He beamed at me. 'It's a classical allusion. To *The Iliad*.'

'*The Iliad*?'

'Homer. The greatest Greek of all – Hector, Achilles, Ajax on the windy plains of Troy, two mighty nations at war for ten years over the hand of beautiful Helen. Quite appropriate in a way don't you think?'

'Are you sure it's a reference to the ancient Greeks?'

'No doubt about it. Book Twenty-four. Achilles and Priam, line 931.'

'It doesn't sound like her.'

'It certainly overturns a lot of previous Myfanwy scholarship, that's for sure.'

'I don't remember her reading much apart from the problem page in *Just Seventeen*.'

'Hidden depths, Mr Knight. Hidden depths. One in the eye, don't you think, for all those who sneered that she was thick?'

I thanked him for his time and just before I left he gave me a photocopy of the essay.

'It might help,' he said.

There was a stretched Austin Montego parked outside with blacked-out windows. I stood and admired and the rear window wound down in awkward jerks as someone inside struggled with a stiff handle.

'It's more impressive if they're electric,' I said.

A man in a Swansea suit and aviator shades stared ahead and spoke to me out of the corner of his mouth.

'Fancy a little ride, peeper?'

'No.'

'Just a little ride and a chat, I've got a message from Ll.'

'From who?'

'Ll.'

'Sorry?'

'Ll.'

'Sorry, I don't understand.'

The stooge turned to face me. 'It's his initial, like "M" or "Q", the boss right?'

'That's not an initial, it's two letters.'

'Not in Welsh. It counts as one.'

'It doesn't, it's a phoneme, it's two.'

'Just get in for fuck's sake.'

'Do I have any choice?'

'We just want a word.'

I walked round and got in the back. The car eased out into the traffic flow and turned left into North Parade.

'So what's his name then?'

'Look, peeper, give us a break from the comedy.'

'Why won't you tell me?'

'Because it's a bloody secret, that's why.'

'Can't be hard to guess if it begins with Ll. Llewellyn?'

'Give over.'

'Lloyd?'

'Not even close.'

'Llunos?'

'That's right. The boss of the criminal underworld is the chief of police.'

'I bet you don't know either.'

'Yes I do.'

'Llyr?'

'Look we're not going to tell you, so give up.'

'Tell me what he's the boss of then and maybe I can work it out.'

'He's the boss of everything. The whole town, now shut up.'

We turned right and followed the one way to the station and then turned into the Devil's Bridge train marshalling yards.

'How come I've never heard of him?'

The car pulled into a dirty red brick engine shed and stopped. They motioned me to get out.

'You're not important enough. He wants to give you a message for Llunos. This thing about closing the town down. It's hurting our business. Tell Llunos we don't know who took Myfanwy and to open up the town again otherwise he'll be wearing a pair of concrete swimming trunks.'

'I'll tell him. Anything else?'

'Yes,' the man in the Swansea suit moved round in front of me and spoke directly to my face. We were alone, the three of us in a vast sooty brick cathedral built in more confident times to house the narrow-gauge trains that brought the lead from the hills. 'Tell the girl to lay off the Nanteos case. She's treading on toes a kid of her age didn't ought to tread on.'

'It's ancient history, why should anybody care?'

'There's no such thing as ancient history. Just call her off or she could get hurt.'

'There's no point me saying anything – it won't make any difference. She never listens to a word I say.'

'Look, peeper, we're serious. If she doesn't remove her snout she'll get hurt.'

'Is there anything else?'

'Yes.'

Clang. It was the noise a shovel makes when it hits a head.

The shadows were lengthening in the engine shed when I opened my eyes. I must have been out about an hour. I ran my fingers over the back of my head. There was a little dried blood and a swelling. And a headache. But all that was good. Normally when you get hit with a shovel you don't expect to have any head left at all. I spotted the sepulchral whiteness of a washbasin glimmering in the gloom and went over to throw cold water over my face. I walked out into a world turning gold with the setting sun.

I drove slowly to Borth, not wishing to put too great a strain on my recently battered head. Allowing time for it to recover. By the time I reached Ynyslas the sky was buttercup-coloured and veined with bars of gold like a butterfly's wing. The silhouette of the Waifery was a dark stain on the wing's edge. I parked in the lane and walked up towards the main gate. The sweet descant of girls' singing drifted on the air like the scent of flowers at dusk. It was accompanied by something I hadn't encountered for many years: the smell of school dinner. Cabbage boiled to the colour of bone; the smell of water drunk from a glass made from car windscreen material; brown food colouring and flour and fat congealing into the brown tapioca that is called gravy.

As I reached the gate, the postman cycled up and asked me to take a parcel. It was addressed to Sister Cunégonde. On the front there was a decorative frank advertising the Shrewsbury Flower Show, and on the back was scribbled the name of the sender. F. Mephisto. The wrought-iron gate squealed like a gull as I opened it and pretended to walk through. I watched the postman cycle away. And when he was gone I went back to the car and put the parcel in the glove compartment. I would be in hot water for this in the next world, that was for sure.

A nun showed me to the corridor and pointed to the end where Sister Cunégonde had her office. The door was slightly ajar and I stood outside with my knuckles poised to knock, but the sound of a conversation from within made me hold back.

'I could have had any man in the village . . . Oh yes I could! They were queuing at the door for me. But oh no! For you I turned them away! For you I spurned their hot desire. Do you hear? For you, you worthless wretch. And now after all I've done for you, I find you going behind my back. In my own house, with one of my own girls! With her of all people! Her! That little trollop . . . that little hussy who doesn't care tuppence for you nor anyone else . . . Oh, you thought I didn't know? Thought I was too stupid to notice? Thought I didn't know about you and your new playmate? Well that just goes to show you're not as smart as you thought, doesn't it? You . . . you . . . twerp!'

The words faded into the squeaky sound of stifled sobs.

I found my head easing quietly forward towards the gap in the door. Who was she talking to? Who was this man for whom she had sacrificed everything, this twerp? Was it Meredith? I eased my head forward with the slow control of a lizard about to shoot its tongue out at an insect. Slowly, slowly, slowly. My eyes cleared the edge of the door and I saw inside. Sister Cunégonde was standing with her back to me in the middle of the room. Her wimple had been cast aside and her silver hair loosened so that it fell across her shoulders like a silver fleece. She was combing it with the air of a miser counting a secret treasure. And I saw with a slight shock that the twerp she was talking to was not Meredith, but someone much older. And made of alabaster, hanging from a cross of wood fixed to the wall.

My foot squeaked on the polished wooden floor and I jerked my head back. The sound of weeping stopped. There was silence and I could tell she was listening, straining her ears to try and divine what the noise portended. I coughed and rapped my knuckles on the door. 'One moment, please,' came the response, and then, 'Come in!' The voice was artificially cheery. I pushed the door open and saw Sister Cunégonde kneeling in prayer before the cross. She looked round from her devotion with an air of deep piety and slight annoyance at being disturbed. She was good, I'd say that much.

I said I'd come back but she waved the suggestion aside and bid me sit across from the desk. The sky in the window behind her head was cobalt blue. The sound of children practising recorders drifted in and soothed my head, which had begun to throb again.

Doe– a deer, a female deer . . .

'It's a contagion, you know,' said Sister Cunégonde, 'worse than German measles.'

'What is?'

'Love, Mr Knight. Trust me, I've seen it. A pathogen in the Petri dish of an adolescent girl's heart.'

She waved an airmail envelope and pushed it towards me across the desk. 'Seren really has gone too far this time. First the nonsense with the locket, and now this. I just don't know what gets into her.'

Ray– a drop of golden sun . . .

I rested my fingers on the envelope. 'What is it?'

'Goodness knows. It's a letter to a someone in South America about a love affair, begging some woman to be reconciled with her estranged husband. Who does she know in South America? Nobody. She doesn't even know anyone in Talybont.'

'Maybe she met someone here on holiday.'

'Nonsense!' She picked up the letter and read. '"To the Mayor of Fray Bentos, please pass on to the French teacher." Where does she get this stuff from?'

Me– a name I call myself,

Far– a long, long way to run . . .

'Where did you get it from?'

'The postman was kind enough to return it. Heaven knows what might have happened if he'd sent it.'

'I thought his job was to deliver them, not intercept them.'

'He just exercised some common sense. It's a pity more people don't.'

'I think it's a rotten trick steaming open someone's mail.'

'I didn't steam it open. It fell on the kettle.'

'All the same—'

'Come on, Mr Knight, you're a private investigator. Don't tell me you've never intercepted someone's mail.'

'No, never. There are certain things I would never stoop to.' My neck felt hot and sticky as I remembered the parcel in the glove compartment.

'Bully for you. What do you want, a medal?'

Sew– a needle pulling thread,

La– a note to follow sew . . .

'She may be just a kid but she has a right to privacy doesn't she?'

'No, actually, she doesn't. Not while she is a pupil at the Waifery. If this had been sent it could have caused all sorts of trouble. Just look at it. What does she mean by it?'

'Why don't you ask her?'

'She refuses to speak. She says I had no right.'

I made no attempt to read the letter. It sat there on the desk between us like all letters that aren't our business – begging to be read. I couldn't see what was so bad about living in a dream world when you're sixteen. Not when you considered what the real one was like.

Tea– a drink with jam and bread . . .

'So now she has to eat bread and water.'

Sister Cunégonde put the envelope in the drawer of her desk and stood up. 'I suppose she told you that as well. It's actually sandwiches and Ribena. That's a lot more than most people in this world get to eat.'

I couldn't argue with her there. I put the locket on the desk. She walked to the window. 'Come and look. See? Out there. Venus hanging low over the sea, always the first star out. I remember watching it when I was Seren's age. How it used to throb and burn. I'm sorry if you find me over-strict. But you don't understand how it is here in Ynyslas, it's different – not like Aberystwyth. Everything seems magnified out here somehow. Everything . . . there's something carnal about the nights here . . . that makes the spirit ache . . . The stars like hot snowballs . . . and . . . and the grassy dunes, like a bearded chin, rasping your thighs as you walk . . .' Sister Cunégonde shuddered and then checked herself and shot me a glance containing a wild untamed fire.

We remained staring at the slowly appearing evening stars. The recorders continued to lay a soothing hand on our troubled hearts.

That will bring us back to doe!

And then there was a scream. Long and piercing, followed by a chorus of more adolescent screams. Then came shouts, the sound of doors banging. Sister Cunégonde and I both spun round to stare at the closed door of her office, as if the explanation might be written on it. The screams stopped and gave way to the sound of general commotion. More doors banging, shouts, footsteps running. Sister Cunégonde ran to the door but not to open it, but to hold it closed. But I got there a fraction of a second ahead of her and as I swung it open she could only grasp the handle and be swept aside. I ran down the corridor, pursued by Sister Cunégonde. Girls stood on the minstrel's gallery looking down, dressed in sheer white nightgowns that shone like spectres in the gloom. They looked on in horror as across the way, outside the door to a dormitory, two sisters wrestled with another girl, whose white nightdress was smeared with blood. It was Seren and she was sobbing. She looked across at me and raised her hands, palms outwards, and there was blood in the palms. Half a second later the two sisters managed to overpower her and drag her into the dormitory and slam the door. But the image of her with bloody palms hung in the air long after the door had been closed, like the spots before the eye that come from staring at the sun. Another sister shooed the awe-struck girls back to their rooms and Sister Cunégonde, seemingly unsurprised at what had just taken place, caught up and planted herself squarely in front of me.

'I think it's time for you to go.'

'What happened there?'

'Nothing happened. Nothing. Please go.'

'Not before I find out what happened.'

'No. Nothing happened. It was nothing. She's had a nosebleed that's all. You must go.'

I was about to tell her to move aside when a flash in a wall mirror caught my attention.

It was a shovel-shaped flash. There was probably a clang when it hit my head. There usually is.

Chapter 10

IT WAS MID-MORNING when I woke up. I was staring at the sole of a shoe. It was resting on a desk and belonged to the desk sergeant of Glanwern police station, probably the same big-belly who had arrested Rimbaud. In between us was the iron grid of the bars that ran from floor to ceiling. There was another man asleep in my cell. He looked like a hobo. I rubbed my hand over the back of my head, and felt two bruises, each about the size of half a golf ball. About average. I stood up.

'That's a nice shoe,' I said.

The sergeant nodded.

'How much longer do I have to stare at it?

He picked up a box of Swan Vestas, took one out and started to use it as a toothpick. He spoke through his cupped hands. 'What were you doing there?'

'Where?'

'The Waifery.'

'I was selling encyclopaedias.'

He sawed away at his gums. 'Selling encyclopaedias. That's good. I like that. Education. Give a man a fish and you feed him for a day; teach him to fish . . . Yeah that's good.'

He stood up, wriggled a light mac over his shoulders and walked out.

The hobo woke up half an hour later. He had been snoring softly for a while and then gave a grunt and a snort, and then a louder snort as if something was stuck in his nose and he was trying to dislodge it and the effort or the noise woke him. He raised his head slowly from a pillow made from his rolled-up coat, swivelled his head round to examine his surroundings, and then nodded as if this was what he expected or was at least fairly accustomed to viewing when he woke up. Then he noticed me. I did a little wave.

'Any coffee?' he asked.

'Sorry. I've been ringing room service for the past hour but there's no answer.'

He stuck out a hand. 'Haywire.'

'Louie. What are you in for?'

'Riding the boxcars. Between here and Porthmadoc. Not many of us left.'

'The world's changing in ways we cannot comprehend. Only the young understand.'

'That's about the way I see it too. What they get you for?'

'Being hit over the head with a shovel.'

'Yeah, that would work, but it's a high price to pay for room and board.'

Haywire reached into his coat and brought out a crumpled paper bag and offered me a gobstopper. I declined and he popped one into his mouth and spoke with a bulge in his cheek like a hamster moving his bedding. For a while I listened to the gentle scrape of gobstopper on Haywire's tooth enamel. Then I asked him if he knew Rimbaud.

'I know him,' he said. 'But he never rides the boxcars these days. On account of he can't get up in time. A hobo needs a train with real wagons and the only one left now is the milk train. That goes pretty early and Rimbaud has demons in his soul that make it difficult for him to respond to the sound of an alarm clock. A psychologist would say that he was blocked.'

'My partner, Calamity, suffers from the same blockage. She used to get it worst during term time. Now she's left school so she gets it all year round.'

'I see I am being mocked.'

'I'm sorry, I just thought it was funny to use a fancy name for something so common as—'

Haywire thrust his arm out and pointed his finger at me, his face hot with anger. 'Did I say everyone who can't get up is blocked? No! I said no such thing. Sometimes I can't get up but I have never entertained the idea that my problem has psychopathological origins. If you had taken the courtesy to mark my words, the actual ones I used rather than your fanciful interpretation of what you imagined I might have meant, and taken the courtesy to inquire into their meaning with an honest disposition rather than the crude desire to mock someone for his erudition, you would know that I never said this phenomenon applies in all cases where someone has difficulties in getting up. Such was your idiotic induction. I simply said Rimbaud was blocked. I took you for an educated man and shared with you some of my great learning. It was a stupid thing to do.'

'You seem to know a lot about psychology.'

'Once long ago I was a neurobiologist. Adviser to the space programme. You remember the monkeys?'

'Funnily enough, I do.

'Perhaps you think a hobo cannot possess great learning?'

'I don't think that at all. Tell me why is he blocked.'

'Because they executed his brother at dawn. And the episode has haunted him ever since.'

'Did he watch?'

'No, he did not watch. But he planned to. Now I know you will probably ask yourself who on earth would want to go and watch his brother's execution? But the problem is, what else are you going to do? It's not like you've got anything more important on at the time is it? So he promises his little brother to be there and kiss him before he dies. But, alas, he oversleeps. He opens his eyes at noon and runs down to the prison but everyone has gone home and all he sees is the mound of lime by the wall giving off steam – that thin evanescence that betokens the departure of his brother's soul.'

'Have you heard about his missing years?'

'Oh yes.'

'Do you know where he went?'

'No. But I wouldn't book a holiday there, wherever it was.'

'Do you think they'll keep us here until after lunch?'

'I hope so. Mondays is minestrone soup.'

Ten minutes later a different deputy walked in with a bunch of keys and opened the door.

'Which one of you is Haywire?'

'He is,' said Haywire, and I walked out. The deputy held out a form for me to sign and I wrote the initials H. W.

The barrel organ was parked outside; the cheap cardboard suitcase stood in the doorway; and Gabriel Bassett's hat hung from the stand. But there was no monkey.

'She's not well,' he said.

I nodded.

'It's because of the shock you gave her last time. Saying you'd seen Mr Bojangles.'

'I can't tell you how sorry I am about that. It was such a blunder.'

'I know it was just a mistake but, you know, she keeps saying, "Maybe Mr Knight really did see him. Maybe he's keeping it secret until my birthday or something."'

'It won't happen again.'

'I've just popped round to remind you – just another week.'

'No problem,' I lied, 'Calamity has it almost sewn up.'

I could tell he didn't believe me so I changed the subject. 'I see you brought the old case along.'

'Yes,' he said sadly. 'I know you think my case is funny.'

'No I don't. I just don't understand how anyone can carry a case round all day and not know what's in it.'

He looked at me but said nothing.

'Aren't you tempted to take a peek?'

'Of course I am, you bloody fool!' he shouted, suddenly

overcome with passion. 'All the damn time! But I can't, don't you see? I damn well can't!'

'But why the hell not?'

'Because I'm too scared.' He looked at me with a fierce anguish burning in his eyes. 'I can't take the risk. Sometimes, late at night when everyone has gone to bed, I stare at it and I stare and it's . . . it's almost as if I can see inside it. Almost as if . . . I . . . I just concentrated a little bit harder, just a tiny little bit harder, I could see inside. Then I'd know. And then I go up to it and put my hand on the clasp to open it . . . and then . . . and then . . . I always stop myself. Always stop, just in time.'

'But there might be something nice inside.'

He looked at me thoughtfully, as if giving this suggestion due consideration. Then he shook his head. 'No.'

'If it was me, I'd look.'

'I did look once, you know. On the day I first got it, five years ago. But I've never had the courage to look again. It almost destroyed my life last time. This time God won't give me a second chance, I just know it.'

'Tell me what happened.'

He stared at me for a second or two, nodding his head slightly – either because he was working out whether I could be trusted or maybe just plucking up the courage to make the leap. Finally he gave a bigger, more affirmative nod, and said, 'It was on a day just like today – in the middle of June five years ago. I was standing at Sospan's stall eating an ice cream and I found to my embarrassment that I had no money to pay for it. There wasn't a single cent in any of my pockets. Sospan said I could pay him later and asked me for my name and address. And I said, "Sure, my name is . . . my name is . . . my . . . er . . . name is . . ." And do you know what? I didn't know my own name. I didn't know who I was or where I came from. I had absolutely no memory at all. I didn't even know how I came to be standing at his stall. I didn't remember ordering the ice cream. It was as if I had just dropped out of the sky or walked through a door from another dimension five minutes previously. The police were called and I was taken to the Enoc Enocs Foundation in Llanbadarn – you know the place I suppose? Where they give distressed gentlefolk a new career by training them to work a barrel organ.'

I nodded. 'When I was in school we used to collect milk-bottle tops to buy a monkey.'

'That's right, everybody did.'

'I could never understand why organ-grinding and not basketry or something more suitable for an old person.'

'It's because they're not allowed by the terms of their charter. Captain Enocs was very particular. He got the idea in Palermo in 1873. The Sicilians told him organ-grinding is the perfect career for people who have fallen on hard times. All you have to do is turn the handle and leave the rest up to the monkey. What could be simpler? They told him an organ-grinder never starves because people will always pay you if they like your music and, if they don't, they will pay you to go away.'

'Seems to make sense.'

'The people at the Enoc Enocs Foundation were very kind to me. They searched my pockets for clues to my identity but all I had on me was my jacket from Gabriel's, the gents' outfitters in Portland Street, and a packet of Bassett's Liquorice All-Sorts. There was just one left – the jelly-centred one with the coating of tiny blue beads. There was also a small red chit of paper in my trouser pocket: a receipt from the left luggage office at the Cliff Railway base station. This was how I came by my name: Gabriel, Bassett.'

'I suppose you're lucky they didn't call you "Lefty Luggage".'

He looked at me blankly and then continued.

'It was arranged for the chit to be redeemed and the suitcase brought to me. A cheap brown cardboard suitcase, scuffed and marked. A bit tatty. And so naturally I opened it. Can you imagine what that feels like? To have no idea who you are, to be totally divorced from that reservoir of memory that constitutes the essence of who you are? And then to open a case containing, or so you believe, the answer to this baffling mystery? To come face to face with a man who is utterly strange and unknown, utterly alien to you, and yet who shares with you the most intimate bond a human being can share with another. Can you imagine that? I'm sure you cannot. But I have experienced it. Picture to yourself the anticipation. With trembling fingers I lifted the lid and looked down and there lying in the case was . . .'

I fell asleep.

Lord knows how I did it. Maybe it was the heat or the hypnotic droning of the traffic like far-off wasps or perhaps it was the after-effect of the knocks on the head, but I awoke half an hour later to find Calamity in a strange pitch of excitement and Gabriel Bassett and his suitcase gone. Calamity was pinning a new card to the wall. She looked at me and then rushed out saying, 'Can't stop, I think we've cracked it!'

With a head stuffed with cotton wool I made a coffee and then walked to the Devil's Bridge train station. I bought a ticket to Nantyronen – the special saver return that includes admission to the Iago Prytherch 'home-stay' – and took a pew on the train alongside the loco-spotters and families on holiday.

At Nantyronen I followed the National Trust signs. They led through the village street and then over a stile and across a field. The track was bounded on one side by a raised earthen bank covered in gorse, and by a straggly wire fence on the other. After a hundred yards or so there was a drystone wall and another stile with a sign that said, 'You are now entering Iago Prytherch Country'. The cottage was further down in the valley. Along the way I passed some sheep who were chewing cud and smelling of dung. The sign in their midst said, 'A few sheep penned in a gap of cloud'. Further on was an arrow pointing west and a sign that read, 'The bald Welsh hills'. Just before the cottage was a ploughed field that I was informed consisted of 'a stiff sea of clods that glint in the wind'. And then I came to the cottage. Chunks of undressed stone beneath a roof of smooth mauve slate. A rusty nail knocked into the wall held the end of a washing line that stretched to a slanting pole in the garden. The sign said, 'Clothes, sour with years of sweat and animal contact'. It began to drizzle and I made for the door and ducked under a low lintel made lower by the sign 'Warning: spittled mirth'.

Iago sat motionless in the chair beside the fire. He fixed me with a stare but said nothing and then leaned slowly across and spat into the flames. There was a little hiss in the grate. Then he resumed his position and stared ahead with a look that had a frightening vacancy, like the hollow of a cave where the wind gnaws on an old bone and where the call of its passing leaves knowledge accreted like scale or scar tissue, its meaning subsisting interstitially, between words, gathered slowly across the centuries like the fat drops of rain dripping from the dead husk of last year's hive. I watched hypnotised. It was amazing how he did it. His witch-black chair extended beneath him like rotting tubers and he clutched with udder-blasted hands to steady himself in the giddying tarantella of the years such that his whole frame trembled like a tree on a ridge, whose sharp twigs scratch the face of the toothless moon. The worn-out rag of his soul was draped on a toasting fork before the fire, in the black-snouted, life-blasting corners of the year, but drew no warmth from the dry brown dregs of summer coughing consumptively in the grate. He turned once more to stare at me, and I beheld not a man but the devil shrouded in the rook's cloak, and wearing Glyndwr's hat. His mouth opened and it was as if the earth was cloven to reveal the grey viscera wherein were interred, gloved in clay and shame-marrowed, the sweet corpses of the men whom Merlin betrayed. No words came, just the chthonic yelp of a heart that yearns for the gruel of love.

'Hello,' he said.

I shook my head and rubbed my eyes to break the spell and, when free of the grip of the enchantment, managed to utter, 'It's OK, mate, you can skip the Iago Prytherch routine – I'm a private detective.'

He jerked with sudden animation, threw his hands up and laughed and said, 'Well bloody hell, a peeper! Why didn't you say?'

'I wanted to ask you a few questions, if you don't mind. You don't have to answer them.'

'I played a peeper once, or rather I auditioned – didn't get the part.'

'Trust me, you wouldn't have enjoyed it.'

'What do you want to know about, then?'

'Some of the work you did before you did this.'

'There was nothing else. Been Iago Prytherch all my life.'

'Sure,' I said and put a fiver down on the kitchen table next to the 'Reluctant Swedes'. 'I hear you did a part in a movie of Myfanwy's funeral?'

'The night club singer?' He reached over and took the money. 'I didn't get the part. Would you like a cup of tea? Sorry the kettle doesn't whine, it just whistles.'

'Whistling's fine.'

He stood up and I followed him into the kitchen. He shoved some root vegetables across the wooden table and fetched down some cups and saucers.

'These are mangels for the cows. I have to dock them with a half-witted grin of satisfaction, but it's not my favourite bit, it feels a bit stagey if you ask me. It was my spittled mirth that got me the job. Would you like to see it?'

I moved back slightly and said, 'Maybe next time.'

He nodded, 'Probably wisest.'

We went back into the parlour and he said, 'They told me it was a movie of her life. They were shooting the funeral and wanted someone to play the gumshoe. Private detectives weren't my strong suit, to be honest, so I rented some Humphrey Bogart videos.' There was a sudden strange transformation of his face as if an invisible hand had stuck a finger in the corner of his mouth and pulled it to one side. He spoke through a mouth shaped like a horizontal keyhole.

'I never met a dame yet who didn't under-shtand a shlap in the kisser or a shlug from a .45.'

I forced a smile.

'Having met you I can see that real private detectives aren't like that, are they?'

'We almost never hit ladies, or shoot them.'

'When I turned up for the audition, I walked in and the director shouted "Next!" "Next," I said, "I haven't done me Bogart yet." "You're too short," he said and then told someone to throw me out on my fanny.'

'What exactly was the role?'

'They said the important thing was not to look too gloomy. I was a bit unsure about that bit because people are supposed to be gloomy at funerals, aren't they? So I asked the agent and he said this isn't a normal funeral and I said, "Oh a modern reinterpretation or something, is it?" And he told me not to say things like that because the director didn't like smart alecks.'

'Who was the agent?'

'I don't know, just a guy I met in a bar. You know how it is.'

'Did the private eye have a name?'

Iago furrowed his brow as he struggled to recall. 'He did, but I'm damned if I can remember it. Began with L. Leopold or something daft like that.'

The fake Iago Prytherch walked me back to the station. 'Thank you for coming,' he said. 'You're a lot more cheerful than the last visitor I had. You probably heard about him on the radio – the war veteran who had the fight with the policeman.'

'You mean Rimbaud?'

'That's the one.'

'What was he doing up here?'

'He's the technical adviser on the project. On account of how deeply he has suffered – he wrote *The Vale of Tears Handbook*. It's our textbook. But the bugger ran into a spot of bother with police down in Glanwern, didn't he? They tried to take him in but he escaped and then baited some traps in the woods with his own pollution, so I heard.'

'Did he tell you about his missing years?'

'He would have done, but to tell you the truth I wouldn't let him. "Oh God!" he said. "Don't make me tell you about my missing years!" And I said, "I wasn't going to." And he looked a bit disappointed and said, "You can if you really want to." And I said, "Actually I don't think I do." It was not long after that he had the fight with the policeman – I guess he didn't want to hear about his missing years either.' We arrived at the last stile and the fake Iago Prytherch stopped and reached me his hand to shake. And then a bright smile appeared on his face. 'That's it! I remember now. Louie Knight! That was the name of the private eye I had to play. Louie Knight.'

I shook his hand one more time and thanked him and just before he turned away he said, 'What did you say your name was?'

'Luggage,' I said. 'Lefty Luggage.'

I went back to the office and opened the book the postman had given me for Sister Cunégonde. It was a biography of Pope Gregory the First, written by someone called Ulricus. Inside it was inscribed: 'To Sister Cunégonde, in the hope that the life of this great man will prove as inspirational to you as it has to me. Fond regards from your loving brother, Frankie Mephisto.'

Chapter 11

THE POOLS AND channels of water of the marsh blazed with the dawn sun as if the ground had torn in places to reveal the fire burning at the centre of the earth. Meredith was already up, and slamming the shovel down into the sodden peat, placing a wellington boot on the rim of the shovel and pushing down, then levering and prising the chunk of turf free like a kid trying to wiggle a milk tooth molar. I stood behind him and watched for a while and then not wishing to surprise him cleared my throat loudly. He eased up and turned to face me. A slight nod of acknowledgement.

'Seen Seren round here recently?' I said.

'No.'

'I was looking for her.'

He nodded as if such a revelation was devoid of significance.

'Thought she might have come this way.'

'Why would you think that?'

'I heard she likes to play over here.'

'I haven't seen her.'

I took a step closer and stared into his sun-burned face, eyes dark as tar. 'Just trying to find out what happened to Myfanwy. They say Seren knows this area well, maybe she could give me some help.'

'She can't help you.'

'Probably not, but sometimes you never know. Kids often see things we grown-ups miss. She might know where they could have taken her.'

'Could have taken her across the water there to Aberdovey.

Could have taken her on the train there to Shrewsbury. Could have taken her back to Aberystwyth in a car. Could have taken her out there to Ireland. Or maybe they didn't take her anywhere, just left her here.' He slung the spade on to his shoulder. 'Don't need no girl to tell you that.'

'Which one do you think it is?'

'I don't.' He made to move past me.

'Seren was in trouble the other night.'

He stopped, but showed no interest.

'I was over at the Waifery. She was bleeding, it looked pretty bad. They told me it was a nosebleed.'

'And what makes you think it wasn't?'

'Blood was all over her face.'

He shrugged and walked past me.

'Thought maybe Sister Cunégonde might have told you what was going on.'

He carried on walking and spoke with his back to me. 'Why would she do that?'

'I thought she was a friend of yours.'

He stopped and turned and took a step up to me. I thought he was going to hit me but he didn't. Underneath it all he was a rough but gentle man.

'We're not friends.'

I considered his answer and then said, 'What's it like to kiss a nun?'

That's when he hit me. He didn't do it immediately. He paused long enough to make it appear that the moment had come and gone and then swung fast and viciously. I lay on the ground, head swimming, my cheek half-submerged in cold wet pond water. He stood over me and looked down. I climbed slowly to my feet, looked at him and said, 'Mind if I get my hat.' He said nothing so I bent down to retrieve it but picked up a wooden stake instead and swung it against the side of his head. It connected but didn't seem to do much. I pulled back for a second blow and swung again but this time he caught the stick in his hand and twisted it out of my grip. It didn't look like it cost him much effort. He dropped the stick and swung the back of his hand into my face. This time I lay with my back in the water and looked up at a man looking down whose shovel was at my throat and whose wellington boot was poised gently on it. One slight heave was all it needed. I swallowed, my Adam's apple grinding against the cold steel edge. He grunted and removed the spade. By the time I got to my feet he was walking back to the cottage with the spade hoisted on to his shoulder.

I followed at a distance and he knew I was there even though he didn't look round. And, since he didn't tell me not to, I followed him into the cottage. He hung up his coat, put the shovel down in the corner, and put the kettle on. I sat at the table.

'Anything going on between you and Seren?'

'Like what?'

'Thought maybe you were sweet on her.'

I tensed in expectation of a fist, but he just sat at the table and said, 'No you don't. Stop trying to bait me.'

I let the tension ease from my clenched muscles. 'Sister Cunégonde doesn't like her much, does she?'

'There's nothing wrong with that girl. She likes to be on her own a lot, so what? So do I. They say she's strange, they say she's awkward and wayward. I don't. She plays truant now and again, but then which kid has never done that? Sometimes she goes out at night, I've seen her in the pub in Aberystwyth on occasion. Probably smokes too. She shouldn't be there, of course. But I used to go to the pub when I was her age and I don't know many people who didn't. Sometimes they catch her and she gets punished, and sometimes they don't. Either way it doesn't stop her and that's hardly surprising either. She tells a few fibs, I know that. So what? It can't be much fun living at that Waifery and if she wants to dress it up a bit, that's fine with me. They say she needs special treatment because she's difficult and has special needs. To me, all it means is she's a normal kid. I like having her around. I wish there were more people around like her.'

It was probably the longest speech of his life. He stood up and walked over to a dresser against the wall. He opened a drawer and took something out. He put it on the table in front of me. It was an old photo, black and white, creased and torn, with a thin white border. It showed a teenage girl being crowned Borth carnival queen. Judging by the parked cars and the hairstyles in the crowd it was taken sometime in the Fifties. It was Cunégonde.

'She was seventeen, about the same age as Seren is now. I was twenty-two, twenty-three.'

'Quite a beauty.'

'Yes, she was. Never seen anyone brush her hair so much.'

'This chap looks familiar.'

Meredith flinched. 'Yes, he's a well-known man in these parts. More's the pity.'

It was Frankie Mephisto, dressed like a backing singer in Bill Haley's band. Hair slicked down, face shiny. And handsome. He had a girl on his arm: the carnival queen runner-up.

'He's changed a lot,' I said.

'This was before he became the big gangster. In those days he was just into small stuff.'

'Did you know Frankie Mephisto was Cunégonde's brother?'

'Yes, I knew. She won't thank you for putting it about though.'

'Who's the girl with Frankie?'

'I don't know. Frankie always had a pretty girl on his arm. He knew how to charm them in those days. I don't know who she is.'

I peered at her. There was something familiar about her. But I couldn't put my finger on it.

'You kept it all these years,' I said, handing it back.

He said nothing. It wasn't a question.

'Were you in love with Cunégonde?'

Again he said nothing. He didn't need to. Why else do you

keep a photo of someone for thirty years? He walked to the back door and opened it in a manner that said he'd talked enough for today. He held out his hand to shake. 'I hope they find Myfanwy.'

The college scarf hanging on the hat stand had alternating stripes of grey, henna and beige. We had a visitor from the college in Lampeter.

'This is Iestyn,' said Calamity. 'He's from the theology college.'

'Always nice to meet a student,' I said.

'The honour is mine, sir,' he replied.

'Is this your first visit to Aberystwyth?'

'How did you know?'

'Just a lucky guess.'

There was a candle on the desk and the inside of a toilet roll.

'Iestyn has been helping me with the case,' explained Calamity. 'We've almost cracked it.'

I sat down. 'We had a client once from your college. Faculty of undertaking.'

'Yes, some of the guys in the third year got the cadaver. "Come to Sunny Aberystwyth" knife lodged up to the hilt between the sixth and seventh intercostal. Nice job.'

'Yeah, well, not all our clients end up on a slab.'

'Oh, I didn't mean to offend, sir.'

'No offence taken. Tell me about the case.'

Calamity pulled a large book out from under the desk and thrust it down with emphasis.

'Item one: Mrs Llantrisant's book on meterology, *Red Sky at Night*.'

'It's an inquiry into the anthropomorphic fallacy in forensic meteorology,' added Iestyn helpfully.

'I know, she wrote it when I was paying her to swab my step.'

'According to this, 1849 was the driest summer for thirty years.

The spinning wheels would have been tinder dry. Neglect to oil one, spin a bit too fast and, presto, you have a stray spark.'

'Where is this leading to?'

Calamity placed her hands on her hips and paced up and down the room. 'The stable boy said he saw burning and climbed up the ivy to save Cranogwen. The peelers say he stole the gems and then set the room on fire. But we already know he couldn't have done that because the gems showed signs of fire damage. So they must have been removed after the fire and planted. But by who? Good question, I'll come to it in a minute. And there's a funny thing about the fire: only the bed burnt. The rest of the room was largely untouched. Except the spinning wheel in the corner.'

'OK, the spinning wheel catches fire because it's tinder dry, a spark jumps from the wheel and sets fire to the bed . . .'

'It couldn't have worked like that,' said Iestyn. 'If the bed catches fire so does the rest of the room. There's only one way the bed can burn and not the room, only one thing produces such a localised effect.'

'And what's that?'

'Spontaneous human combustion,' said Calamity.

'It's my specialist subject,' added Iestyn. 'Look!' He moved over to the table and picked up the candle. 'See this? It's a candle made from human tallow.'

He took out a lighter and lit the wick. 'The wick's made from a gauze taken from the mid-section of a lady's combinations *circa* late 1840s. And that's the key, you see. The wicking effect. A light summer corset wrapped round a lump of fat makes a pretty good candle.' The candle had fizzled out, but not without filling the room with the odour of singed flesh. 'Now normally, as you see, nothing happens. The fire won't catch. You need something to get it going. A catalyst. And what do you think that could be?' He looked at me. I shrugged and Iestyn picked up the toilet roll tube. 'Tra-la-la!' he shouted in a lame attempt to invest the proceedings with an air of drama. 'Her stovepipe hat!'

I shot Calamity a glance. She was striving for an air of nonchalance as if this was all purely routine.

'Stand back, now,' said Iestyn. 'And look what happens.' He lit the candle and then brought the tube of cardboard down over the flame. Instead of standing back we both leaned in closer. And then we jumped back as a blinding flash shot up the tube and burned with a fierce white flame like magnesium in a school chemistry lab. 'See!' Iestyn shouted above the roar of the flames. 'It acts like a flue! Pretty impressive, huh? It's the same process as a Bessemer converter used for smelting iron – but then I expect you already know that.' He drew the flue away and the flame subsided. There followed half a second's stunned silence and then Calamity said, 'Open and shut case.'

'All right,' I said. 'The fire started accidentally, spontaneous human combustion. The stable boy saw the flames and climbed up to save the girl. He didn't touch her gems, someone else planted them after the fire to incriminate him. So why does the ghost finger the kid by writing *comes stabuli*? She must have known he didn't do it.'

'Easy,' said Calamity. 'There was no ghost. The writing was done by a member of the household to point the finger at the kid. That's why the writing stopped appearing after a while and then started again this century. If you compare the handwriting of the ghost on the tea towel which is taken from the appearance in 1923 it's clearly a different hand from the original sketches done in 1860.'

'Are you sure about that?'

'I spoke to a graphologist.'

'Where did you find one of those in Aberystwyth?'

'Llunos knows one.'

'First I knew.'

'He said they are clearly different hands. I reckon the new owners are doing it. A decent ghost can add another twenty-five quid a night to the cost of a room.'

'OK, the ghost is a phoney, I buy that. That means the stable boy was set up. By who?'

'Still working on that,' said Calamity 'But it has to be someone who understands Latin so my guess is the physician Dr Weevil.'

Later that morning I saw Gabriel Bassett walking into the Pier and I followed. He moved with the blinkered swiftness of someone who knows exactly where he is going, who has come to still a craving rather than for mere pleasure. He moved through the machines and took a seat at the bingo game towards the rear. I sat next to him and put a couple of coins into the electro-illuminated screens.

'Didn't expect to find you here, Mr Knight,' he said.

'It's not one of my regular haunts.'

The caller invited us to focus our attention on the game by the time-honoured manner of casting down our eyes and looking in. She reeled off the numbers and Gabriel talked to me and slid the doors across on the screen without even looking at what he was doing.

'Not long now,' he said. 'Just over a week.'

'We'll be fine, we're almost there.'

He nudged me slightly in the ribs as if making a lewd remark. 'Care to give me a little foretaste?'

'Calamity will have to take you through the detail, but we're pretty certain the ghost is a phoney—'

He jumped in surprise. 'A phoney? My word you surprise me!'

'It looks that way.'

'But how can that be? The medium I spoke to contacted her not two weeks ago.'

'How much did you pay the medium?'

'Only two hundred pound. You're not suggesting she was a charlatan are you?'

'I never met one yet who wasn't.'

'She seemed very honest.'

'Believe me, that's not always a reliable indicator.'

'She even gave me some ectoplasm. Look.' He took out an old tobacco tin – St Bruno Ready Rubbed Flake – and opened it. The heady sweet sharp perfume of tobacco rose up but otherwise the tin was empty.

'It's a nice tin, Mr Bassett, but it's not worth two hundred pound.'

'Oh dear.'

A woman shouted 'House' and everyone looked round with hate in their eyes. The numbers were checked, the call confirmed, the next game began.

'Lucky bitch!' said Gabriel. 'I was almost there and all.'

I put a shilling in to light up his screen and he started mechanically moving the little plastic doors.

'How can you be sure the ghost isn't real?' he said.

'We had the handwriting analysed. It's not consistent. We think originally someone had it in for the stable boy and tried to point the finger at him.'

'You don't know how happy this news makes me.'

'Care to tell me why it makes you so happy?'

'Oh no, I couldn't possibly do that. It's a long story anyway and you'd probably fall asleep.'

I apologised for falling asleep midway through his story about the suitcase.

'It was rather strange, I must say.'

'I was suffering from the after-effects of being hit on the head with a shovel. Concussion.'

'You know what it reminded me of? The way you dropped off like that? It was like those people in the audience at Mr Evans's hypnotism show. That's what it was like, like you'd been hypnotised. Anyway,' he added, kicking the case under the bingo console, 'I don't blame you for falling asleep. The story of my case isn't very interesting.'

'It's not boring at all, I was fascinated. What did you find when you opened the case?'

'I found a pair of Breton fisherman's trousers and a pile of old letters tied with a ribbon.'

'Is that all?'

'There was also a photo of a little girl. The darlingest little girl ever: standing in the Jardin du Luxembourg in winter as snow fell, wearing a pillar-box-red coat. The letters were in French and I had to get them translated. They told the story of a love affair between this girl's mother – Evegnie – and a Breton fisherman. Evegnie had lived a sheltered life, brought up by her aunt who was a strict and puritanical woman and saw to it that her niece remained untutored in matters of the heart. I'm sure you can guess the course the affair took: the man swore that he loved her and when he had robbed her of that treasure that it is a young maiden's shame to lose, he abandoned her. He left her with child by him and as a consequence her aunt called her a tramp and cast her out. She went to work as a seamstress in Paris where the child was born. I suspect you will have guessed by now that this fisherman was none other than myself in the pre-Gabriel-Bassett days. Yes, I was that fisherman. Which is surprising because nowadays I only have to look at a boat and I get seasick. Naturally, I was appalled at what I had discovered. To think that I could have been responsible for such cruelty! Her letters were written in a simple, disarmingly frank and childish style, and leavened with many beguiling touches. And as I read I found myself growing increasingly fond of this girl: of her candour, and open-hearted wonder, the sensitivity of her soul revealed in a thousand light touches, the charming childishness of her handwriting and even the cheapness of the perfume with which she daubed the paper – it all conspired to win my heart. What a paradox, you may think, that the story of her suffering, that I myself had inflicted, should now melt my heart. And then I thought of the little girl in the red coat. My daughter? What an astonishing thing! To think that I had such a lovely daughter here on this earth.

'And so I wrote to Evegnie telling her all that had befallen me.

At first, of course, she refused to acknowledge my letters. But I persisted, writing again and again and repeating over and over the simple truth that I was a changed man. Until eventually she started to write back. In time I managed to win her trust and convince her of my sincerity. I dared to inquire if there was another man in her life. She told me that there was not, that there never could be, that she was capable of giving her heart away but once in this world. And then I took the boldest step of all and asked whether I might be permitted to visit her and my daughter. I waited for her reply with my heart in my mouth. What might she say? Would she spurn me like I deserved or would the light of Christian charity that shone so clearly through her letters look kindly on my request? Suddenly the humble postman had acquired the power to transfigure me with joy, or crush me utterly with despair.'

Bassett stopped and sighed and said, addressing the bingo console, 'I guess some of us were never meant to achieve happiness in this world.'

'But what did she say?' I asked. 'Did she refuse to see you?'

'No.' He shook his head. 'No. I sat by the front door for days waiting for her reply. And then finally when I thought my heart could take it no more, when I thought that it was surely too late and that I was destined not to receive the reply I craved, I saw the postman turn into our street. He was wearing the uniform of the special delivery corps and he was carrying something. It was a box of some sort. I watched him walk up and stop outside my house. He checked the number against a slip of paper that he carried, then walked up to the door and rang the bell. I opened the door before his finger had even reached the bell. I looked at his face and then cast my eyes down to the box standing next to his shoe. It was a suitcase, a tatty cardboard suitcase very similar to mine. And then I saw that I had been deceived. It was not the special delivery postman, it was someone whose uniform was similar. It was the man from the left luggage office. He told me there had been a mix-up and they had given me the wrong case. He had come to exchange them. He gave me this one, the one I carry around now, the one I have never dared open. And he took away the case containing the record of my love for Evegnie and the beautiful daughter I thought for a while was mine.

'But what did Evegnie say?'

'I don't know. I never contacted her again. How could I? She was a stranger.'

'But the love was real.'

He looked at me, pain etched into the crevices of his face. 'Yes, the love was real. But it wasn't mine. It belonged to someone else and I just picked it up and wore it for a while the way you wear someone else's hat by mistake.'

I gave Bassett another shilling for the bingo and walked down to Sospan's and ordered an ice cream.

'Penny for your thoughts, Mr Knight,' said Sospan.

I shook my head. 'I was just wondering. Do you ever think you might have chosen the wrong career?'

A look of deep earnest furrowed the ice man's brow. 'To tell you truly, Mr Knight, it's difficult to answer that question in the terms in which it is asked. Being an ice man is not a career as such, more of a calling.'

'You didn't choose it then?'

'Not really. I was called to it.'

'Did you get to choose to do it in Aberystwyth or was that part of the calling?'

'That is the question that should never be asked.'

'All I'm asking is what made you come to Aberystwyth.'

'Let's just say I came for the water.'

'The seawater?'

'No! Not the seawater. Whoever heard of going somewhere for that. I mean, you know, the water. Like in that film with what's-his-name, the bloke whose photo they've got on the wall in the Cabin.'

'Humphrey Bogart.'

'Exactly. The guy asked him what brought him to Casablanca and Humphrey Bogart said he came for the water. And the guy said but there is no water in Casablanca and he said, "I was misinformed."'

'He was misinformed?'

Sospan gave me a bright insistent nod and said, 'There you go.'

But I was baffled and asked him to explain. He frowned with annoyance. 'I shouldn't have to spell it out, it's perfectly clear. Saying he came for the water was his way of saying "mind your own business" wasn't it? He didn't want to tell him, you see, because his past housed a ghost, a source of pain that he preferred not to think about.'

'And there's a ghost in your past like that?'

He raised his index finger and pointed to a fine jagged scar that meandered down his cheek just in front of the ear. 'Never ask how I got this in the days before I came to Aberystwyth. I'll say no more.'

Chapter 12

I THREW MY HAT across the room and missed the hat stand.

Calamity looked up from a sheaf of papers on the desk. 'Nice walk?'

'It was OK. I was thinking about various things and one thing that I got to thinking about was the incident board. Covered with clues and facts and statements, and I was wondering about where you are getting it from—'

'From my sources.'

'That's right: from your sources. Or maybe that should be your source.'

'More than one.'

'I got to thinking about something else too. Have you noticed how I keep falling asleep? It's not really like me.'

Calamity looked at me slyly. 'It's probably the strain about Myfanwy, preying on your mind. It's surprising how tired a thing like that can make you.'

'Yeah, that's probably it. But I've noticed that every time I wake up, you have a new clue on the wall.'

She looked at me, eyes narrowing and then said with exaggerated casualness, 'No I don't.'

'You do.'

She shrugged.

'But what really got me thinking was something Gabriel Bassett just told me. He said when I fell asleep halfway through his story it was like I'd been hypnotised. And of course the funny thing is, I have been hypnotised, haven't I?'

Calamity concentrated hard on her notes.

'Have I been talking in my sleep?'

'No.'

'No?'

'No.'

'No?'

'No.'

'No?'

'No.'

'No?'

'No.'

'No?'

'No.'

'No?'

'Not much.'

'Calamity!'

'Well, it's not my fault if you fall asleep and start talking in the voice of the lamplighter. What am I supposed to do?'

'Wake me up, that's what. Not pump me.'

'I didn't pump you.'

'What do you call it then?'

'Overhearing.'

'You did more than that. You asked questions didn't you?'

'Just a couple. The stuff he was giving me was so useful that—'

'It's not useful, it's an end-of-the-pier party trick. You can't use the people as a source of evidence. They're dream figures.'

'So why are you dreaming suddenly about Gwylym?'

'Who's Gwylym?'

'The lamplighter?'

'I thought his name was Pigmallow.'

'It is. Gwylym Pigmallow.'

'It's got to stop. It's not genuine evidence. He's a Freudian figure, dredged up from my subconscious: he's symbolic of illumination you see, a lamplighter, shedding light—'

Calamity made a farting sound with her lips. 'Who told you that?'

'Meirion.'

'What does he know?'

'You've got to stop it, Calamity. Do some real detective work – forget about Pigmallow the footpad and Captain Poxbag the pirate and Whisky Williams the smuggler? OK?'

'Hmmm.'

'And another thing, where were you earlier before I took a walk?'

'Out.'

'Sure, but where?

'Just out.'

'You were supposed to be manning the phone. What if Myfanwy has been trying to ring?'

'I only went out for a little while – I needed to get some more tacks.'

'More tacks?'

'I dug up a few things at the town library and . . . did you get anything?'

'What does that mean?'

'Nothing, just asking.'

'No, I don't have anything to pin on my side of the wall if that's what you are asking.'

Calamity made as if to speak and then decided against it.

'And another thing, don't think I haven't noticed what you've done to the line.'

'What line?'

'The dividing line on the incident board. You've moved it.'

'No I haven't!'

'Originally it was straight down the middle. Now it's more over to my side.'

'But I only moved it an inch because my side was full.'

'It doesn't matter whether it's an inch or a mile.'

'An inch or a mile.'

'It's the principle. We share things down the middle in this office. You don't like it, you know what you can do.'

Calamity stood up and walked over to the incident board. She unpinned the black dividing line and moved it over two inches nearer to her side.

'That makes me feel a lot better,' I snarled.

'Well, we probably don't really need it any more because the case is solved.'

'Solved.'

'I was going to tell you but you didn't give me chance.'

I said nothing. Calamity went and sat down and stared at nothing.

'Aren't you even going to ask?' she said finally.

I sighed. 'You solved the case, great. Tell me about it.'

'Not if that's your attitude.'

'Just tell me, damn you!'

Calamity jumped at the fierce tone in my voice. Her eyes misted – I don't think I'd shouted at her before. Not like that, not in three years together.

'I'm sorry,' I said. 'I . . . I . . . you know . . .'

Calamity nodded. 'It's OK. This thing about Myfanwy is doing you in. It would do anyone in.'

'Tell me what you've turned up,' I said gently, my heart still sick.

'To tell you the truth it wasn't me really, it was Iestyn. He phoned a while ago. He worked it out.'

She went over to the kitchen and brought back two glasses and some ginger beer. She filled the glasses and explained.

'Remember I was saying the ghost was a phoney? Whoever wrote the ghostly words *comes stabuli* was just trying to make it look like a ghost to point the finger at the stable boy.'

'I remember. The only problem was, you couldn't work out who had it in for the kid, but thought it might be the physician because he spoke Latin.'

'Yeah, well it looks like I was wrong and right at the same time. I still think the ghost was a phoney, I still think it was the doctor who wrote the words, the bit I got wrong was the "keeper of the stables" bit. According to Iestyn, *comes stabuli* comes from Roman times, and means the guy who took charge of the emperor's horses. But the point is, he did a lot more than that. He had to look after all sorts of things, he was a sort of Roman cop. And that's where we get the modern word constable from. *Comes stabuli*, y'see? *Comes stab- comes stab- comes stab-ul.* Constable. Whoever wrote the words was not pointing the finger at the stable boy, but at the policeman. The peeler. You see, the fire was an accident but they suspected it was murder so the peeler planted the evidence to help get a conviction. Dr Weevil must have guessed what had happened.'

I said nothing, just screwed up my brow as the impact of what she was saying sank in.

'Anyway, I'll just finish writing up my report, get Llunos to sign it, and I'll be sending it down to Swansea to get my badge.' She raised her glass for a toast. 'Cheers!'

I didn't move.

'Cheers,' she repeated.

I still didn't move.

'What's wrong?'

'Nothing.'

Calamity put the glass down very slowly. 'There's something wrong.'

'Everything's fine.'

'Now I know you're lying.'

I let out a long deep breath and said, as gently and with as little accusation as I could muster, 'You're not serious?'

'About what?'

'You're going to ask Llunos to sign that?'

'I have to, otherwise I can't submit it to the Board in Swansea.'

'I know that but—'

'But?'

'Llunos?'

She didn't answer, just stared silently with that inner rage that starts to build up when you start to defend a course of action you weren't really sure about in the first place.

'It was his great-grandfather, Calamity.'

'I know.'

'He worships his memory.'

'I know that too.'

I made a dismissive gesture as if washing my hands of it. 'Fine.'

'You expect me to do what?'

'Whatever you like.'

'Don't try and get out of it. You don't think I should tell him what we found out?'

'As I said, it's up to you, but personally I wouldn't tell him that we found out his great-grandfather, whose memory he venerates as the inventor of the principles of policing that have served Cardiganshire for 150 years, was bent. That the paradigm of model policing he established includes falsifying witness testimony, lying on oath, planting evidence and that he probably connived at the hanging of an innocent boy. No, I don't think I would tell him that. Perhaps I'm too sentimental for this job.'

'And why wouldn't you tell him that?'

'What good would it do? Think what it would do to his reputation.'

Calamity screwed her face up in disbelief. 'Reputation!? What sort of crap is that? We're detectives, aren't we? It's our solemn duty to bring truth to light no matter whose reputation it hurts.'

'Where did you get that from? A dime novel you picked up in Devil's Bridge?'

'I got it from you.'

'Oh . . . Yeah?

'Yeah.'

'Well, sometimes I say things that don't always apply in all circumstances equally.'

'And you get to choose where they do and where they don't.'

'If I did say that, I'm sorry. I should have qualified it. We were talking about a different sort of case. In this situation nothing useful will come of publishing what you found. You won't help the stable boy. He's been dead 150 years and if he isn't happy now then he'll never be. All you'll achieve . . . all you'll do, is crush Llunos. I know you want to publish your first case, I want you to, I really do. But I just want you to think about the consequences, it's the first rule—'

'Yeah, I know, of being a private eye. How many first rules are there going to be?'

'All right it's the golden rule. Think of the consequences. You know what consequences are? They are the things you can't put back into the bottle once you release them.'

'I still don't get it. What's the point of doing all this if at the end we keep schtum? We might as well not have started in the first place. I thought we were the guys in the white hats.'

'In Aberystwyth there are no white hats, Calamity. Grey is as good as it gets. Just a dirty old grey hat that gets kicked about the floor a bit and has a footprint on the brim. That's all we've got. We're not saints, and we're not knights like it says in the stupid sign on the frosted glass. We're not engaged on some noble quest to uncover truth for its own sake, we just try to make things better than they were when we started. Sometimes that's damned hard. But we try and sometimes we get it right. But that's all it is. If you want to walk around with two shoe boxes marked "good" and "evil", join the Church. I'm not trying to interfere in your decision, whatever you decide I'll support you. Just think about it that's all.'

'My hat doesn't have a footprint on it.'

Ten minutes later Llunos walked in. I held up the rum bottle but he shook his head, he was just dropping by. He walked over and put a hand on Calamity's shoulder.

'How's the case coming along, sleuth?'

She looked up. 'Solved.'

Llunos did a pantomime of a man stepping back in amazement. 'Solved!'

She shot me a glance that was so swift it almost never happened. 'Yeah, I reckon the boy was innocent all right. It's pretty certain.'

'Innocent, was he?' The voice was pure frost.

'Pretty sure. He was fitted up. They changed witness statements, planted evidence, lied under oath. A real can of worms.'

Llunos took his hand off Calamity's shoulder and said very quietly. 'Who did?'

The pause lasted the length of a long breath. No more. 'Syracuse did.'

He looked down at Calamity but she avoided his gaze. She avoided my gaze and busied herself instead with tidying the papers on the desk. They didn't need tidying. Llunos walked slowly to the centre of the room and stopped. He rocked back on his heels and seemed to be lost in thought. Then he said to no one in particular, 'You're going to send a report to the Bureau in Swansea saying my great-grandfather was a bent cop?'

Calamity shrugged weakly, the blood draining from her face. 'Yep.'

'I see,' said Llunos. He nodded to himself and said again, softly, 'I see.'

'She has to, Llunos,' I said.

He jerked round to face me, 'She has to?'

'What's she supposed to do?'

'She could try minding her own bloody business for a start!'

'Oh sure!' I cried. 'Mind her own bloody business. What sort of thing is that to teach her? She's trying to be detective, she's not supposed to mind her bloody business. She's supposed to dig and probe and snout about and make a bloody nuisance of herself until she brings the truth to light.'

'Truth to light!'

'And if it upsets people that's just tough.'

'She's got a lot to learn if that's what she thinks.'

'I'm sorry, Llunos!' I shouted. 'Round here you either wear a white hat or you don't. There's no grey, no in-between, you either play it straight or . . . or . . . or . . .' I hadn't a clue what to say next.

Llunos walked to the door and stopped and turned. 'You and me aren't supposed to get on, you know that? We're supposed to be adversaries because there's a stupid book somewhere that says snoopers are jerks who need to be kicked out of town. But I threw that book away a long time ago. For a long time now I've loved you like a brother, you know that? I never say it because blokes like me don't. That's the way I was brought up and it's too late to change now. But I did . . . and now . . . I can't believe what I've heard here today, I really can't. After working this festering moral sewer together for fifteen years, you throw the white fucking hat crap at me?!' He turned in disgust and walked down the stairs shouting as he went, 'White fucking hat!'

I ran to the door and shouted down the stairwell, 'It was a miscarriage of justice, Llunos!'

'So?!' he shouted back.

'So? I suppose she should have kept it to herself and hoped no one noticed!'

'Why not?' he shouted now from the street level. 'That's what I did when I found out!'

For a while I stayed there staring down at the empty stairwell and then walked back inside.

'Sometimes it's hard to do the right thing,' said Calamity.

'Well, you sure failed today.'

I walked to the window and stared out at Llunos turning at the junction with Great Darkgate Street. After a while the distant hum of the traffic outside faded and I became aware of a soft squeaking sound, the noise of stifled weeping. I turned and walked over to Calamity and knelt down. She looked at me, eyelashes heavy with tears like raindrops on a branch. 'Oh Louie, what have I done?'

Chapter 13

MOMENTS WHEN I felt no fear:

At night, in the gaps between dreams, where time is extinguished.

Emerging from sleep – that instant of awareness before opening the eyes. I have learned you can prolong this instant in the same way yogis can lower their body's metabolism.

Two occasions when people knocked me unconscious with a shovel. I must remember to write and thank them.

And, sometimes, under the ocean.

The caravan was warmer than blood when I got back. There was a parcel on the caravan step. It was from Siop-y-Pethe – a translation of Brainbocs's 'invented language'. I left it untouched on the table, put on my swimming trunks, and left the doors and windows open to clear the air. The sand was hot under foot and the wind warm and blustery, heavy with grains of salt. The tide was out, and the high-water mark demarcated by a wavy line of wet sticks tangled with blue nylon netting, plastic bags, and shampoo bottles from which all the writing had been washed away. I dropped my towel on the hot stones and walked through avenues of evaporating jelly fish. My feet hissed on the sand like a snare on drumskin, and then I reached the silver film of water, waded in and lay back. The water dancing next to my ears tinkled like a xylophone. And then I went under and the world was removed, sounding far away like the thumping of someone moving boxes in a cellar.

After my swim I returned to the caravan and began to read. The accompanying note explained that it appeared to be the beginning of an epic poem about Myfanwy and, although it was always difficult rendering poetry in a different language, they had done their best to capture the mood.

Cider with Myfanwy

Like to the dog hit by the truck whose leg is withered
I scavenged at the bins of her love . . .

Note: this part has been crossed out, with the words, Damn! Damn! Damn!

Neither ask me about the colour of her hair,
Demand instead the conker—

This part is also crossed out

As the unclaimed coat left hanging on the pegs
Half an hour after the 4 o'clock bell
Does she esteem me . . .

The attempted poem is abandoned here and turns into a letter

Mama,
I watched from the Prom, once, as she wrestled in the sea with a boy. She was fifteen. Her bikini top came off and she brought her forearms forward and huddled inside them, and the boy tried to prise them apart. They both laughed so much. They did not know it at the time, and perhaps it would take a lifetime for them to grasp the truth of that hour. But it was available to me in its entirety as the gift of the outcast. I knew then that this was a moment that comes but once in a lifetime; this was the day they drank their cider with Rosie. And there would never be such a moment for me. Never anything sweeter than Lucozade.

I gathered the sheaves of paper together, lifted them and banged them on the table to align the edges. Myfanwy had sat at a table like this a few summers ago. We had played ludo and she told me between interminable waits for her first double six how Brainbocs had haunted her steps, smitten beyond the power of words to describe. Smitten with a depth of suffering that carefree Myfanwy whose life had been anointed with the love of others freely given couldn't even begin to imagine; his torment a country she had never visited and which I had occasionally glimpsed in the eyes of the people who sat on my client's chair. The seekers after benediction who, when the priests failed them, came to haunt my door and begged me to damn them with the truth about their cheating spouse. They would take out the sixpences collected in coronation mugs and spread them on my table and say, 'Take it all,' as if the silver mined from twenty years of Christmas puddings was a fortune too great for mortal men to count. Take it, and find out.

I can't bear it any longer, it's torture.

You think so? What do you know about torture? Have you ever been to a museum and seen an iron maiden? They used them for entertainment in the Middle Ages – a great time to be alive. A nice big metal sarcophagus that they stuck you in if they didn't like you, with vicious inward-pointing spikes on the door. They made them shaped like a woman, too, which was a nice touch. And, when they closed the door, two spikes pierced your eyes and one went through your heart.

Is it worse than that?

Yes, it is.

The knock on the door was so soft it barely rose above the hiss from the gas lamp. I stopped breathing and listened. It came again. It couldn't be a twig brushing against the aluminium skin of the caravan because it wasn't loud enough. Maybe a dandelion had been blown against the door. I stood up, walked slowly across and opened the door. Sister Cunégonde stood there and whispered, 'Can I come in?'

I nodded and stood aside and went to put the kettle on. I also unscrewed the top of the rum bottle.

'Nothing stronger than plain old tea for me,' she said.

I took the tea cups over and put them down.

'Seren's gone,' she said.

'Gone?'

'Run away.'

'I haven't seen her.'

She nodded.

'Tell me what happened to her the other night.'

'Which other night?'

I spluttered with the scorn that had been simmering near the surface for too long. 'Oh let me see!' I cried. 'Which one could it be now? Oh, I know! What about the night when I came round and heard a girl screaming and saw Seren covered in blood fighting with two nuns and someone hit me over the head with a shovel?'

'It wasn't a shovel, it was a warming pan. And, anyway, I told you, she had a nosebleed – someone punched her on the nose.'

'So why was she struggling?'

'She was hysterical. She gets fits, you see.'

'I don't blame her.'

She shot me a glance and then looked down and pretended to be coy. 'It's partly your fault too.'

'That's a good one!'

Sister Cunégonde hesitated and looked down at the cup, then bit her lip.

'I wouldn't give you fifty cents for your acting.'

'Sometime last year the girls played truant and went to Aberystwyth. They went to see that spot down at the harbour where the prostitute was killed. The stain in the tarmac that they can't wash out. You know what adolescent girls are like.'

'Not really, it's been too long.'

'Are you always so dark and bitter?'

'Mostly.'

'I'm sorry we hit you with the shovel.'

'Don't worry about it, being clouted with garden tools is my latest hobby. Tell me what adolescent girls are like.'

'Highly impressionable. They think there is something romantic in such squalid stories.'

'What stories?'

'A lady of the night being murdered. Her lover, a handsome private detective – oh yes we read all about it in the newspapers. The girls knew instantly who you were that night you came round. They weren't fooled for an instant by my story about you being from the gas board.'

'If you're talking about Bianca, I wasn't her lover.'

'It's all one. The newspapers said you were. They said a lot else besides. Then when you started showing an interest in Seren the other girls were jealous.'

'Since when have I taken an interest in her?'

'She met you down at Meredith's cottage, didn't she? It's OK, you don't have to say anything, I know she probably asked you to keep it a secret and, like the gallant private eye that you are, you agreed. She thinks old Cunybongy is old and stupid and doesn't know what's going on. But I know she goes down there even though I've told her not to. The sand down there is a different colour, you see, and someone is traipsing it in to the Waifery two or three times a week . . .'

'Maybe you should examine the bottoms of your shoes first.'

She winced. 'What do you mean?'

'You're not averse to the odd midnight visit either, are you?'

She stared at me in genuine surprise and then hissed, 'I s'pose I should have expected something like that from a . . . a . . . snooper!'

'I wasn't spying on you. I saw you by accident. It's none

of my damn business and I don't care tuppence where you go or what you do. As long as it remains not my business. Trouble is I'm starting to think there's something funny about you that is my business. And before you start hatching any nasty little thoughts in your busybody mind, there's nothing between me and Seren. Nothing that anyone has any call to hide from the light of day. I met her at Meredith's, that's all. It was a harmless meeting. I don't know what she told the other girls but—'

'Yes, yes, of course. I wasn't suggesting anything like that. Not suggesting you did anything to encourage her or anything . . . it's just that the story no doubt got embroidered a bit in the telling, and the other girls were jealous, that's all. I mean I expect so. I don't know. I'm just guessing but it's not hard to guess sometimes how things are. I was her age once as well, despite what people think, and I wasn't particularly different. I was just as good at climbing the wall, thinking no one knew. I wonder if there ever was a time when no one knew . . .'

'So one of the girls thumped her.'

'She was boasting that she was your . . . your friend and a fight broke out. As I've told you, she's not particularly popular at the best of times. The fight caused her to have a fit. She has them sometimes. That's all it was.'

'All it was.'

'Yes.'

'I'm glad we cleared it up. Two girls fight over some petty squabble, one gets a nosebleed, and then a fit. So naturally the only thing to be done is hit me over the head with a shovel.'

'We didn't know what to do.'

'You're a lousy liar, Sister Cunégonde.'

'You must think what you wish.'

'And now she's run away.'

'Yes, it seems so.'

'You don't seem too bothered.'

'It's not the first time. She normally comes back after a few days.'

'So where does Frankie Mephisto fit into all this?'

'I've no idea what you mean.'

'Stop trying to take me for a fool. Frankie Mephisto is a gangster serving time in Shrewsbury jail. He's just your type actually – a good Samaritan. They say he's got a little sideline helping people in trouble. But every time he does that he stores up a debt for them in a little bank account in the name of Faust. Folk say he's about to be released. He did the crime, he did the time. Now he's on his way to Aberystwyth. Some people say he's already out. I wouldn't know. They say he's planning one last, final job. His swansong. I wouldn't know about that either. And frankly I wouldn't care. Except that the girl I love went missing from Ynyslas and, for some reason that no one has been able to explain to me, one of the girls at your Waifery planted a locket on the dunes meant to throw the search off the scent. And I might be able to not care a damn about that too, might be able to put it down to a silly adolescent prank, but then you come into the picture and every instinct I've got tells me you are one strange kettle of fish. And maybe I could manage not to care about that if it wasn't for this awkward fact that Frankie Mephisto is calling in the favours, drawing cheques on that account marked Faust, and something tells me you are one scared old woman. Any of that mean anything to you? It doesn't make much sense to me at the moment. Maybe you can help me work it out?'

'I don't know what you're talking about.'

'So why is he sending you books from Shrewsbury library?'

She looked shocked. 'He isn't!'

I took the book out of my bag and threw it on the table. 'He is.'

Her mouth opened and she popped her hand to it.

'Pope Gregory, whoever he is.'

'H . . . how did you get it?'

'The postman asked me to deliver it. I forgot. Then it fell on the kettle. You know how easily that can happen.'

'You had no right!'

'Don't give me any crap about rights. I had about as much right as you had to read Seren's letter.'

'It's not the same. The girl is sixteen. I'm her guardian.'

'So what's so special about Pope Gregory?'

'Why don't you ask Frankie Mephisto?'

'Oh that's good!' I laughed in scorn. 'A minute ago you didn't know who he was. Which is a bit surprising because I hear he also happens to be your brother, although I can understand why you would want to disown him.'

'You think you have all the answers, don't you?'

'On the contrary, all I have are questions. You're the one who knows the answers. Why would Frankie Mephisto send you a book on Pope Gregory?'

'I don't know.'

'Like hell you don't!'

'I don't.'

'What's he got on you? What are you scared of?'

'Nothing. I'm not scared of anything.'

'He's got something on you. I can see it in your eyes. Guy like him doesn't send people bedside reading. He sends them an Aberystwyth overcoat. You know what that is? It's made of pine. He's got something on you, I can smell it.'

There was a stand-off. Sister Cunégonde stared at her lap. And then looked up at me and said quietly, 'Can I have a rum?'

I walked over to the kitchenette to fetch the bottle and a glass for her and poured us two generous measures. She lifted the glass and looked at me over the rim, her tongue making a slight dart along the dry pale lips.

'Chin, chin,' she said and knocked it back.

At that moment she just looked like a sad and broken woman. She hiccupped on the scalding rum and said, 'I can't tell you what he has on me. I can't. It's too . . . too terrible. Please don't ask. I'll never say.'

'So what does he want from you? Normally blackmailers want money, but it can't be that.'

'No, he doesn't want money.'

'What then?'

'He wants me to do something. Something for him. Something soon.'

'Something like what? A favour?'

She turned the glass round in her hands. 'Yes, a favour. But I don't know what. He hasn't told me.'

My eyes narrowed slightly as I took that one in. I hadn't been expecting it.

'But he will. Oh, he will. And the only thing I know,' she added, her voice quivering on the threshold of tears, 'is that, knowing Frankie Mephisto, it will be something terrible. Something really, really awful. Horrible. And . . . and . . . worst of all . . .' She looked up at me and the tears were curving down in snail trails either side of her sharp red nose. 'Worst of all, I know that, whatever it is, I'll do it.'

Chapter 14

THE INCIDENT BOARD was in the bin next morning. Nothing was said about it, and nothing was said about the dossier on Nanteos that had found its way to the top of the cupboard in the kitchen.

I spent the rest of the week walking up and down the Prom. Two or three times a day I would run into Eeyore and ask how the search for Miss Muffet was going. He'd say it was going well and ask about Myfanwy. I'd say the signs were hopeful and I had plenty of leads to chase. But he knew that couldn't be true because if I did, why wasn't I chasing them? And I knew things weren't looking good for Miss Muffet either. Normally when they ran away they turned up again after a few days, dusty and hungry and in need of a good brush. Usually, too, they had a sort of chastened air about them that said the big wide world was not such a great place after all. But when a few days passed without news you tended to fear the worst. You normally didn't hear anything for a few months and then a friend would tell you how he'd been browsing in a bookshop in the red light district in Amsterdam and saw a donkey on the cover of a magazine that looked like her.

In all that time we didn't see anything of Gabriel Bassett either but I was glad in a way. On the Monday evening before he was due round I ran into a Cub Scout as I was leaving the office.

'Bob-a-job, mate?'

Green jumper, green and yellow cap, neckerchief, freshly scrubbed face glowing with youthful idealism. 'Is it bob-a-job week already?'

'If you've got a bob and a job it is.'

'Sorry, son, the last Cub Scout I invited in stole the umbrella stand.'

'You need an umbrella stand? Why didn't you say, I can supply.'

'Poxcrop! Is that you?'

'Doing my duty for God and the Queen. Not necessarily in that order.'

'How did you get the glow of youthful idealism?'

'Saddle soap.'

'Even your own mother wouldn't recognise you.'

'That's truer than you think, Mac, I just washed her dishes for fifty pence.'

'You did a bob-a-job for your own mum?'

'I admit she wasn't wearing her glasses. All the same. Didn't even know me – her own flesh and blood. She said I should come back later and meet her son, we'd get on well together. Imagine that! As if I were the type to make friends with a lousy Cub Scout. After all these years, that's how much she knows me.'

'Bit of a mean trick to play on your own mum.'

'What about the one she was going to play on me? Me, the little guy who suckled at her breast, she makes wash up for nothing. Some kid in a green and yellow cap turns up and she gives him fifty pence. She doesn't know him from Adam. Where's the justice in that? And then she says if only the Lord had sent her a little boy like him. I said, "Woman, behold your son."'

'So what have you got for me?'

He pulled out a box of papers from under his arm and held it out. The sheet on the top said, *Llanbadarn Parish Bugle.*

'I think you must have got your orders crossed.' He lifted the top paper to reveal a periodical beneath. *Journal of the Proceedings of the Myfanwy Society.*

'Complete set, pristine condition, all sixty issues including the special commemorative edition to mark the monkeys in space.'

He put the box down and added, before walking off, 'I've also heard a whisper about the singer.'

'Myfanwy?'

'Just a whisper.'

'What is it?'

'They say a special nurse has been engaged to look after her – Frankie Mephisto's old *consigliere*.'

'And who's that?'

'No one knows, Mac.'

I left the box with Calamity and arrived at the office next day to find her asleep with her head down on the desk. A flask of coffee was next to her and the periodicals were scattered over the desktop and littering the floor. She flinched when she heard me walk in, jumped slightly and made a soft groan. I nudged her awake.

'Hi!' she said, peering at me through eyes gummed up with sleep. 'I've been manning the phone.'

I smiled and gave her shoulder a soft squeeze. 'That's good, but you don't need to do it all night.'

'You never know. If Myfanwy was trying to ring she might have to wait until a strange hour.'

'I see you started on the periodicals.'

'Uh-huh.'

'Found anything?'

'Uh-huh.' She nodded towards the wall. One of the journals was pinned open. 'Remember you telling me Frankie Mephisto had a . . . a . . . whatchamacallit in prison, that made him go all religious?'

'An epiphany. The day he walked with Jesus and saw the wonder of his works.' I walked over to the wall. 'Maybe we should clear some of this mess up before Bassett comes. Today's the big day.'

'He's not coming.'

'No? What makes you say that?'

'Just a hunch.' She nodded again at the wall.

The periodical was opened to a black and white photo of Myfanwy aged seven or eight, maybe nine, sitting on a man's knee. She was wearing a party frock and hair in cutey-pie pig-tails. The man was wearing prison uniform. He smiled the beatific smile of one who is undergoing an unexpected epiphany. The caption read, 'Even notorious gangster Frankie Mephisto is not immune to the charms of Myfanwy's "Good Ship Lollipop".' Calamity came over and stood next to me.

'It's a Sunday school trip to sing to the prisoners, about fif-teen years ago.'

I looked at the face of Frankie Mephisto smiling into the camera and the hairs on my neck prickled as I experienced my own epiphany. I remembered where I had seen him before, why he had struck me as vaguely familiar when I went to visit him at Shrewsbury. He was the granddad parked next to us the day Myfanwy and I ate our last ice creams together at Ynyslas. The man whose beatific smile had misled me and caused me to reflect that the lustre of his forehead was the glow of avuncular phi-lanthropy when in fact it was nothing more than the patina that comes from a lifetime of hitting noses.

'Look at the guy standing behind him,' said Calamity.

It was Gabriel Bassett.

Gabriel Bassett was due round at noon but we decided in the light of this new discovery that we couldn't wait. Instead, we put on our coats and walked down to Harbour Row to pay him a call. The sign in the window said 'No Vacancies'. I stood on the step and rang the bell. Like all the B&Bs along Harbour Row, the house fronted almost directly on to the street, separated from it by a stretch of yard about a foot wide which meant that I was almost brushing up against the bay window and could clearly see Mrs Gittins sitting in her front parlour, wearing a housecoat. She was warming herself in front of a gas fire, even though it wasn't cold out. But, though I could see her, and she could see me, some strange protocol demanded that I pretend not to be able to see her and she pretended not to see me. She was knitting. After we got bored of the charade, I tapped on the window and pointed at the door. Mrs Gittins looked up with an expression of fake surprise, then stood up gingerly as if her joints had grit in them. She padded to the door in fluffy slippers. She opened the door a few inches and said, 'No vacancies.'

'Mrs Gittins, we've known each other ten or fifteen years. You see me every week somewhere in town. Do you really think I need a room?'

'That's what people normally come to a guesthouse for.'

'I want to talk to you about Gabriel Bassett.'

'He's not home.'

'Can we come in and chat? I'll pay for the gas.'

Inside the small parlour, the gas fire hissed, and the air was hot and fuggy with stale frying smells and the cloying absence of a husband, now long gone either to his grave or some illusion of a better life in Shrewsbury. Somewhere in the direction of the kitchen there would be a sitting room preserved in silence, as little visited as a sealed pharaoh's tomb, and reserved for special occasions the like of which never came to anyone who lived on this stretch of the Prom.

'Is he a friend of yours?'

'Yes, sort of.'

'Hmmmm.' She bid us sit down on the sofa and frowned deeply at the revelation that Gabriel Bassett had a friend. Normally, the lonely human flotsam that passed through her establishment seldom had such luxuries, especially ones that came visiting.

'Hmmm, I'm not sure.'

I took out a pound coin and let the Queen's face catch the light. 'As I said, I'll be happy to pay for the gas.'

She tilted her head back slightly and looked down her nose at the coin, nodding methodically as if slowly parsing the thought that my business with Gabriel must be respectable if I was willing to throw money around after it. In truth, the opposite was more likely to be the case. She took the coin.

'I'm afraid you're out of luck for all your fancy money, I haven't seen him for a few days.'

'How many days?'

'I couldn't say for sure because he has his own key, but it must be getting on for a week. I wasn't too worried because he pays in advance. That's partly why I let him take the room. Of course, if I'd known the sort of company he would keep I might have thought twice about it.'

'I would have thought he would make an ideal tenant.'

'That's what I thought, too, but anyone can make a mistake. A man is judged by the company he keeps is what my late husband always used to say. Only intelligent thing he ever said.'

I took out another coin. 'Did he keep company, then, Mrs Gittins?'

'No women if that's what you're thinking. I run a respectable house.'

'Of course you do.'

She took the coin. 'If I'd known he was going to receive visits from people like that, I never would have shown him houseroom.'

'People like what, Mrs Gittins?'

'That fellah that robbed the Cliff Railway. Frankie Mephisto. They let him out early, didn't they? Only been in twenty-five years, not much of a price to pay for a young girl's life is it?'

'I expect it feels a lot longer on the inside.'

'Should have sent him to the gallows. I'm not a vindictive person, Mr Knight, like some of them other women in this street, but I'm a mother and I know how I would feel if I lost my daughter like that. She was only seventeen when it happened, still a child. Ever such a nice girl she was. Just like her mam, Mrs Prestatyn.

Lord knows how she has suffered over the years. I know some people says she's a bit sour now, but can you blame her? She never used to be like that I can tell you. She had a good heart she did. Worked her fingers to the bone for the St John's Ambulance. Makes you wonder, doesn't it? If this is her reward. Spends her life teaching the kiss of life and going to church every Sunday and the Lord takes her daughter from her and won't even tell her where the poor thing is buried. And this gangster, Frankie Mephisto, comes over all repentant at the last minute so he can sweet-talk his way past St Peter. She says she's going to bite his tongue out like in that movie in the Turkish prison. That'll stop him. And I wouldn't blame her neither.'

'So Frankie Mephisto came to see Mr Bassett?'

'That's what I said, didn't I?'

'And when was this?'

'Maybe three weeks ago.'

'Do you know what they talked about?'

'Of course I don't. It was a private conference between the two. They even made the monkey leave the room. I didn't like it much, though, I can tell you.'

'But you don't know what they spoke about?'

'The door was closed.'

I reached into my pocket and pulled out a fiver. 'You couldn't overhear anything on purpose, but sometimes you can't avoid it, if you happen to be cleaning near the door. Not that you would want to listen, of course, but sometimes it can happen by accident. Especially if you were cleaning the keyhole. Most people don't bother but I can see how spick and span you keep this place, Mrs Gittins, so I suspect you're not the type to neglect a detail like that.'

'I do like to keep a clean house, if that's what you mean.' She took the fiver. 'It's the little things like that that make the difference, isn't it? A dirty keyhole is like grime on the cuffs, or not polishing the heels as well as the toes. A dead giveaway.'

'That's what I thought.'

'Sometimes you can't help but hear what goes on.'

'Exactly.'

'Even when you'd really rather not. But what choice do you have? You can't close your ears like you can close your eyes, can you?'

'So what did they talk about?'

'I do seem to remember Frankie Mephisto had a big box with him covered by a cloth so you couldn't see what was in it. It seemed quite important. Frankie Mephisto was saying how he had a job for Mr Bassett only he didn't call him that, he called him Eli. And Mr Bassett said something like "Oh, I don't know what you are talking about, I don't know you, you must have made a mistake. My name is Bassett." But, of course, Frankie Mephisto wasn't having any of that and I don't blame him neither, because, if he didn't know who he was, why did he let him in and send the monkey out of the room?'

'Good point, Mrs Gittins.'

'So then Mr Bassett says, "What you got in that box under your arm, then?" And Frankie said, "I don't want to show you what I've got in this box. And what's more I won't need to because you are going to help me on this job without me having to show you." And Mr Bassett said again he didn't know what he was talking about and Frankie laughed and said, "I don't believe you, Eli. Old Frankie is not a mug. People who take a favour from Frankie Mephisto are warned in the clearest possible terms of the consequences of their debt. No escape is allowed, including loss of memory, feigned or real. The only loss of memory that has any currency is if I lose mine. And then you are all off the hook. But my memory is functioning perfectly and I remember you Eli Cloyce as if you were my brother. So my recommendation to you is, if you have lost your memory you had better find it again quick. And I make this recommendation safe in the knowledge that your loss of memory is bollocks, the oldest trick in the book, a book that Frankie Mephisto read cover to cover years ago and threw in the bin." Well, of course, those aren't the exact words but near enough.'

'And then what happened?'

'Then Mr Bassett started sort of pleading with him and saying things like, "No, no, Mr Mephisto, you have made a mistake, I am not the man you think I am, I can't help you with this job." And Mr Mephisto said . . . he said . . .' Mrs Gittins frowned as she hammed up the posture of a woman struggling to remember. 'Now what did he say, let me see, what was it now?'

I tucked another fiver into the breast pocket of her housecoat. 'I hope your memory is better than your acting, Mrs Gittins.'

'Oh yes, now I remember, he said, "Eli, look at me, Frankie. Frankie, remember? All those years we spent together, don't try and tell me you don't remember Frankie Mephisto, because he remembers you and he has a job for you." And Mr Bassett said, "I can't do it, Frankie, I can't." And Mr Mephisto said, "If you won't think of yourself, Eli, think of the little monkey who is sitting so patiently outside this door. Do you really want to hurt her? That nice little monkey?" And Mr Bassett said, "No, you leave her out of this, Frankie." And Frankie said, "Well, Eli, I don't want to bring her into this, God knows I don't want to hurt the little monkey, but what choice do I have? I've tried being nice but it doesn't seem to be working, so why don't we have a look in the box? The box I had so hoped we wouldn't have to look in. But, ah, such is life. What are we all but poor wayfarers on the Via Dolorosa?" And there was a pause and then Mr Bassett cried out and Frankie said, "Everything's arranged, Eli. My boys will collect you. And please don't insult me by trying to leave town." That was it really.'

We thanked Mrs Gittins and walked back along the Prom towards the Pier.

'So what have we got?' said Calamity.

'It looks to me,' I said, 'like we now have the set. I'm not sure what it's a set of, but I'm sure it's a set of something. We have Frankie Mephisto smiling beatifically at Ynyslas the day she disappeared. I suppose he must have slipped away from his community service at the library to drive there. And we have him experiencing an epiphany in the presence of Myfanwy fifteen years ago. We have Sister Cunégonde at the Waifery who is Frankie's brother and is being blackmailed by him. And we have a man turning up in our office the day Myfanwy disappears, a strange man with an even stranger request, to solve a mystery which he is willing to pay five hundred in cash up front to have solved by a certain date. The mystery seems to concern a crime committed 150 years ago involving a bent cop. It turns out our friend Bassett is an old friend of Frankie Mephisto. And, although he pretends to have lost his memory, he nonetheless seems to remember this acquaintance. The man we need to talk to is Mr Gabriel Bassett. Clearly he knows more than he is saying because so far he hasn't said a damn thing.'

'What if he doesn't want to talk to us?'

'Then I am afraid it is time for us to take off our white hat, Calamity, and put on the grey one with the footprint on the brim.'

How could we find a way to lean on Bassett? It was simple really. Just ask Torquemada. Bassett loved Cleopatra and she loved her missing son, Mr Bojangles, and the person who might be able to tell us about him was Professor Haywire – hobo, neuroscientist at the college, and one-time adviser to the space programme. I'd seen him recently working at the crazy golf as the resident pro. I wasn't sure how we would make him talk, but one of the golf clubs might come in handy. We walked down to Smith's in Terrace Road to pick up a Stanley Gibbons catalogue and then doubled back to the crazy golf course.

He put clubs and score cards on to the counter without looking up from the book he was reading. Behind him hung the tattered placard, 'Aberystwyth Crazy Golf. You don't have to be mad to work here but it helps.'

I cleared my throat. 'Professor Haywire?'

He looked up, his old watery eyes slightly bewildered at being called professor after so long.

'It's fifty pence each. No reductions for minors.'

'We don't want to play, we wanted to ask you some questions.'

'Questions is it? What would they be about then?'

'About the old days, working on the space programme.'

He looked at his watch with the vain air that it might be lunchtime. It was 10.30. The worst time of all for a man like Haywire: too late for breakfast, too early for lunch. A time when only bank tellers eat.

'Answering questions is hungry work,' he said.

'These aren't hard questions.'

'That's for me to decide.'

'It's not really a mealtime at the moment, though.'

'Elevenses.'

We walked to the Cabin and ordered some sandwiches and listened patiently as he spoke through mouthfuls of food.

'I guess you want to hear about the monkeys. Most people do. "Can they really talk?" they ask.'

'It is hard to believe.'

'Of course. Some people say impossible. The people from the philosophy department certainly did. They used to say, "Imagine we made a machine with three buttons: one red, one green and one blue. Then we teach a dog to press the buttons with his paw. Now imagine he presses on the green, the red and the blue in that order and nothing happens. Then he presses on the blue, the red and the green and the machine gives him a bone. So he does it again. And he gets another bone. After ten tries he knows the only sequence worth a bone is blue, red, green. Now you write the words Give, Me, and Food on the blue, the red and the green. Someone else comes in and sees the dog press out the sentence 'Give me food' and the machine feeds him a bone. Hey presto," they said, "he's learned to speak. But does he really understand language or have you just trained him to make noises that sound like speech?" They were a bunch of gits in that department. We said, "OK, smart alecks, why don't you make your little machine and see what you get?" And they said, "Oh, we don't need to, it's a thought experiment." And we said, "Sure that's always the way with you people, isn't it? You sit around jabbering all day asking things like how do I know the colour I see as green in my head is the same colour that you see as green in yours? Whereas we go and make our machine and send it into space." Assholes.'

'Did all the people working on the project know sign language?'

'No, we had Mrs Watkins from the deaf school working with us at Mission Control. She translated. The wise-guys from the philosophy department gave us a hard time about that too. They said, "You're breaking the frontiers of science here, going where no man has gone before, making new discoveries that may change our understanding of the Cosmos for ever, but how do you know Mrs Watkins isn't a liar?"'

Haywire shook his head in frustrated recollection and then bent down towards the plate and scooped the last crumbs into his mouth with his fingers.

I took out the Stanley Gibbons catalogue and opened it to the commemorative stamp of Major Tom. 'Do you remember this little guy?'

He glanced down at it. 'They all look the same in them suits.'

'We know it's a long time ago, but if you could just try.'

He considered for a second and then gave a slight shrug. He picked up the plate and licked it clean, saying, 'He never made it back. Oxygen ran out.'

'How can you be so sure?'

'Oxygen ran out on all of them. It was designed that way.'

Calamity gasped. 'But that's horrible. Why couldn't you give them some oxygen to come home?'

'I know. To a lay person it doesn't make sense. You'd think the trip back would cost the same as the outward journey, just like the train to Shrewsbury. But it doesn't work that way. It's all to do with the weight of the payload, and the weight of the fuel, every extra gram you want to send up, every extra second it has to be there, the costs rise exponentially, which is a mathematical term meaning "a fuck of a lot". Add a few more kilos of fuel, plan for the return journey, and well it turns out cheaper to get a new monkey. We never told them that, though. It helped having monkeys who knew about sign language rather than maths.'

'So, they just run out of air?'

'It was the only way. Even if they'd come back what were we supposed to do? Send an aircraft carrier to the South Pacific to pick them up? Read your history – all those dogs and chimps the Russians and Americans sent up in the Sixties, how come none of them made it back? It's all about money. Research always comes down to that in the end.'

'Seems a crummy way to treat the little guys for all their loyalty and hard work,' I said.

The old professor flinched, 'I'm not proud of it, but I don't spend the long winter nights grieving about it neither, my life's already lousy enough. And, if you really want to know, it was a pretty crummy way to treat the humans as well. Look at what happened to me: world-renowned neuroscientist, and now scratching a living on the crazy golf circuit. At least when the project was wound up they sent the chimps for vocational training. What did I get? A letter saying I had to clear my desk by noon.' He stood up to leave and I grabbed the sleeve of his coat. 'Major Tom had a son called Mr Bojangles. Do you know what happened to him?'

He jerked his sleeve free and walked briskly past us and through the door, snarling, 'Even if I did, why should I give a damn?'

Chapter 15

THE DONKEYS WERE tethered to the side of the kiosk but there was no Eeyore. Cadwaladr was there instead, putting nose bags on them. He told me that Eeyore had rushed off when he received word that Miss Muffet had turned up at the stable. She was a bit bedraggled and thinner, he said, and had lost an ear in a fight but otherwise she was OK. And best of all, she was with foal.

'Never guess who else was here yesterday,' Sospan said over his shoulder as he watched the fluted torrent of ice loop and twirl into the cone. I wondered what they put in it to make it so shiningly, translucently white, whiter even than Dulux gloss paint. Whiter than the smiles of the starlets in the What-the-Butler-Saw movie studios. It had to be a chemical, nothing natural ever looked so pure.

'Surprise me then,' I said.

'Frankie Mephisto, the gangster. Came up to the kiosk cool as you like and ordered an ice. Said he'd been waiting twenty-five years for this moment. Dreaming of it every day.'

'And I bet you gave him credit, didn't you?'

Sospan looked a bit uncomfortable. 'What would you have done?'

I bought an ice for Cadwaladr and went to lean against the railings and savour the bright windy day. For once I wanted to think about nothing. Nothing at all. Like a donkey with its face in the bag.

The stiff breeze raised goosebumps on the flesh of my arm and some quality in the glitter of light on the sea brought unbidden the soft melancholy of summer afternoons in childhood. That moment when the heat loses its edge and with a stomach sick with ice cream, and hair lank with salt, you roll up wet trunks in a soggy, gritty towel and climb the steps home. At the top you always paused, like Lot's wife, and something about the late afternoon light on the sea, whose shade of blue had inexplicably deepened, would catch at the heart and whisper of pleasures still to be sucked from the rind of the day. Perhaps that was how Brainbocs felt from that vantage point on the Prom. The day that still haunts him when he saw Myfanwy in the soft love-play of adolescence. Who could blame him if his heart had never recovered from the blow? There was a basic design flaw in the universe: God had ordered something strong and durable to create the human heart, like carbon fibre, or polypropylene, and they'd sent flesh by mistake. Just a mix-up in despatch. No one was to blame, could have happened to anybody.

Cadwaladr joined me and placed his elbows on the railing.

'When are you going to tell me?' I said.

'Tell you what?'

'Where Rimbaud went during his missing years.'

'Didn't I tell you that?'

'No.'

He nodded and thought for a while. And then he said, 'He went to see the widow. The widow of the man he slew in the ravine. Remember me telling you that story? That's who he went to see. The guy's widow.'

'What for?'

'Don't know. These things happen that way sometimes.'

'How did he know where to find her?'

'I don't suppose he did. But he had all the time in the world. Probably just wandered around for a while. Then one day he arrives in some dusty, sun-beaten one-horse town. The sort of place you might stop to get a glass of water but not much else. And maybe buy some feed for your animal. He left his mule with the ostler and went for a walk and as he passed the town library a woman came out of the revolving door carrying some books under her arm. She dropped one and bent down to pick it up and, without thinking, so did Waldo. Their hands met on the book for a second and she pulled her hand back and Waldo picked up the book and handed it to her. It was a collection of poems by the French symbolist, Rimbaud. The lady took the book and at that moment Waldo, or Rimbaud as he was just about to become, looked up into her face and gasped. Her skin, he said, was the colour and sheen of a freshly opened bar of the finest Swiss milk chocolate; her eyes deeper and darker than a moonlit pool. Eyes so big and so pure and clear that you couldn't look at them without wanting to swim in those depths and never return to the shore. She was the most beautiful woman he had ever laid eyes on, he said, the most beautiful woman it was possible for a mortal to lay eyes on: and, if that wasn't enough, she spoke French. After she took the book from the thunderstruck Waldo she did a little curtsey and said, "*Merci, monsieur.*" And then she left and Waldo stood staring at the empty street for the next ten minutes. He sold his mule to the ostler, sold his saddle and the two little pouches of prospected gold and went to the inn. "How long you planning on staying?" they asked, and he said, "However long it takes."

'He knew without needing to be told that the divine vision he'd seen on the library steps was the local French teacher so he signed up for some lessons. You will have guessed by now who the woman was: the widow of the dead soldier, of course. But it was quite a while before Rimbaud guessed and by that time it was too late. Her name was Isabella. I mean that's what they all called her, I don't know her real name. It's not important. When she saw Rimbaud at her lesson the following week she thought it must have been a coincidence ordained by fate. A belief only further reinforced when she found out his name was Rimbaud. Well, he had to tell her something, didn't he? But that's my favourite poet! she said in delight. How amazing, said Rimbaud, it was my mother's favourite poet, that's why she named me thus. And Isabella laughed. For the first time since the news of her husband's death reached her, she laughed. Laughed with childish delight at the silly coincidence of their names. Perhaps if she had been a little better versed in the ways of the world she might have known that the likelihood of someone from Bala being named Rimbaud in honour of his mother's favourite poet was not high. But she didn't. Soon they were best of friends. And not long after that they were more than just good friends. So it is between a man and a woman the whole world over. And has been since this world was made. The townspeople were also pleased. Isabella was a popular girl and had shown the correct amount of piety that decorum demanded after the death of her brave husband. But life, as we all know, must go on and we must go on with it. They rejoiced when they saw the burgeoning relationship with the stranger in their midst. They could see he had brought joy back into her life, and laughter into the lonely home where the daughter, Carmencita, was growing up into a fine child. Before long, Rimbaud moved into the house and the little Carmencita began to call him "Dad" and the townspeople were doubly pleased. Because it is not right for a child to grow and not know a father. And, though he had slain her dad, it did not stop him loving her as if she were his own child. Rimbaud didn't intend any of this. It just happened, like it could have happened to any of us. And when he found out the identity of the woman he had fallen in love with, what could he do? He tried to explain things to Isabella, he told her he was a Welshman, of the same blood that slew her husband, but she wouldn't listen. Perhaps she should have taken the bit about the same blood more literally. "I don't see a Welshman or a Patagonian, or a Spaniard, or a mestizo," she told him. "Just another human being who has suffered, but whose heart is big." And then she added, "You know, I think Salvador, my poor departed husband, would have liked you."

That was a moot point, of course. But she seemed convinced of it. "Sometimes," she added, "I can feel his presence, guiding me and telling me that you are a good man. When I get this feeling, it is never wrong." Before long they were married and farming llamas and the wounds for both of them were healing fast. The man called Waldo had gone from this world and in his place was Rimbaud, a man who was nowhere but had come home. Together they set up a charitable trust in the name of her dead husband, Salvador. And, to his credit, Rimbaud worked tirelessly for the memory of the man he had savagely murdered. For the first time in his life Rimbaud was happy. He had a beautiful wife, an angel of a daughter, and a respected position in society because to the simple farmers who comprised the townsfolk he was the living embodiment of a Christian parable. The priest even alluded to it from the pulpit: the spirit of Jesus was walking among them in that town, he said, a town they had all wrongly supposed to be too humble and mean to be worth his notice. His spirit had walked among them and touched the hearts of two people who had been bitter foes and had now filled them both with love. And this bond of love between them was thus a symbol of reconciliation and His greater redemption. *Amor vincit omnia.* Love conquers all. And the good priest even went so far as to hope it would not be long before this blessed union was consummated with a child whom they could all love. And the congregation smiled and Isabella reached across and squeezed Rimbaud's hand.' Cadwaladr paused and spat on to the rocks below.

'So how did it end?'

'Novocaine. He needed some root canal treatment. Talked in his sleep.'

I returned to the office and found Calamity who had been to Gabriel's, the gents' outfitters in Portland Street. Gabriel's was old school and specialised in serving gentlemen who like to keep abreast of fashion, as long as it was the fashion of fifty years ago. They were not cheap and they were not quick and nothing was off the peg. Even the handkerchiefs were bespoke. But, interestingly, they kept detailed records of their customers; normally they would have been too discreet to divulge particulars to a stranger. But a case in which one of their coats might help a man recover a lost memory was different. They were quite helpful, even intrigued, when Calamity explained the purpose of her visit. From her description they thought the coat sounded like the one they made for Dr Galbraith from the Clinic for Women's Problems on Laura Place. The poor doctor had been found dead recently; cause of death an excess of fluid on the lungs.

'What sort of fluid?' I asked.

'Seawater.'

'Hmmm. That's quite a common cause of death round here.'

'Found on Aberdovey beach, body been in the water two or three days.'

'OK.'

'I also tried the Enoc Enocs Foundation but all their records were destroyed in a fire about five years ago.'

'You've been busy.'

'There was one other thing I found out.' She looked hesitant.

'Go on.'

'It's a bit . . . er . . . sort of . . . I don't know how to say it. I followed a hunch.'

'Nothing wrong with that. Where did it take you?'

'I was thinking about the lawn out at the Waifery, the one where the grass won't grow. I had a chat with the grass seed expert at the Farmers' Co-op. He said that, according to the Borth Birdwatcher's Society, birds won't sing there either.'

'Really!'

'He seems pretty sure it's something to do with metal deposits in the soil.'

'Either that or it's cursed.'

'I tried to find out when the pond was filled in and it seems to have been about the time of the Great Cliff Railway Robbery. And I thought, if you buried some loot in the pond that would count as a metal deposit wouldn't it?'

'It would. That's quite an intriguing thought.'

'Especially as they seem to have acquired a new roof for the Waifery around the same time. Anyway, I sort of borrowed one of those five-pound notes in the petty cash and paid Poxcrop to go and have a dig.'

'You borrowed it?'

'He's given us a receipt.'

'That's all right then. And what did we get for our five pounds? The long lost buried Cliff Railway loot?'

Calamity shook her head. 'No, something else. It's better if I show you.' She walked across to her old school PE bag and unzipped it. Then she took out a skull. 'I think it might be a monkey,' she said.

I sat in the corner of the Castle pub next to the switched-off fire and sipped my pint. The lounge bar had a sad, mid-afternoon emptiness. Just me, two students playing pool, and an old man making his pint last all day. The door swung open with a faint squeal and Llunos stood framed in the doorway surveying the room. There wasn't much to survey and within a second and a half his eyes lighted on me. It was one of those moments – we hadn't spoken since the men in white hats argument a week ago. When I telephoned him he had been gruff but listened. I told him about Bassett and he said he would bring him in for questioning along with Professor Haywire. He made a slight jerk of his head, walked over. He pointed at my glass, took my answer for granted, and went to order two pints. When he returned, I said I was sorry about the argument and he said, 'I was out of line, too.'

'No you weren't. Everything you said was true – about the white hats and all that.'

'You were just sticking up for Calamity. I saw that afterwards. I wouldn't have respected you if you hadn't of stuck up for her.' He took a drink and said, 'Syracuse wasn't a bent cop like Calamity thinks. You have to understand how it was in those days.'

'Of course.'

'The Squire was a powerful man. Syracuse was just a nobody.'

'I can see that.'

'I wouldn't blame you if you didn't. I don't know the truth of it myself. I just know after thirty years doing this job that no matter what you do, right or wrong, no one gives you any credit for it. It's always wrong. You let a guy go, you're too soft. You give him a slap, you're too brutal.' He sneered. 'These people don't know what brutality is. They should try doing my job for a month, then they'd know. Most of the time we're just trying to sort things out. Ask your dad. He'll know what I'm talking about.'

'What you said on the stairs when you left – it sounded like you knew all along.'

'I did. I found out a long time ago. And a few other things besides. There's a lot I find out about that I don't publicise. All I'm saying is, we don't know what goes on. He probably did his best in the circumstances, and now we don't know what the circumstances were. I'm not going to judge him. If Calamity wants to, that's up to her. One thing she'll find out though, the only thing I know for sure and it took me a while to learn it – is things are never what you think. Tell her to send the dossier round and I'll sign it.'

'She threw it in the bin.'

'There was no need for that. She's earned that badge. Take it out and I'll sign it.' He paused and took a long slow drink. 'Haywire's down the station. We couldn't find Bassett but we got the monkey. I've sent a car down to the deaf school for Mrs Watkins. She can translate. I thought we'd do the interview together – hard cop, soft cop.'

'I really appreciate it.'

'Don't bother. I owe you one.'

'What for?'

'I can't tell you but, trust me, I do. Let's see the skull.'

I dragged the bag across to his side under the table and unzipped it.

'We thought it might be a monkey.'

He glanced down and shook his head. He dropped his index finger into the bag and drew it along the outline of the brow. 'You'd get more pronounced prognathism if it was an ape . . . It's human. An infant.'

'You seem pretty sure.'

'I've seen some like this before. How good's your memory?'

'So-so.'

'Drink up, I want to show you something you'll never forget. And then I want you to forget it.'

Chapter 16

SOMETIMES, THE SUN sinking out in the bay beyond the rocks was a cool silver penny like the moon, and sometimes a Spanish doubloon that sizzled and threatened to turn the sea to steam, but today it was the colour of a crimson rose petal, the image repeated in every window of the seafront hotels. We drove along the Prom and pulled up outside the old police station annexe, five doors down from the precinct station. It had been locked and unoccupied since the flood. Llunos jumped out and climbed the stone steps to the doors which were secured with a thick chain from which hung a big old-fashioned padlock. He brought out a set of keys and tossed them around in the palm of his hand until the one he wanted became evident.

'Don't forget to forget you were here. We're going to have a conversation that never took place and quite possibly we'll share a phantom tot of rum.'

He unwound the chain and gave the door a shove with his shoulder. The air that puffed out smelled of wallpaper paste and seaweed. We walked in and closed the door behind us. We were in the old station foyer and it had that same atmosphere you get in rooms that have been suddenly abandoned and remain preserved for ever at the moment of sudden crisis – like the excavated dwellings of Pompeii, or those images of wrecked ships taken by underwater robot cameras. Must and damp and mildew spores filled the air, and timbers fallen from the ceiling lay aslant the dust-covered desk in which the hinged section was raised and would always remain that way.

'Spooky, huh?' said Llunos.

He jumped over the desk and opened a small door in the wall. It was a utility cupboard and he reached inside with a practised hand and flicked down the electrical circuit switches. A thin hum started from somewhere and in the ceiling above us a fan started to spin slowly, causing bits of insulation fluff and scraps of newspaper to dance along the floor.

'Come,' said Llunos.

I followed him down gritty steps and along a corridor to some some more steps. We arrived at another padlocked door and Llunos found the key on the ring and opened it. He flicked a light switch on the door jamb outside and walked in. I followed.

'Not many people have seen this room,' he said, 'even when the rest of the place was occupied. Don't forget, you haven't seen it either.'

It was a lumber room. Most of the floor space was filled with discarded office furniture. Shelves along one wall were piled with books and papers, not in any order but simply thrown there by people who didn't care and weren't expecting anyone to come along and inspect their handiwork. Three heavy filing cabinets stood in the middle, positioned as if they were having a conversation. Behind them were two desks, one empty, one laden with old typewriters. They were Remingtons, heavy-duty and robust as iron stoves, with carriages and bells louder than on a district nurse's bike. Some of the carriages still had sheaves of paper in them, sheaves made up of five or six sheets with carbon sheets sandwiched in between. Dust gave everything a uniform grey coating like volcanic ash and spiders hung on threads and eyed us without blinking. Llunos lifted two chairs from a stack, gave them a quick dusting with his hands, and set them either side of the empty desk.

'I come here sometimes,' he said simply.

He took out a hip flask, unscrewed the top, and poured out a shot into the cap and set it down on the desk in front of me. He took a drink from the flask and raised it and made a circular motion. 'Hear that?'

'What?'

'Listen.'

We both stopped our breaths and listened. I became aware of a distant rhythmic sighing sound, a susurration that seemed to come from nowhere and then from everywhere, and then sometimes it seemed to come from inside my own head and I wondered whether it was the sound of my soul inhaling and I myself had died.

'Sounds like breathing, doesn't it?' said Llunos. 'Sounds like the whole place is alive and breathing.'

'What is it?'

'Spooked?'

'No.'

'It's the sea.'

I looked surprised. Llunos took another swig from his flask and raised it towards the ceiling. 'Right up there.'

He pulled open the drawer in the desk and reached in. He took out a small skull and placed it on the desk. Then two more and set them beside it.

'They're human. Infants. All less than a month or two old.'

'Where are they from?'

'The pond. We've got a collection, been handed in over the years. Folk at Borth reckon they're pixies. Calamity was a bit out in her dates – the pond was filled in two years before the Cliff Railway robbery. The loot's not buried there. And I've already examined and discounted the theory that Mrs Prestatyn's daughter is buried there, in case that's what you are thinking. The story of the pond is much older than that. Seven hundred years older.'

'So what does it mean?'

He stood up and walked over to the shelves and took down a book and brought it over to show me.

'Ever seen this before?'

It was Ulricus's *Life of Pope Gregory*.

'Frankie Mephisto sent a copy to Sister Cunégonde.'

He opened it and began leafing through the table of contents like an old scholar.

'Pope Gregory the First is usually known as the guy who thought up the seven deadly sins. But there is a far more interesting, less widely known story about him. How's your Latin?'

I laughed. 'About as good as my Greek.'

Llunos took out a pair of reading spectacles and set them on the end of his nose. He began to intone in Latin.

'*Memorabile quod ulricus epistola refert Gregorium quum ex piscine quadam allata plus quam sex mille infantum capita vidisset . . .*' He looked up and slapped the book shut. 'Ulricus is discussing the subject of celibacy in the holy orders. In particular he describes the day when Pope Gregory drained a fish pond near a nunnery and found six thousand infant skulls. Soon after that he rescinded the decree forbidding priests from marrying. Better to marry than burn. By all accounts this was not an uncommon discovery in medieval times. Luther records a similar finding in the basement of a nunnery at Neinburg in Austria. More recently, workmen excavating the foundations of a convent at Avignon found a similar cache. It seems that wherever you get a lot of healthy young women living together, it doesn't matter what vows they take, or how strong you make the lock on the door, that old master locksmith, Mother Nature, will find a way in. The Sisters of Deiniol founded the original convent in twelve seventy something, about the same time as Aberystwyth Castle. After the chapel and the kitchen, the ornamental fish pond was the first thing they built. The skulls have been there a long time. It's just that they keep turning up from time to time. The earth moves a lot next to an estuary apparently. My guess is they're probably not too proud of them down at the Waifery, and Frankie Mephisto was threatening to publicise their little secret.'

He put the book back on the shelf and said, 'Come. Let's go and do some interviews.'

* * *

We walked the five doors down to the precinct station and found Haywire waiting for us in interview room one, looking scared. We sat across the interview table from him and Llunos said, 'Do you know why you are here?'

Haywire shrugged.

'This man says he went to see you earlier today and asked you some questions about a certain monkey called Bojangles. He says you weren't very helpful. This man is a friend of mine, so if he wants to know what happened to the monkey, so do I. The only difference is I'm not so politely brought up as he is. Do you understand?'

'But I don't know this guy called Bojangles.'

I squeezed my eyes together involuntarily. That was not a good way to answer a question from Llunos.

'Sure you do,' said Llunos. 'You've seen the chap wheeling the barrel organ round town? You've seen the little monkey on top? Her name's Cleopatra. Bojangles is her son. But she hasn't seen him for fifteen years. He was born up at the college during the space programme but we don't know what happened to him. Now you used to work up there at that time, so we thought we'd ask you. Am I making myself clearer, or do you need a truncheon in your mouth to help you concentrate?'

The old professor swallowed hard, his eyes brightening with fear. He nodded anxiously; the nod that says, You don't need to take out the rubber hose, I'll tell you what you want to know. The pointless look of supplication. The people with the rubber hose already know you are going to tell them everything. They know from long experience that outside the movies there isn't anyone tough enough to take what they have in their power to give. And you're going to feel the rubber hose anyway, not because it's necessary but because they like it. It's that simple.

Llunos pulled a cassette tape recorder across the desk. 'This here is to ensure that you get a fair hearing and that no unfair pressure is applied to you during the interview process. Do you understand what I am telling you?'

Haywire nodded.

The policemen pressed down the record button and spoke gruffly. 'Interview with Professor Haywire. Present are me, Haywire and a few other people. The witness has been advised of his rights and declined the presence of an attorney.'

Haywire looked surprised to hear that but chose not to say anything.

Llunos flicked the lid of the cassette player open and replaced the tape with another from his pocket. He pressed down the play button and we found ourselves listening to Mantovani. Llunos stood up, walked over to Haywire, grabbed his lapels, hoisted him to his feet, and threw him violently into the corner. Then he walked over to that corner, grabbed Haywire and threw him into the next. This procedure was known as the suspect falling off his chair. After Llunos had helped Haywire fall off his chair a few more times he put him back in the chair, sat down and turned the volume down. 'As you can see, it's not infallible.' He put the original tape back in and began the interview.

'OK. What happened to Bojangles?'

Haywire paused while he collected his wits and then said, 'I want you to know it wasn't my idea—'

Llunos leaped forward, veins throbbing at his temple, 'I don't give a fuck whose idea it was, you idiot!'

Haywire threw his hands out as if shielding himself from a bright light. 'OK, OK, OK. We called it sending them to Timbuktu. You see, we had a lot of monkeys born on the project so we had to get rid of them. It got to be pretty distressing, you know, taking the kids away from their mothers, so we invented this thing. We told them the kids were going to be research fellows at a foreign university, the University of Timbuktu, that way they would be sort of proud of their kids, you see. We even had a little "going away" suit made with a University of Timbuktu badge on the pocket. And a scarf and a bag. It was always the same suit, of course, but they never noticed. We'd have a little going away party and all the chimps would gather at the door and wave the little fellah off. Then when the door was closed we took his suit off and took him down the corridor to the animal behaviourists where they were conducting research into resistance to fear-extinction in primates—'

'What's that mean?'

'Oh, you know, the usual questions of whether phylogenetic and ontogenetic stimuli are comparable once the orientation and aversive consequences of the ontogenetic FR stimulus are taken into account. That sort of thing.'

There was a second's silence in the room as Llunos blinked and the thought dawned on Professor Haywire that he might have said the wrong thing.

'What,' said Llunos in a slowed-down voice, 'the fuck does that mean?'

Haywire turned pale and Llunos looked at me, bubbling with rage. 'Did you understand a word of that?'

I wanted to say yes to spare Haywire but there wasn't a lot of point.

'Look, Haywire, you're not up at the Arts Centre now with the rest of those dodos in their corduroy jackets, talking hooey in front of a canvas that looks like someone has thrown a tin of Dulux at it, do you understand? When I ask you a question you'll answer in words I can understand.'

'OK, OK,' said Haywire. 'Basically it means they were conditioning monkeys to be scared of flowers.'

Llunos grabbed the arms of his chair in disbelief.

'They did what?!'

'Conditioned them to be scared of flowers,' said Haywire weakly. He could tell this wasn't going very well.

'How can you be scared of flowers?'

'That's just the point. You can't, normally. But if you give the monkey an electric shock every time he sees one, well, I mean you can make him terrified of anything. We even made them scared of toy rabbits.'

For a while Llunos was too astonished to speak. Finally, he said, 'B . . . b . . . but what's the point?'

'It's to find out whether fear of things like snakes and things is innate.'

'Where the hell's that?'

'No, it's not a place. Innate. It means built-in. Look, I didn't like it either, I was just doing what they told me.'

'Oh right, you were following orders, just like Klaus Barbie. Look pal, this is Aberystwyth not Nuremberg.'

Haywire wisely kept his own counsel and there was silence in the room for a while as Llunos cogitated. An air of calm slowly took over but you could tell it wasn't real calm, it was a thin layer over a boiling fury. He looked at me and I turned to Haywire.

'Do you know anything about these postcards from Timbuktu?'

He nodded weakly. 'I didn't mean any harm. I was just trying to spare their feelings. You know, pretend the little guy was still alive.'

I stood up to leave, I needed some air.

'So what happened to Bojangles then?' said Llunos.

I paused in the doorway to listen to Haywire's answer.

'We sold him to the holiday camp out at Borth: they had a travelling booth in those days that they sent round the country trying to drum up custom. You know – to agricultural shows and fairs and things. They took him along to entertain the kids. His first gig was Shrewsbury Flower Show. Died of heart failure.'

The last thing I heard as I reached street level was the sound of Haywire falling off his chair again.

When I returned from my walk, Haywire was gone and Cleopatra was sitting in the chair. She looked scared. The chair was too low and some phone books had been placed under her, but even so her chin was barely above the table top. Two tiny paws clutched the top of the table. Mrs Watkins was wearing the hat she normally wore to weddings and christenings. I explained the procedure to Cleopatra in a soft patient voice. And I asked Mrs Watkins to make sure she got the soft patient bit in the sign language.

'Now look, Cleopatra,' I began. 'No one wants to hurt you, you understand, we're your friends and we want to help you.' I stopped to let Mrs Watkins catch up. Cleopatra nodded.

'But we need you to help us and then everything will be all right, do you understand?'

Cleopatra nodded again, still wide-eyed with fear.

'All you have to do is tell us where Mr Bassett is.'

'She says she doesn't know,' said Mrs Watkins.

'All right,' shouted Llunos, 'that's enough of the pussy-footing about. I want answers and this mangy little fur-bag is going to start singing.'

Mrs Watkins sat there immobile, looking shocked.

'Well, what the hell are you waiting for?' he demanded.

'You want me to say that?'

'What do you think I brought you here for? Flower arranging? Just tell the monkey it's time to cut the crap and start singing. Or signs to that effect.'

'I'm not saying that!'

'Saying what?'

'Profanity. I won't translate profanity.'

Llunos started to get annoyed, the genuine variety as opposed to the dissembled stuff. That was always the way with 'bad cop': you forgot you were acting. 'Look, Mrs Watkins, I haven't got time here to dance round your sensibilities. You either do what I tell you or I subpoena you and send you down somewhere you'll hear enough profanity to blow your hat off.'

Mrs Watkins turned reluctantly to Cleopatra and translated.

Cleopatra answered and Mrs Watkins turned to us. 'She says she understands.'

'OK, ask her again. Where's her master?'

'She says she doesn't know.'

Llunos slammed his fist down hard on the desk. Both Cleopatra and Mrs Watkins jumped. He got up and walked round and thrust his face up close to the monkey.

'Right, listen to me good, fur-bag. We can do this the easy way or the hard way. Play ball with me and you walk out that door right now. You want to play silly buggers, go ahead, see where it gets you.' He reached into the monkey's jacket and pulled out a little plastic bag with some white powder in it. 'What's this? Drugs, is it? Are you a dealer, are you? Is that your little game?'

'I saw that!' shouted Mrs Watkins. 'You planted it on her.'

Llunos turned the colour of a plum. He spun round and shouted at Mrs Watkins, 'What was that!? You want some too, do you?'

He thrust the bag of narcotics under her nose, pulled off her hat and then dipped his hand in and pulled the bag of powder out. He tore the bag open, dipped his finger in and tasted.' I can't believe it! Mrs Watkins from the deaf school is peddling snow.'

'I . . . I . . . I want a lawyer,' stuttered Mrs Watkins. She was trembling violently and it smelled like she had involuntarily urinated. But it could have been the monkey.

Llunos paused and wiped the sweat off his brow. 'What the hell are you talking about? You're here to translate, you don't need a lawyer.'

'Well, stop bullying me then.'

Llunos spat on the floor and Mrs Watkins gasped. 'We're doing our best,' she said.

'Like hell you are.'

He looked at me and I took over.

'Look Cleopatra,' I said gently, 'I don't want to see you get hurt. This mess is none of your making, you're just an innocent monkey caught up in it. I want to help you, really I do. But you need to help me. You understand? I know you had nothing to do with the cocaine they found in your pocket, but who's going to believe me unless you help me first? You have to tell me where Mr Bassett is then we'll speak to the DA and see if we can cut you a deal. All you have to do is tell us where he is.'

Mrs Watkins answered, 'She says why should she trust the word of a lousy cop.'

Llunos rushed over again and grabbed the monkey by her Ardwyn school tie.

'Because I'm all you've got, fur-bag! I'm the only thing standing between you and zoo-time, do you understand? I got enough to put you behind bars for the rest of your life. And I'm not talking about a safari park here or an open-plan place. I'm talking about one of those mangy cheap places in a holiday camp where you spend your days in a concrete room with a rubber car tyre hanging from the ceiling that's supposed to be a tree in Africa. You want that, do you? You know what happens to animals in zoos like that? They get so bored they chew their own paws off. I've seen it happen. Now you think about that.'

He stormed out of the room and I followed him. Outside, we looked in through the two-way mirror. Cleopatra sat in a pose of utter dejection, her head resting on her paws. Mrs Watkins was sobbing.

Llunos drank coffee from a plastic machine cup. 'Do you think I'm riding her too hard?'

I shrugged. 'Hard to say.'

He screwed up the cup and threw it with a metallic clang into the bin. 'Come on, let's get it over with.'

Ten minutes later a man in a fifty-dollar Swansea suit turned up and said he was the attorney for the Mephisto family and we were illegally detaining one of his clients. We had to let the monkey walk.

Chapter 17

THE PAPERWEIGHT WAS still lying on top of the ring-binder files where Llunos had left it. I picked it up and shook. Snow fell above Aberystwyth at Christmastide. Just like it did that day in June when Myfanwy begged me to take her away from Aberystwyth. The day I needed more time – the myth that cripples all our attempts on happiness in this world. The day it snowed in June, big feathery flakes falling from a grey summer sky like tufts of kapok from inside a broken old teddy, a bear with one eye and stitches for a nose like the old streetwalker, Lorelei. I pulled a bottle of Captain Morgan out of the drawer and filled a tumbler. I drank slowly, thinking about things, shaking the paperweight idly now and again. Gradually, the room grew darker, the level of amber in the bottle descending gently like the sun, sinking like the level of oil in a lamp. I put on my hat.

Cambio, *Wechsel*, change . . . tickets for the continent . . . The Cliff Railway station had that time-worn, forlorn air of railway termini everywhere, places that offered the illusion of escape, a door to a new life. The rails dropped from the sky, like the lowered ropes of a rescue party at the bottom of a collapsed mine shaft. I stood in the darkness of the doorway and stared.

It had a ticket counter with an arched window, a snack bar where you bought your beer or tea and stood at a chest-high table that had no seats; it had a departure board and a clock; a crumbling lattice of ironwork in the ceiling supporting filmy grey pieces of cracked glass, dirt and droppings, and brooding gulls. It had a shoeshine machine and an empty fibreglass kid, dressed like a refugee from an Enid Blyton book, politely soliciting donations for a children's charity; usually too there would be one or two women of the night soliciting with varying degrees of politeness; but what it didn't have was a left luggage office. I felt a fool. I turned and headed down the Prom.

The lengthening shadows signified a change of shift as eternal as the reversing tides. Bathers scurried off to the sanctuary of their homes and the people who wandered the beach now had ugly coats and unwashed hair and were laden with bottles of sherry of a type unknown to the men of Jerez. The scent of fried onions began to impregnate the breeze – the perfumer's sizzling overture to the coming night. At Sospan's, the townsfolk gathered for a last ice like wildebeest at dusk round an African watering hole. Yet here they licked a nectar far sweeter than the brackish waters of a lake where hippos swim. Vanilla: the analgesic of the heart, the scent of lugubrious South Sea lagoons, and of the nursery. I ordered one. A workman stood on the roof of the kiosk fixing the illuminated cone and its neon motto, *Et in Arcadia ego*, and we watched him work for a while because there was nothing else to watch.

'Let the lamp affix its beam,' quoted Sospan to anyone who wanted to listen. 'The only emperor is the emperor of ice cream.'

I took my ice and continued walking, filled with soft envy for the donkeys that drink from the waters of the Lethe at either end of the Prom, and thus begin every journey bright with hope, while we all struggled to escape the snare of the past and the power of events from long ago to blight us. I thought of Brainbocs, who had been crucified by a vision of play on a summer's afternoon; the simple image of a girl that lodged in his heart like shrapnel. And I remembered Rimbaud, haunted by acts that time would not give back; the albatross of his missing years weighing so heavily precisely because the years were not missing. They never are, except perhaps for Bassett for whom fate has devised another torment: a choice. Knowledge or oblivion. To throw away his past, never discover it, or to take the risk and look inside and be for ever stained by what he saw. He was doubly cursed. Damned if he opened and damned if he forbore. And I thought of Sospan and of the hidden sting in the tail of his Latin motto. Eeyore had explained it to me once. He said most people misunderstood it; the '*et*' meant 'even' and not 'also' as was commonly supposed. Not 'I too was in Paradise', but 'I was even in Paradise'. A subtle but crucial difference because the speaker was Death. Eeyore insisted that the ice man as secular priest was aware of the true meaning but I could never make up my mind. How much did Sospan really know? Did he receive that pale zigzag scar down his cheek from a brawl in a dark harbour-front bar in Marseilles? Or did he just fall on a cornet? Maybe his was the cruellest fate of all: that his soul was a blank; that he went into *gelati* to forget that he had nothing to forget.

I continued walking around castle point and chanced upon Lorelei sitting on one of the benches set into the wall below the war memorial. I said good evening and sat next to her. Her face was hard and shrivelled like last year's conker, toughened by the vinegar of the years and the perennial diet of mockery and rejection. Poxcrop had said a nurse had been engaged for Myfanwy by whoever had kidnapped her, and that was good. But he had also said it was Frankie's old *consigliere* and no one knew to this day who that was. But there was one source of information in this town, one oracle, that went back further even than the Orthopaedia Britannica. The girls who used to pull the tricks. No one, not even Meirion, knew more about the ancient criminal fraternities of Aberystwyth than Lorelei and so I asked about Frankie Mephisto and she seemed to recall the name from long, long ago. But since it's thirsty work remembering that far back we went round the corner to the Castle pub and I bought her a pint of Guinness.

'There was never such a thing in all the world as a good pimp,' she said, 'but Frankie Mephisto was worse than most.'

She sat wedged into the corner next to the jukebox, her white jowls curving along the collar of her charity-shop coat, the line of bright red lipstick, only a lazy approximation of a mouth.

'I didn't know he had been a pimp.'

'He won't thank me for telling you. He'd prefer to be remembered as the train robber. But I remember what he did before that. He used to make his girls do tricks with men they didn't want to go with. That was always the taboo, you see. The girl should always have a choice.' She drank slowly from her glass, the foam adhering like a false moustache. 'I see his sidekick is back in town, too. Using a different name naturally. But you can always tell.'

'Who's his sidekick?'

'Eli Cloyce.'

'You know the barrel-organ man?'

'Long time ago. He used to be a burglar, stately homes and things. Did some work for Frankie. Went to prison for a while. Didn't see him any more after that.'

The pub began to fill. Townsfolk and students, and bands of kids who were too young to be there legally. Like newly emerged butterflies gathered on a branch, the teenage girls huddled in groups and discussed the myriad melodramas of their lives. I watched in fascination the strangely choreographed pantomime of cigarette smoking: eyes closed, smoke drawn in with a look of deep ecstasy, a pause, the head tilted back with feigned insouciance and the smoke expelled in a sort of world-weary sigh. All an elaborate assay on sophistication that revealed an innocence more fragile than a wren's egg. Lorelei watched, but didn't seem to see. Perhaps she had long ago lost the capacity to notice the teenage soap opera: the fighting and coupling and betrayals and heartbreak; the arguments that seem so vital but are so trivial; the livid declarations and the postmortems; the infidelities and tales of hearts given to the unworthy, taken back, then given again; perhaps she had gone beyond the ability to see the liaisons, affairs, betrayals, jealousies, threats, plots of vengeance, pregnancies and abortions, and tears, always tears . . . Which one of them would it be tonight? The pretty blonde girl, perhaps, leaning on the corner of the pool table? She was about sixteen, her hair jaggedly cropped and the mascara pasted on so thick – thicker than mascarpone cheese – it made her look like a blue panda. Her porcelain skin was still unblemished, like freshly fallen snow before the first tracks are made in it, but would soon turn to slush. And there are few things viler in the world than slush. The kohl was applied fiercely around the eyes, a wise precaution. There were so many heartaches lying in wait to wash it away, so many crises ready to send rivers of soot surging down and leave trails like the legs of a bird-eating spider. Tonight I felt sorry for her, and yet strangely loved her for all her woe to come, this girl whose freshly minted fate was already as old as time, annually reissued by the printing press of the years. None of it was her fault and yet there was no remedy . . . And then I realised it was Seren.

Lorelei noticed my expression and followed my gaze.

'It's the girl from the Waifery,' she said.

'I heard she was missing.'

She nodded. 'Reckon I'd run away if I lived there too.'

'Do you know Sister Cunégonde?'

'Used to. Haven't spoke to her for twenty years or so. Maybe more. The times I do see her she doesn't see me. Or pretends not to.'

'Do you know why she resents the girl?'

'She resents everybody.'

'I heard it was because folk think Seren is the illegitimate daughter of Meredith. I heard she used to be sweet on Meredith herself.'

'That's what they say. But it's not true, just gossip.'

'Sometimes gossip is true.'

'Sometimes. But not in this case.'

'You seem pretty sure.'

'I used to know them well, when Cunégonde was crowned carnival queen; they were just kids, her and Meredith. Then something happened, the sort of thing that often does in situations like that. Cunégonde got pregnant. The Mother Superior at the time made her break if off with Meredith. He was devastated and I'm pretty sure he's never been near another woman since.'

'What happened to the baby?'

'Don't ask.'

We spoke no more for a while, and then it occurred to me how it was she knew so much about Cunégonde. I turned to her and said, 'You used to be Frankie's moll, didn't you?'

She narrowed her eyes at the memory and said, 'How did you know?'

I told her about the photo that had lain all these years in the vault of Meredith's heart, a cracked and faded photo of a carnival queen and a young hoodlum called Frankie Mephisto with a girl on his arm who had struck me as vaguely familiar. And now I knew, thirty years on, I was sitting next to her.

She nodded. 'I was his girl for a while, before he got tired of me. I knew them all. Cloyce, Frankie, Cunégonde . . .'

'Do you know who the *consigliere* was?'

'Of course.' She took a last sip of her drink and said, 'Mooncalf.'

I lifted the ragged curtain aside and looked out. The aluminium window frame was cold and dripped condensation. The sky was translucent indigo like an insect's eye. Away towards Dovey Junction the milk train bellowed, but outside there was no other sign of life. I was sitting at the caravan table where I must have fallen asleep last night. I was still in my clothes; my head throbbed and there was a tender lump on the side of my head. I tried to touch it but I couldn't raise my hand. It wouldn't move further than six inches from the table. I looked down and focused on a pair of handcuffs attaching my wrist to the leg of the table. The knuckles of my hand were raw in the way they get sometimes when you've hit someone. I shook my head to clear the cobwebs and started to piece together the jigsaw of fragmented recollection. The image of the face I had punched took form. It was a policeman. And these were his cuffs. A policeman with a friend's face: Llunos. Oh God.

The events of the night before started filtering back to me. After I left the pub I had driven over to Clarach to kill Mooncalf. It was a bad thing to do, I knew, because I was over the limit. There was no doubt in my mind about the deed, the only uncertainty was about how slowly he should die. When I got there I found I couldn't do it. He was already dead. Some men in a black Morris Minor, like the one Frankie Mephisto drives, had driven up earlier and torched his trailer. It was still smouldering. Llunos was there and he told me to go home and wait. We disagreed about that; he insisted, we disagreed some more, and the exchange got quite heated. We really couldn't find any common ground so I took a swing at him and he hit me with his truncheon.

After a while I gradually became aware of something scotch-taped to my shoe. It was an envelope. I bent down and retrieved it and found a key inside and a short note from Llunos. It said, 'There's no need to explain.'

I brewed a cup of tea amid a fume of camping gas and took it out to the dunes and sat watching the stars retreat and the windows across the water in Aberdovey begin to gleam with pale gold. A car arrived. Eeyore got out and struggled up the sand to join me, his progress made difficult by the tumbling sand and by something heavy he was delivering. I'd had it on order for a while now, and finally here it was. My cross.

I held out my hand to help him and he sat beside me. 'Don't jump the gun, son,' he said. 'Just listen to what I have to say.'

I didn't jump the gun.

'There was a lot of embalming fluid under the van,' he said, unaware of the irony. 'It all went up. And in that shed at the back, where he kept the dog . . . the one that was always whining . . . they found the charred remains. Only it wasn't a dog. It was . . . it was . . . a person. A girl. Chained up.'

I nodded. It was probably OK to jump the gun now. 'It's Myfanwy.'

'We don't know that, son, we don't know that. It's probably someone else.'

'It's Myfanwy. Mooncalf was the nurse.'

'We don't know that . . .'

'It was her and she was crying; they thought she was a dog.'

'We don't know that, we don't know that, son, it's too early to . . . they're doing tests . . . on . . . on . . .'

Now it was Eeyore who whined like a chained-up dog, his voice began to rise and rise, getting squeakier like an adolescent boy.

'It could be . . . could be . . . anyone . . . in fact, I'm sure it's not . . .'

'I threw her a bone.'

His voice rose up the scale and disappeared in a final squeak, like a protesting teddy bear. 'No!'

'It's OK, Dad, it's OK.' I put my arm round his shoulders and drew his head on to my chest. He was weeping and I hugged him to comfort him, and told him it was OK, everything was going to be all right, the way he used to do to me when I was small. It's OK, everything will be all right. Everything is just fine now.

I felt strangely calm. My fear had gone. Myfanwy was dead.

Chapter 18

I DROVE ROUND FOR most of the day, listening to a tape of Myfanwy – *Live at the Moulin*. I didn't expect to find Gabriel Bassett but late in the afternoon, and much to my surprise, I did. He was leaning on the railings, looking out to sea. I parked some distance away and crept towards him as quietly as a cat stalking a bird. He looked round and registered my approach and then made the subtle sideways glance of a man checking his escape route. Some instinct told him he was in trouble. Maybe he was clairvoyant. Or maybe it was the look on my face. Most of us have never seen the look in the eyes of a man who wants to kill us, but we would probably recognise it, if we did.

I rested my arms on the railing next to him and followed his gaze out to sea. I could hear the soft glug of a man swallowing in fear. I reached across and gathered the fabric of his Gabriel's coat in my fist, and inserted an arm inside his and locked him in place so there was no chance of him making that escape.

'Lovely day, isn't it?' I said.

He swallowed again, and nodded. 'Beautiful.'

'Take a good look. It's the last one you're going to see.'

'I . . . I . . . don't know what you mean.'

'No one's that stupid. Least of all you. Choose a stone.'

'I beg your pardon?'

'Down there on the beach, pick a stone. A man who is about to have his skull stoved in like a boiled egg at least has the right to choose the spoon.'

'What do you want?'

'I wonder.'

'I don't know anything.'

'It's too late for that, Eli. Too late.'

'My name's not Eli. I keep telling people. But they won't listen. It's so galling.'

'I understand. It's not a problem. Let's go for a walk.'

I pulled him away from the railing and dragged him along the Prom.

'Where are we going?'

'We're going to see Llunos. He's better at asking questions than me. He's got a cleaner paid for out of the rates to mop up the blood. You can start talking now, if you like.'

'What about?'

'Oh I don't know.' I pulled him closer, tightened my grip and turned my face towards his. So close the white bristles above his ear were scratching the end of my nose. 'You could tell me what the fuck you are doing in my life.'

'I was scared of ghosts.'

'Lots of people are.'

'Always have been.'

'That's tough. You're going to be one soon.'

'I loved the monkey.'

'Of course you did, she's a sweet little thing. I'll make sure she finds a good home. Testing cosmetics for a lab somewhere. You know that one where they pour shampoo into their eyes all day long to see how long it takes for them to get cancer. She'd be good at that.'

'Frankie was going to tell her what happened to Mr Bojangles. It would have broken her heart.'

'He's a wicked man is Frankie.'

'When I met Cleopatra she kept asking about her son, so I went back to the Enoc Enocs Foundation and looked into the records. It was all there: experimental subject made to fear flowers, sold to Kousin Kevin's Komedy Kamp, died of heart attack at Shrewsbury Flower Show. I couldn't tell her that. She was all I had in the world. So I torched their records room. Told her he was still studying at Timbuktu. Then, one day, Frankie's boys came to see me and said they had a job for me. I didn't know what they were talking about – this amnesia, it's genuine. They had that dictionary with them and told me to find the word "no". Well, of course, I couldn't, could I? They'd cut the bloody thing out. They said it was an easy job for a man of my talents. A stately home blag. They wanted me to steal the Nanteos Cup. But still I told them they'd got the wrong man. My name was Bassett not Eli. So then a few weeks later Frankie came round. He had a glass case under his arm – Mr Bojangles stuffed. He found it in the natural history section of Shrewsbury library. I still insisted I didn't know who he was. Really I didn't. But he wasn't having any of it, and the funny thing was, even though I didn't know him, there was something about him, something that said here was a figure from my past. That night I dreamed about him, and it all started coming back. How I used to do some work for him, as a cat burglar, specialist stately home blags. How we'd done time together in Shrewsbury prison. How I got into a spot of bother there with one of the other inmates and Frankie helped me out. That was his style, you see. Help someone out and hold it in reserve for the day he would come and call in the favour. And, just to make sure, he would take out some insurance against the intermittence of memory. Human gratitude was a feeble thing he would say. Straw in the wind. That's why he spent all the time looking for the skeleton in your cupboard. I guess that's how he found out about Mr Bojangles. I was with him the day Myfanwy sang to us and he had his epiphany. Even tough old Frankie Mephisto was touched. From that moment he could think of nothing but the day he was released and came to Aberystwyth to hear her sing at the bandstand. Of course, then she got sick. Frankie didn't like that. After all those years of waiting it struck him suspiciously like someone was taking the piss. And no one does that to Frankie Mephisto. Not even God. He demanded to know what was wrong with her and they told him what folk in Aberystwyth were saying, that her illness might have something to do with what Brainbocs did. And then, by coincidence, Brainbocs turned up in prison. Frankie summoned the boy and gave him an ultimatum. He said, since you're the one who made her sick, you had better find a way to make her well again. That is, if you don't want to spend your days here as someone's girlfriend. Brainbocs said it would take a miracle to save her and Frankie said, so make one. Then they gave him a chamber pot and locked him in the tower. That's how he came up with the idea about the dinosaurs. When Frankie's boys approached me I said, "What about the ghost?" In the old days we always had a ghost-layer as part of the team. They gave me a lot of money, expenses, and said sort it out yourself. So I went to see a medium and she got in touch with the ghost. The ghost said she'd stop haunting if the police reopened the case. Well, you need fresh evidence for that, don't you? That's why I approached you. But then you showed me the ghost was a fake. That's why I didn't need to come round with the money. I can still give it to you if that's what you're worried about.'

'And you stole the cup?'

'Yes.'

We stopped across the road from the public shelter and Bassett said, 'Do you mind if I take a wee?'

I looked at him, my face clouded with suspicion.

'Please. I'm getting old. I find it difficult to . . .'

Still arm-in-arm I walked him across the crossing to the shelter. Outside, we stopped. 'I'll be right outside. Before you go in, tell me what you were going to do with the cup.'

'Well it's supposed to be the Holy Grail, isn't it?'

'You really thought drinking out of that would cure her?'

'Oh no, not like that. She wasn't going to drink out of it.'

'What then?'

He bit his lip and glanced up and down the street in a piece of acting even phonier than Sister Cunégonde's.

'I'll whisper it.'

I shrugged and he leant in close to my ear. And then he sank his teeth into the side of my neck and bit me like a dog.

You can kill a man doing that if you get it right. They say it's the best way to fend off a rapist. I wouldn't know. But I know I was incapacitated by pain for a second and a half. And that was all he needed. He broke free of my grip, turned and ran up the steps into the hotel. I ran after. The entrance is a little porch of two doors and once inside the first he turned and let down the rimlatch on the outer door and then ran on. It gave him five more seconds' grace as I banged on the door and demanded someone open it. But no one did. Instead, a group of old ladies in the bay windows dropped stitches and stared in astonishment.

'Open the fucking door!' I shouted and more stitches were dropped.

I took out a handkerchief and wrapped it round my hand; smashed the glass with my elbow and then reached in and released the lock. I ran through the bar and into the dining room. It was mid-morning, breakfast had been cleared and the tables were being set for lunch in the endless ritual of seaside hotels. In the kitchen, the chefs would be standing in front of a bubbling vat into which had been thrown every conceivable type of vegetable leftover, and wondering what to call it. In the office, an old woman would be typing the lunch menu on a typewriter older even than her, the keys for c.o.n.s.o.m.m.é. so badly worn soon they would have to buy a new typewriter or change the soup. The manager's son stood as an eternal sentinel, polishing a glass at the bar. From far away and up above, girls from distant grim cities would be hoovering their way through last night's hangover in preparation for the next. It was a marionette show that never changed from day to day or season to season. Except for today when an old man ran through their midst chased by a younger man who was going to kill him. At the entrance to the dining room, Bassett made a split-second tactical decision guided by instinct, or just plain luck, and twisted to his right and ran down some stairs that a sign indicated led to the Grill. The steps down twisted and turned in near-darkness like the stairs to Fagin's cellar. Every ten or so there was a sort of landing covered in some furry smear that might once have been carpet in a previous century and from there the steps led off at a different angle. It was like running through an Escher engraving. At the bottom I saw the tail of a Gabriel's coat disappearing through a swing door. It led through to a dim, small dining room full of cheap furniture making a desperate attempt to look chic enough to justify the extra expense of dining in this subterranean vault. The room smelled of lavender polish and last week's grease and the only light came from the skylights that led to the street. It was like the nave of a cathedral where they worshipped stale food. A girl in a waitress's uniform had a cigarette in one hand and was laying out cutlery with the other, the box of spoons and forks balancing in the crook of the arm that held the cigarette. She looked up. 'Sorry we're not open yet.'

'Where did he go?'

'Who?'

'The old man?'

'The boss?'

'No, not the fucking boss! The old fellah in the Gabriel's coat.'

'Look mate, we're closed—'

I ran past her towards the doors leading to the kitchen.

'Oi!' she shouted. 'You can't go through there!'

But I had already gone. The doors swung open and swung closed and I found myself in a cabbage-coloured corridor, narrow, low-ceilinged and claustrophobic. Rooms so small they were really just alcoves off the main corridor. In the first, a man was bent over a sink of grey sud-less water rubbing with a piece of ragged abrasive plastic at the egg stain that had been fire-baked on by the washing-up machine. He glanced over his shoulder.

'What's the quickest way out of here?'

'Food poisoning.' He laughed.

I ran down the tiny corridor towards the kitchen, past shelves laden with battered silver pots and Cona jugs sooty with years of stewed coffee. Two chefs were at work in a kitchen so small it could have been on a submarine. They turned to look at me as the waitress from the Grill appeared in the doors behind me and shouted 'Oi' again. The chefs barred my way. 'You can't come through here mate. It's private.'

'I'm looking for my dad.'

'Diddums.' He pointed with a knife. 'The way out's down there, the way you came in.'

'Don't fuck with me,' I said.

The two chefs were slightly taken aback, but only for half a second. They exchanged interested glances. Two young men in their mid-twenties. From somewhere in northern England judging by the accents. Sous-chefs wandering the country, migrating to the coast for the summer season because that's where the fun is and the girls are. A long summer of beer and chasing women, punctuated by occasional fights in night-club car parks. This was un unusual development, but one they would enjoy. Normally they were required to defer to a guest no matter what the provocation but being told to fuck off by one was clearly an exceptional circumstance. The first one stepped forward and grabbed me by the throat and I shoved him back against the eye-level grill and then the fight erupted and we careened wildly about the place as if the submarine galley was now under assault from depth charges outside. We ricocheted from side to side into pots and pans and fridge doors like the ball in a pinball machine. Alerted by the noise, two more chefs and the washer-up appeared out of nowhere and I fell beneath the onslaught of their fists and the pans that they were banging on my head. The mêlée surged under its own momentum along the corridors like water through pipes, up some steps and we emerged blinking and still fighting in the car park behind the hotel. More blows were landed on me for good measure until it was clear that for the time being there was no more fight left in me. They stopped and stood back as I sat in a pile of cardboard boxes left out next to the reeking bins. They watched me cautiously, calculating whether this was a situation that required the intervention of the police and when it was clear that I was no longer in the mood for trouble they grabbed me and threw me through the gate. I picked myself up off the pavement, brushed myself down, and made for the rear entrance to the public shelter.

I walked back to the car, climbed in and checked my appearance in the rear-view mirror. My face was bruised and cut and flecked with blood. I'd seen worse. I turned the ignition and the engine made that coughing sound it makes when it has no intention of going anywhere today. I tried a few more times and then gave up. I climbed out and started to trek up the Prom to the harbour. Far off, from somewhere in the direction of the railway station, came the sound of an ambulance.

It was heading to an address on Harbour Row.

Chapter 19

THEY WERE LOADING Bassett into the back when I arrived. He was staring up at the sky wide-eyed with shock, panting like a dog.

'Just came straight out at me,' the driver of a car explained. 'Ran straight out of the house, like a madman, didn't look nor anything.'

Mrs Gittins was standing in the doorway drying her hand on her pinny. She looked at me, her face white with shock.

'How was I to know?' she wailed. 'I just signed for it and told them to take it up. How was I supposed to know?'

I followed the direction of her gaze to the upstairs bedroom window and then ran into the house. The door to Bassett's room at the top was ajar. Inside, the floor was littered with packing materials – brown paper and polystyrene and bubblewrap. You can't be too careful when transporting a museum case. It was standing in the middle of the room; a stuffed monkey, a glass case. The brass plaque read, 'Mr Bojangles, died of heart failure.' And next to it amid the torn paper was a card that said, 'Compliments of Mr Mephisto'.

Mrs Gittins stood behind me in the bedroom doorway, continuing to wail, 'How was I supposed to know? I just signed for it and told them to take it up.'

'Where's Cleopatra?'

She didn't answer but stared at the bathroom door and I walked across and pushed it open. It banged against something, something heavy and inert. I squeezed round the door.

'How was I supposed to know?' came the refrain.

The bathroom was small and there was only room to get my body half in but it was enough to see what was blocking the door. It was swinging from the light fixture, hanging by an old Ardwyn school tie that was knotted into the fur under the left ear. A monkey, with fur turning white around the muzzle and deep sad dark eyes, like two wishing wells that hadn't seen a penny in years.

I ran out and down the stairs and jumped into the back of the ambulance as they closed the doors.

'He's my brother,' I said.

'He's not my brother,' said Bassett weakly.

I put on a pained expression and looked at the medic. 'Even after forty years he still won't forgive me.'

'It's OK, mate, don't upset yourself. It's the shock, it makes them say things they don't mean.'

'I do mean it,' said Bassett. 'He's not my brother. I haven't got a brother.'

'That's it, Sebastien!' I snarled. 'Even now deny the people whose only crime was to love you!'

I covered my face with my hands. The ambulance raced along the Prom, siren wailing. The medic patted me on the back. 'Sit down, mate. I'll see if I can find you a little sedative.'

'Is he going to be all right?'

'He should be. I don't think the guy was driving very fast, lucky for him. He's broken some ribs, and maybe a hip, we'll need to see.'

'The hip?'

'Easily done with a man of his age. A fall off a stepladder will do it.'

'Is it painful?'

He looked uncomfortable. 'We're doing the best we can.'

The ambulance turned into North Road.

'He's not my brother,' said Bassett.

'Which is most painful, a broken hip or broken rib?'

'About the same I think.'

'Hmmm. I think he needs more air, it's stuffy in here.' I shuffled to the back and opened the door. 'That's better.'

The medic shouted, 'Hey, don't do that, you could fall out.'

He tried to close the door. I said, 'I want you to know I have the greatest admiration for people like you and I'm really sorry about this.'

'About wh—'

The end of his sentence was lost as he bounced down the road.

I walked over to my brother and looked into the terror-filled waters of his eyes.

'Hip or rib?' I said.

'Huh?'

I punched my fist down into the fractured ribs above the heart. I could feel them give. At the same time I shoved the palm of my hand down on his mouth to stifle the scream and all the force that should have emerged from his throat was diverted and made his eyes bulge out like a frog's. For a second, the pain forced him up, off the bed and he pressed with all his weight against my hand. And then he collapsed back on to the cot.

I kept my hand in place and said, 'Want another?'

I punched him again and the same power levitated him but this time it was weaker and I could see that the next one would take away his consciousness or even his life.

'OK,' I said taking away my hand. 'What was the point of stealing the cup?'

He looked straight into my eyes and said, 'He got the idea from that movie about the dinosaurs.'

'What do you mean?'

'It was for the girl, Seren.'

'What about her?'

'She was going to have a son, one who could save Myfanwy.'

'You mean a doctor?'

'Sort of, a healer. A saviour.'

'But how?'

'You know the legend of the Holy Grail? It was used by Joseph of Arimathea to collect the blood of Christ on the cross. Think about it. Blood in a wooden cup. With a bit of luck you could extract DNA from that.'

'And?'

'And . . .'

'And!?'

I raised my fist above his rib cage once more. 'And do what?'

He paused for another quarter beat and then sort of collapsed with a puff of air and said, 'Have you ever seen the movie, *Jurassic Park*?'

At the end of North Road, the ambulance slowed down and a car pulled alongside. The driver told him something had fallen out of the back. Something like a man. I jumped out and ran through the bowling green to Stryd-y-Popty.

Seren was sitting on the client's chair, drinking tea. 'Hi!' she said and smiled. I slumped into the chair opposite.

'I've run away.'

'If you're thinking of seeking your fortune in Aberystwyth, I wouldn't advise it.'

'I'll probably go to Africa or something.'

'That's a good idea.'

'I can't go back anyway, Frankie Mephisto is looking for me. He offered some of the other girls money to tell him where I was. But they wouldn't. There was a bloke in a wheelchair with him.'

'This bloke in a wheelchair, was he a little skinny runty sort of boy, a real egghead clever clogs by the name of Brainbocs?'

'I don't know. He was just a boy in a wheelchair. I don't have to go back, do I?'

'Not for the time being.'

'Cunybongy is going to kill me.'

'Why?'

'She's found out I'm up the duff.'

'So where have you been this past week?'

'What do you mean?'

'Half the county has been looking for you.'

'I had a blackout. I get them sometimes.'

'So, where did you go?'

'I don't know.'

She brought out from her lap a scrap of newspaper. It looked a few days old. She pushed it across the desk and I read the headline. It was about the hunt for Rimbaud. 'I found this on the floor of the bus shelter. I wanted you to know they're looking for the wrong man.'

'I don't think you need to worry about that.'

'But I do, don't you see? He's innocent, and they're hunting him like a dog. It's not fair.'

'Seren—'

'I won't stand for it.'

'What makes you so sure he's innocent?'

'I'm just sure that's all. People are saying he kidnapped your girlfriend, but he had nothing to do with it.'

'If he gave himself up he could put himself in the clear.'

'Don't be silly! He'd be stupid to do that.'

'We just want to ask him some questions.'

'Why? What makes him so important?'

'He was the last person to see Myfanwy before she disappeared.'

'You don't know that, you're just guessing.'

'We've got a photo that shows him next to the car.'

'Rimbaud would never do a thing like they're saying he did.'

'Tell me what makes you so sure.'

'I just am, that's all.'

'You know where he is, don't you?'

I looked her in the eye and she looked quickly away.

'No! I've no idea. How should I know?'

'You know where he is.'

'Don't.'

'I tell you what. If you take me to where he is so I can talk to him I promise not to give him away.'

'Yes you will, you'll tell the police and they'll all come . . .'

'Where?'

'I don't know.'

'He's hiding somewhere down by the estuary, isn't he?'

'How would I know?'

'Do you want to know how I know?'

'No, it's not of the slightest interest to me.'

'OK.'

I didn't say anything more. Seren tapped her fingers on the desk. Then reached out and took the scrap of newspaper and then thought better of it.

Then I said, 'You wrote to the French teacher, didn't you?'

She was pretending to be interested in the top of the desk but her face shot up when I said that.

'Who told you I wrote to her?'

'Don't kid me any more, Seren.'

'I'm not kidding you, I didn't write to anyone, I've no idea who you're referring to.'

'And you've never met Rimbaud.'

'No, never.'

'So, why do you care?'

'I . . . I . . . I just hate to see the innocent persecuted that's all.'

I picked up the phone and dialled directory inquiries. 'The number of Sister Cunégonde's Waifery please. Thank you.' I wrote it down and replaced the handset.

'What are you doing?'

'I'm turning you in.'

'Why? I came here because I thought I could trust you.'

'You can, but I can't trust you, you're lying. You know where Rimbaud is—'

'But you really mustn't worry about Myfanwy. She's all right, I saw her in my dream. She's fine. I saw her in a house and there was a dog in the garden, and a chocolate tree . . .'

I nodded seriously. 'OK.'

'Yes, I know, it sounds daft. But my dreams are special. They come true. She'll be fine.'

'Thanks, it's a comfort.'

'I know you don't believe me.'

'What happened when I was at the Waifery last time, the blood?'

'My stigmata. It happened after Cunybongy cut my hair.'

'Are you serious?'

'Yes. I get it now and again. It started when I went to see the place where that girl died by the harbour – Bianca. I dream about her now and again, too. Cunybongy thinks I'm faking it to get attention, but I'm not. Really I'm not.'

'Why did she cut your hair?'

'She found my application form for Kousin Kevin's Karnival Kween. She cut it while I was asleep.'

I nodded and absorbed the information. It could be true. It could be nonsense.

'Rimbaud didn't hurt Myfanwy.'

'Just tell me what you know.'

'I found him . . . he was in Meredith's stable . . . he was hurt. He said he'd done his ankle in and couldn't walk. So I took him some food and medicine. He was scared at first, he thought I would give him away to the police. But I didn't. I used to go and see him every few days and take him food and things.'

'For how long?'

'About six weeks.'

'Is he still there?'

'Yes, but you mustn't go. He's made a man-trap. He showed me. It's got three sharpened sticks like they used to make in Patagonia.'

'What was he doing near the car the day Myfanwy disappeared?'

'I told him not to go out, that there were men looking for him, but he . . . I don't know . . . he couldn't bear it hiding all the time in the stable so he went for a walk. That's all.'

'But he spoke to Myfanwy.'

'Honestly, all he did was try and bum a cigarette. That's all he did.' Seren stared down at the hands in her lap, hands that were fumbling nervously.

'You can do better than that.'

She looked up, and wetness formed and sparkled in her eyes, and suddenly I knew.

'He stole the locket didn't he?'

She didn't say anything, just sat there like stone, the only movement the tears that brimmed over, the meniscus of water held suspended for a second like a bubble which then burst and a tear darted down each cheek like rain drops falling.

'He stole the locket,' I repeated, more to myself than to Seren. She nodded.

She ran the back of her hand across her nose and snivelled into it. Then she said, 'It was because I was so kind to him . . . he came back from his walk and gave me the locket as a present. Then, when they started looking for Myfanwy, I knew what he'd done. I knew he must have stolen it . . .'

'So you planted it on the dunes to send us all in the wrong direction and give him time to get away?'

She nodded. 'So he could cross the bridge to Aberdovey.'

I walked round the desk and offered her a handkerchief. She looked up, cheeks glistening and said, 'I'm so sorry.'

'It's OK.'

'Are you going to arrest me?'

'I'm going to take you somewhere where you'll be safe. Where's your coat?'

'I gave it to Calamity.'

I blinked. 'What?'

'When I told her Frankie Mephisto was looking for me she asked if she could borrow my coat.'

Chapter 20

'In such a night as this . . .' said Llunos.

> 'When the sweet wind did gently kiss the trees
> And they did make no noise, in such a night
> Troilus methinks mounted the Troyan walls . . .'

He sat slumped lazily into the seat of the prowl car, one hand resting on the gear stick, the other resting on the door handle with his fingers holding the edge of the wheel. He squinted into the night, cars coming down Penglais, forgetting to dip.

He hummed a bit and then said, '*Jurassic Park*. It was the one with the dinosaurs, wasn't it? They found the dinosaur DNA in a mosquito trapped in amber and cloned a dinosaur.'

'That's right.'

'And you're saying they're going to clone Jesus?'

'Yes.'

'To save Myfanwy.'

'Yes.'

'That's quite a scheme.'

'I know. Frankie Mephisto tells Brainbocs to save Myfanwy. He says it will take a miracle, and Frankie says, so make me one.'

'Then what?'

'Bassett says Seren was chosen to give birth to the baby. I don't know why they chose her. I'm sure Brainbocs had good reasons, he normally does. Maybe because of her blackouts. My guess is they drugged her and then did some sort of IVF pregnancy – performed by that doctor whose body was washed up on Aberdovey beach.'

'The guy from the Clinic for Women's Problems.'

'Yes.'

'OK, so Frankie Mephisto has engineered the second coming, what do you want me to do?'

'Arrest him.'

'For what? Cloning Jesus? I'm fresh out of forms for that.'

'I'm glad you think it's funny.'

He darted a look across. 'Trust me Louie, this is not an example of me thinking something is funny.'

We drove on in silence for a while and the police radio ran a report of a disturbance outside Meredith's cottage. News that Seren was pregnant had spread and the gossips, unaware of the divine explanation, had accused Meredith of responsibility. And, of course, the same gossips alleged that he was her father too, so it was sort of bingo for the gossips. Meredith had lain with his own daughter and sired a child by her, an abomination. Although probably good fun to get upset about. A deputy had been despatched to disperse a stone-throwing mob that had broken some of Meredith's windows.

'How did they find out she was pregnant?' I asked Llunos.

'She told her best friend in secret and she told her best friend and she told her best friend and so it went on until it reached the ears of a best friend that didn't also happen to be a best friend of Seren, and she told her mum, and she told a neighbour who told the rest of the village. I expect news has reached Hawaii by now.'

We skidded to a halt outside the entrance to the Waifery and sprayed the walls with loose gravel. The sister on the door said they were not admitting visitors tonight and Llunos flashed his buzzer and said something rude. Her jaw dropped but no words came out. Sister Cunégonde was in her office, sitting at her desk doing nothing, just staring gloomily at the door as if she'd been expecting something to come through it that wasn't nice. She looked pale.

'He's not here,' she said. 'He was here earlier, but he's gone.'

'And who would that be?' said Llunos, sitting himself down on the corner of her desk.

'Frankie Mephisto. That's who you want isn't it?'

'Maybe,' said Llunos. 'How's the fish pond?'

She winced.

'You wouldn't know, would you?' I said. 'You wouldn't know about Pope Gregory and the six thousand skulls.'

Llunos picked up a set of knitting needles lying on the desk. Two little white woollen things hung from it. Booties.

'Expecting a happy event, are we?' he asked.

'Well, you can't expect the poor mite to go barefoot.'

'Why not? It wouldn't be the first time.'

'What do you want?'

'We want to know where Myfanwy is.'

'How should I know.'

'Frankie Mephisto knows.' I said, 'I thought he might have told you.'

'He doesn't tell me anything.'

'That's right, I forgot. He's been blackmailing you for weeks now and forgot to tell you why.'

'Oh, he told me that.'

'Maybe you'd like to share it with us.'

'He wants to adopt Seren's baby.'

There was a pause. No one had thought of that.

'This would be the infant Jesus, I take it,' said Llunos.

'That's right. I laughed in his face when he told me about the crazy scheme he cooked up. I told him it was the stupidest thing I'd ever heard. He said it wasn't stupid, Jesus was going to save Myfanwy. Oh yes, I said, what if He doesn't feel like it? He said, He'll feel like it all right, He'll do as He's told. No's not in my dictionary. I said I can't imagine what makes you think Jesus will help you. I've been married to Him for forty years and He's never lifted a finger to help me.'

I cast a look up at her alabaster husband. It was probably my imagination but I'm sure He rolled his eyes and I heard a disembodied voice in my head saying, 'Women eh? Can't live with them, can't shoot 'em.'

'Anyway, I refused. I said I wanted nothing to do with it. I sent him packing.'

'How noble. It's never too late, I suppose.'

'Yes, you can sneer. I know everyone thinks I'm just some dried-up, mean, scornful old woman with no more charity in her heart than . . . than . . . a crow . . . yes . . . not like her, not like Miss Sweetness and Light, she can do no wrong can she, the little hussy. Think what you like. See if I care.'

'Where's Frankie?'

'I told you, he's gone. And I wouldn't be in a hurry to find him if I were you. He's furious because he found out he's been double-crossed. He said he was going to do Mooncalf and then the guy with the monkey. And a lot else besides. He always did have a temper.'

'Who has double-crossed him?'

'I don't know. Everyone, I suppose. It was because of what I said. He was telling me about this ridiculous scheme and saying how they did it last week and I said, it doesn't make sense to me, someone must have got the dates wrong. And he says it all makes perfect sense. And I said, so you say, but I know for a fact that the girl is two months gone. And he looked a bit taken aback to hear that and said that was impossible they only did it last week. And I said well you can say what you like but she's missed twice now and he called me a stupid old lying bitch and I said yes I may be stupid and dumb and anything else you care to call me but there are a few things that I do know about and I'm telling you Seren is two months gone. And he looked really angry now and asked how such a thing could have happened. And I said, she probably did it the same way everybody else does it, no need for Divine intervention, it's quite a popular pastime in Borth, so I'm told. And then he demanded to know who the father was. And I said how should I know. And he said he'd kill whoever did it. So I told him, you'll have a long list of people to kill. Who did it? he asked. And I said I really had no idea, she doesn't tell me anything, but judging from the way she puts herself about it could be anyone, it could be the postman for all I know. Of course the fools from the village are all saying it is Meredith—'

And as she said the word her hand shot up to her mouth and she said, 'Oh my God!'

'In such a night as this . . .' said Llunos.

We walked along the ridge of a scree of stones beneath a sky of violet stained glass. Away to our left, the lights of Aberdovey scintillated on the dark waters of the estuary. Somewhere there, too, was a beach which we couldn't see. But it had to be there. It was yesterday.

'When the sweet wind did gently kiss . . .'

The stones gave way in a noisy cascade and the movement impelled us down to the sand and the invisible sea that never stopped sucking the detritus off the beach. A meteor fizzed like a fairy's wand across the night sky. We walked along the water's edge.

'I've got a confession to make,' said Llunos.

'Oh yes?'

'You remember those guys who took you to the engine sheds to give you a message from Ll and hit you on the head with a shovel?'

'Yes.'

'Ever wondered who Ll was?'

'Yes, I have.'

'It's short for Llunos.'

'Funny, that's your name.'

'Yes. I'm sorry. They were working for me. I told them to put a fright into you, not knock you unconscious with a shovel.'

'Since it's the night for confession, would you care to tell me why you did such a strange thing?'

'I wanted Calamity to stop investigating the Nanteos case.'

'Did the reputation of your great-grandfather really mean so much?'

'Actually, I didn't give a damn about him.'

'So why did I get a sore head?'

'It was because of my mam. You've met my mam?'

'Once or twice.'

'She's a good sort. Getting on a bit, but a heart of gold. Never says a bad word about anyone. That's rare round here.'

'Rare anywhere.'

'She's never really had much out of life. Doesn't complain about it but, you know, she's never really had much. She doesn't have any fancy things, or anything like that, you know.'

'I can understand that.'

'Except one. It's a . . . it's a . . . it's a necklace.'

'Oh really?'

'She adores it, only nice thing she's got. It's a bit of a family heirloom.'

'Oval, flat-cut garnets set in gold with close-backed foil collets, concealed clasp and pear-shaped garnet drop?'

'Yeah, something like that. A beauty it is. I'd hate to have to ask her to give it back.'

I laughed. And then he began quoting again.

> 'In such a night
> Did pretty Jessica, like a little shrew,
> Slander her love, and he forgave it her.'

Across the dark water the car headlamps flashed in Aberdovey and an answering voice came from the blackness that was the sea.

> 'I would out-night you, did no body come;
> But, hark, I hear the footing of a man . . .'

It was a boy's voice. Coming from the direction of the water. We stopped and peered into the darkness. Llunos took out a flashlight and wafted the beam across the surface of the water. The shaft of light picked out a dark shape that shouldn't have been there. It moved.

'Louie,' a voice said. 'What an unexpected pleasure.'

It was Dai Brainbocs wearing a thick fisherman's jacket, up to his chest in the water.

'What are you doing here?'

'Dying.'

'Where's your wheelchair?'

'I'm sitting on it.'

'Is Frankie Mephisto here?'

'I saw him about two hours ago. With a shotgun. I'd steer clear of him if I were you, he's not in one of his best moods. Who's that with you?'

'Llunos.'

'Good evening, Llunos,' said Brainbocs.

'I'll go and get help.'

'No point, Louie. The chair has sunk into the quicksand up to my waist.'

'We could get a boat.'

'There isn't time.'

The water had reached just below his shoulders and as we spoke there was a black invisible surge that took it to just under his chin.

'But you'll drown.'

'I hope so.'

'You've caused a lot of trouble, you have,' said Llunos.

'It's no use you trying to throw a guilt-trip on me, what was

I supposed to do? Frankie Mephisto was going to make me someone's girlfriend.'

'But what about the poor girl, Seren?'

'I wouldn't worry too much about her. Mooncalf says the doctor from the clinic refused to have anything to do with the plan. He said it was against every imaginable ethical and moral principle. Mooncalf killed him and fed the DNA mixture to that feral donkey that's been hanging around. The one with a missing ear.'

'Come on,' I said. 'There's a deputy on guard outside Meredith's cottage – he can radio the coastguard.'

'Please don't trouble yourselves, Louie. I don't want to be saved. I want to die and join Myfanwy.'

Sister Cunégonde beat us to Meredith's cottage. We saw her disappearing through the front door when we arrived. The light was on in the kitchen but there was no sign of the deputy. I knocked on the door and a voice shouted from within.

'Yes?'

'We need to use the phone, there's someone in trouble – in the water.'

The voice said, 'come in' and we pushed the door open and walked in.

Meredith was sitting on the floor of his cottage with his back pressed against the wall. The coarse grey plaster above his head was smeared with his blood. It began midway up in a blob and then slalomed down in a wide, drunken stain, as if someone had thrown a flan against the wall and it had slithered to the floor. 'Welcome to the party,' said Frankie, cradling a pump action shotgun in his lap like a favourite kitten. He jerked the shotgun to indicate that we should walk over to join Sister Cunégonde at the table. One of the tough guys I'd seen on the platform at Shrewsbury stood next to Frankie, also holding a shotgun.

'Need to use the phone did you say? Who's in trouble?'

'Brainbocs,' I said stupidly.

Frankie aimed the gun casually at the phone and pulled the trigger. It was one of those old-fashioned phones with a dial and a braided black cord. It disintegrated in a shower of bakelite fragments.

'We've been trying to work out who got the girl up the duff,' said Frankie. 'This chap says it wasn't him.'

Meredith made no acknowledgement but there was still a gleam in his eyes, the last embers of consciousness or maybe just the torch of the caretaker locking up as he left. Frankie looked accusingly at Sister Cunégonde.

'I never told you it was him.'

'You never told me it wasn't either, did you, you stupid bitch?'

He walked over to Meredith, hefted the shotgun, looked inquiringly at Sister Cunégonde and said, 'So who was it?' He rammed the butt of the gun down into the side of Meredith's head. He let out a soft groan. Sister Cunégonde jumped up and ran at Frankie Mephisto and he casually swung the gun round and caught her on the ear with the end of the barrel. She stopped in her tracks and fell to the floor and then started crawling towards Meredith. Frankie put the sole of his foot on her and shoved her across the room.

'So who?' he said again.

'Does it matter?' asked Llunos.

A spasm flashed in the muscles of Frankie's face. He turned a gaze of withering intensity on Llunos and whispered, 'Don't you tempt me, copper.'

'No one knows who the father is,' said Sister Cunégonde. 'Only Seren.' There was a deep gash above her ear and the side of her head glistened wet in the dimly lit kitchen.

'That's a lie for a start. Even I know it takes two.' He kicked Meredith in the chest wound where the shotgun discharge was concentrated. Everyone in the room winced. Frankie chuckled. 'Give us a clue, Cunybongy.'

'I swear on everything that's holy—'

This time he stamped. Meredith let out a low agonised howl like a bull sinking beneath the lances of the toreador. 'Swear on something you care about. I know what. Swear on the pond!' He laughed.

'We know all about it, Frankie,' said Llunos. 'Your little tricks won't work.'

Frankie looked puzzled for a second. 'All about what?'

'The book by Ulricus. Pope Gregory and the skulls. It's ancient history, nothing to do with her nor anyone else. All forgotten long ago.'

The look of bafflement hovered over Frankie's features, the look of a man trying to make sense of a puzzle. Then he burst out laughing. 'Is that what she told you? Is it? Said she was ashamed of all those old skulls left in the pond?'

'You shut your wicked mouth, Frankie Mephisto!' Sister Cunégonde hissed.

He laughed again. 'Oh no, it wasn't ancient history she was afraid of, was it?'

Cunégonde picked up a garden fork and lunged at Frankie Mephisto. He stepped out of the way and cuffed her again with the gun and swung it round to train on me and Llunos. The whole movement was done with the easy grace and fluidity of a ballet dancer. It looked as if he'd been born holding that shotgun, or had played out scenes like this a thousand times before. You could see he was enjoying it. He laughed again. 'Why don't you tell everybody the truth? Why don't you tell them what you were really ashamed of?'

The kitchen door banged open and we all looked across. Mrs Prestatyn stood framed in the doorway. She was wearing one of those transparent plastic coats that fold up into a purse but which always look crumpled. Her hair was tied up in a headscarf and in her hands was a shotgun. She looked like she'd received the news midway through doing the washing up. 'Stick 'em up!' she said.

'Who the fuck are you?' said Frankie.

'Drop the guns,' she said uncertainly.

Frankie laughed. 'What if I don't?'

'I'll shoot you.'

'Which one, me or him?'

'I mean it!'

'Sure you do. I'll make you a deal. You shoot me and Brother Grimm here will shoot everybody else.'

There was a pause. Mrs Prestatyn kept the shotgun trained on Frankie but the barrel was wavering, hands trembling.

'You don't impress me, Frankie Mephisto.'

'I'm not trying to. Who the fuck are you anyway?'

'And we'll have less of the profanities if you don't mind.'

'Oh!' said Frankie. 'Frightfully sorry. Have we been introduced?'

'My name's Gaynor Prestatyn.'

'Did we go out together or something?'

'You killed my girl.'

The light of understanding crept over Frankie's face, the corners of his mouth slowly lifting. 'You should thank me – you've been dining out on that for twenty-five years.'

'I'm going to shoot.'

'Well, get it over with then.'

'Don't think I won't. You killed my girl.'

Mrs Prestatyn stood as someone facing a chasm too broad for leaping. In the stricken look on her face I knew she would never pull the trigger. Not even to save her own life.

'Shoot him, you stupid bitch,' said Sister Cunégonde.

'Oh yeah,' laughed Frankie. 'I bet you would, wouldn't you? You'd happily watch me die.'

'I'll shoot you, Frankie Mephisto,' said Mrs Prestatyn. 'You killed my girl.'

Frankie Mephisto laughed and played his trump card. The one no one even suspected he had. 'What makes you think she's dead?'

There was a moment's stunned silence. And he made a noise that was like laughter but which froze the heart. 'Go on shoot me, you silly bitch, then you'll never know, will you? Maybe it's better you don't. There are fates worse than death you know. Ask Mooncalf.'

A look of despair swept over Mrs Prestatyn's face. She let the gun fall and looked across at us. 'I'm sorry . . .'

Frankie's sidekick retrieved the gun and Frankie jerked his in our direction. Mrs Prestatyn duly obeyed and walked over to us.

Frankie walked over to Meredith and crouched down beside him. 'Where were we? Oh yes, Cunybongy's little secret. You'd like to know Cunybongy's little secret, wouldn't you?'

'You bastard,' said Sister Cunybongy. 'A dying man.'

But Frankie just smiled. It was clear he held no especial reverence for dying men. And probably not live ones either.

He looked up from his crouch and said, 'I want the name of the father.'

'I've told you I don't know. I swear. You know what she's like. Why would she tell me?'

'She wouldn't have to tell you. You'd know all the same – you know everything else that's going on, you nosy bitch.'

Sister Cunégonde made another desperate attempt to run over and shut her brother Frankie's mouth. The sidekick slammed the barrel of his shotgun into her ribs and she fell to the floor and this time stayed there, holding her chest with one hand, supporting herself with the other and gasping for breath.

Frankie shook his head in mock sadness. 'You never told him, did you?'

He turned to Meredith and grabbed his chin and pulled it round to face him. 'She never told you, did she? That wonderful summer when she won the carnival queen. Why she sent you the letter and told you never to see her again. Broke your fucking little heart, didn't it?'

Sister Cunégonde sobbed.

'She was carrying a child, you see. Oops! Did I forget to mention that? Don't ask me where it ended up.'

'She was just sixteen,' said Mrs Prestatyn. 'Poor mite. She did nothing wrong, it was the Mother Superior who made her get rid of it. Made her write the letter.'

Frankie spoke again to Meredith. 'You never knew, did you? Never knew you had a child?' He grinned sourly.

And Meredith parted his lips and formed the silent shape of a word. Frankie bent down to listen. 'What was that?'

Meredith formed the voiceless word again with the last few ounces of strength left to him. Frankie bent his ear next to his mouth. 'Say it again, son.' And Meredith took a slow final breath, his eyes half-closing as waves of pain racked him, and he groaned the words which, this time, everyone in the room could hear. 'I knew.'

Even Frankie looked surprised. He shrugged and stood up.

The kitchen door swung open again and this time a girl stood in the doorway, a girl wearing the coat of the Waifery.

'Why don't you ask me who the father is?' she said. 'It's my baby.'

Sister Cunégonde looked up from her kneeling position and gasped, 'Seren!'

But I could see that it wasn't Seren. It was a girl who'd borrowed her coat.

'Is this the girl?' said Frankie.

'He's down there.' Calamity pointed in the direction of the stable. 'It was Rimbaud.'

'Who's Rimbaud?'

'The man who's been on the run. He's been hiding in the stable.'

A sly grin stole over the face of Frankie Mephisto. He walked sideways like a crab across the kitchen and grabbed Calamity. He pulled her in front of him with the shotgun now held against the side of her head. Again it looked as if he'd spent his lifetime rehearsing manoeuvres like this. He nodded to the sidekick. 'If anyone moves, shoot them.' Frankie and Calamity walked slowly backwards towards the stable. We watched them both disappear down the rough path leading to the shed and then go inside. There was more silence. The sidekick eyed us warily. He didn't feel so sure of himself on his own. There were a lot us. And it takes time to reload. The thunder of gunshot came from the shed, and the slate tiles of the roof shattered and flew up in fragments. The gunshot was followed in the next instant by a young girl's scream and the long-drawn-out moan of a man in great pain. Instinct overcame caution and we all rushed outside. Calamity ran out of the shed, her face and coat spattered with blood, she ran up to me and buried herself in my arms and I could see the blood was not hers. The sidekick looked on bewildered. A man stumbled out of the stable wading through the air as if through treacle. His progress was made slow and difficult by the strange wooden encumbrance he had acquired and by the difficulty in catching one's breath that comes from having three sharpened stakes of a man-trap stuck in one's chest like a giant fork; three chest wounds that froth and suck. His mouth was open wide and blood slathered down his chin. He cried like a newborn infant and slowly pirouetted and sank to the sandy floor; his bellows and groans ebbing and getting softer and softer until they were no more than tiny moans and he finally lay back on the ground and said no more.

No one said a word. And then, suddenly, from nowhere, a woman in a plastic fold-up coat and headscarf rushed past us and over to the body of Frankie Mephisto. She threw herself down into the sandy grass beside him and bent down over him. Her mouth met his in that most intimate of communions and we watched in disbelief his cheeks quiver as if being kissed and probed with her tongue. I saw her jerk her head back, arch her back and pull away and gasp for air. She threw me a glance, her lips smeared with Frankie Mephisto's gore, and then dived down and pressed her lips to his again like Juliet in the tomb. And it was only then as she blew, withdrew and pressed her ear against his chest that I realised that she was not fulfilling that long sealed promise to bite out his tongue. She was giving him the kiss of life.

I walked over and knelt down and placed a gentle hand upon her back. She looked up from his lifeless chest and shook her head to communicate to me that Frankie Mephisto was dead. And then a strange look disfigured her face as perhaps she realised the full enormity of what she had just done and she opened her mouth, still covered with blood, and made to speak, but she couldn't think of anything to say. And then the spell was broken again and the sidekick hefted his gun but that was as far as he got because the sound of a shovel hitting a head, a sound that had become so intimately familiar to me, clanged on the night air and the sidekick slumped to the ground. Sister Cunégonde stood over him and looked down to make sure that she had put him beyond the capacity to act and then threw the shovel to one side. And a second later cheers erupted from the bushes and a troupe of girls in Waifery coats stood up and out from the shadows and applauded, shouting 'Bravo for Cunybongy!'

Dawn broke upon an estuary so quiet and glass-smooth that, like a mirror, it contained the sky. Two skies separated by the hills above Aberdovey. The only blemish in the wide mackerel-silver surface was the wheelchair of Dai Brainbocs, left there by the receding waters like the rotting piles of an old jetty, or a sunken ship. Like Jonah, he had been swallowed by the sea and with him had passed, it seemed, the last custodian of the secret of Myfanwy's last resting place.

Chapter 21

SISTER CUNÉGONDE DROVE us back to Aberystwyth in the Waifery minibus. Llunos followed in the prowl car. No one spoke. The door to Eeyore's cottage was ajar, the kettle warm, but no one was around. I walked through the kitchen into the stable. Miss Muffet was licking a newborn foal – all white like a unicorn still waiting for its horn. She looked at me and there was fierce pride in her eyes. I continued on out the back and found Seren sitting on a lobster pot cradling a mug of tea with both hands. She looked up at me and smiled.

'Eeyore had to go out. He got a call earlier on. He said he wouldn't be long.'

I nodded. 'This dream you had about Myfanwy. How did it go again?'

'A chocolate tree and a dog called Hector. And a Kerplunk set and a view of Ynyslas from the window.'

Sister Cunégonde joined us saying, 'I didn't know you could get albino ones.'

'Eeyore said it's the first he's seen in forty years,' said Seren.

'The Lord moves in mysterious ways,' said Cunégonde.

There was the sound of a car pulling up and I walked back through the cottage. Up by the main road I saw Eeyore and Llunos engaged in conversation. I walked up the path and Eeyore came up to me with a heaviness to his step. He looked deeply unhappy.

'I've got some good news for you, son.'

I waited. He didn't look like a man with good news.

'The charred body they found at Mooncalf's, it's not Myfanwy. Too old.'

I said nothing, waited. He sighed. 'Just wish telling you didn't make it the hardest day of my life. Looks like I've got to go and tell Mrs Prestatyn we've found her daughter.'

I took Eeyore's car and drove back to the office. There was a letter addressed to Calamity lying on the mat. It was from Swansea and contained her detective's badge. I put it on the desk and opened the drawer and took out the photocopy of the stolen essay. Myfanwy's idea of heaven. I guess if you are going to resurrect someone you need to pay some attention to details like this, where they open their eyes. You don't want them panicking and thinking they've gone to the wrong place. Some people can be quite literal about these things. I skimmed the essay again. A chocolate tree; Kerplunk; a view of Borth and Ynyslas across the water; the white bones of Hector. It was quite simple really. Where else can you enjoy a view of Ynyslas across the water? Not in Ynyslas that's for sure. I went back to the car and drove to Woolies and made a small purchase and then drove up Penglais to Borth.

I turned left at the top to take the slow route. I was in no hurry and I always preferred to go this way when there was time. A road full of happy memories, of a time far away when Myfanwy and I drove together up and down the green dales like a ship tossed on an ocean of grass. A journey on a day that you could say was my idea of heaven. If anyone ever wants to go to the trouble of creating it for me. But I'm happy to wait. The same cows as before, or maybe their descendants, chequer-boarded the fields, and every so often there was the same tantalising glimpse of Borth down below, beyond the hills, stretching north and away to Aberdovey. I drove in a dream, my spirit dancing away in the past where the best things are kept as well as the shadows that haunt us. I pulled up on the sands of Ynyslas and drove up to the water's edge. A man stood with his back to me and turned round at the sound of the car door. His army greatcoat flapped in the wind and wild hair splayed out across his shoulders. He was holding a tin of creosote.

'I was just wondering where I was going to get the price of a cup of tea,' he said, 'and they sent you.'

'Price of a cup of tea for the ferryman.' I put fifty pence in his hand and stepped into the boat.

Cadwaladr rowed me across and I sat in the stern and stared at the Loothouse across the water. There was a flash from the upstairs balcony, the sort that a pair of binoculars might make in the sharp morning light but which was actually the morning sun flashing on the silver top of Brainbocs's cane. We hit the jetty with a gentle thud and I climbed ashore. Some wet clothes were hanging on the line – small sizes that would be suitable for a boy of about Brainbocs's build. And there was something that I had mistaken in the dark last night for a heavy fisherman's coat but was actually a life jacket. I walked up the garden, past a tree with what looked like chocolate bars taped to the branches. A dog barked and bounded up to me and placed his paws on my chest. 'Down Hector,' I said. 'Go back to Troy.' French doors were opened and I walked into the lounge. A video of the children's TV series *Hector's House* was playing on the TV and on the table next to it was a brand new Kerplunk set, still unopened. Also next to the television was a What-the-Butler-Saw machine and, lying on top, a tape labelled, 'My Funeral'. I guess that's one of the best bits about dying – seeing who comes to the funeral. And hearing all the nice things they say about you. It's the only time in your life you can guarantee that people won't say a bad word and that's quite ironic, since it's not in your life.

From somewhere in the house came the sound of mice squeaking. I walked through into the kitchen and then into the hall and up the stairs. The noise of the mice grew louder. At the front was a bedroom overlooking the estuary, a view of Borth and Ynyslas. The rhythmic beeping of mice came from a medical machine with an oscilloscope display. Next to that was a bed.

Myfanwy lay attached to a weeping willow of wires and drips that shone bright silver in the morning light, falling like creepers in an enchanted bower above the place where she slept. She was smiling. I kissed her and she sighed in a dream. Her cheek had lost its former pallor and in its stead was the soft translucence of honey.

Brainbocs was sitting in a wicker bath chair on the balcony. He was wearing a well-cut tweed shooting jacket and holding a cane between the fingers of his small hands. The early morning sunshine looked delightful. I walked out and he looked up as if he had only just noticed my presence, even though he had been following the progress of my boat the whole time.

I said, 'You thought up all this on your chamber pot?'

Brainbocs smiled. 'Sherlock Holmes would have called it a three-pipe problem. I came to regard it as a "three-pot problem". Considerably more than three actually.'

'Did you really think you could save her?'

He didn't answer for a while but regarded me with a look of piercing intensity. Then said, 'Maybe I have.'

I looked back to the beeping mice and he added, 'To tell the truth, it wasn't really my intention to save her. Not really, not deep down. Deep down I had something else in mind.' His voice drifted away slightly as if he had forgotten I was there.

'Tell me, Louie, have you ever wondered what place there could be in a benevolent Father's world for such a cruel device as unrequited love? Or for deformity?'

I looked down at him with pity and he said, 'But of course you don't. You never do. I know these things mean nothing to you, Louie. You are like Cadwaladr painting his bridge. You get to the end and look back and you see that it needs doing all over again, all your efforts have been in vain. And yet somehow you are not dismayed by this. You start again. You place your palms on the rock and start rolling. I admire you for it and yet sometimes I despise you also in the midst of my admiration. Because being undaunted is easy for a man like you. Myfanwy looks at you and smiles. Yet for me she reserves the worst fate of all. Far worse than hate, or scorn or contempt. Far more cruel. For me she smiles too. But it is a smile born only of pity. And pity can never turn to love. Pity is withering to behold in the eye of one's beloved because it makes clear for all time and irrevocably that one is but a cur in her eyes. A cur with a withered hind leg that limps and which she feeds because if she didn't the other dogs would kill him.'

Tears appeared in his eyes.

'Tell me, Louie, how does the Lord decide on the basis of a life not yet lived who should be blighted?'

'I don't know. I'm sorry.'

'No, you don't know. No one does.'

'You tried to bring Jesus back to us and you didn't want to save her?'

'Being saved or not saved, who cares? It's beside the point. The more I sat on my pot and thought about it, the more I came to realise how unimportant is the hour of our doom when set against the simple fact of it; the fact that we are doomed at all.'

'So what was the point of all this?'

'I wanted to ask Him a question.'

'Jesus?'

'Yes, Jesus.'

Brainbocs dipped his hand into a bowl of dried bluebell florets.

'I love bluebells, the same way some people love snow. You awake one morning and the world is blue. Danycoed Wood transfigured by blue frost. The dreary grim lacklustre world made sublime with their fire. All the litter, the crisp packets, the cigarettes, and all that foul dross left behind by lovers who go there to couple in shame, all obliterated. There is no light more beautiful than the glow that suffuses the woods that week. It is like the intense distillation that shines through the stained glass in medieval cathedrals, the ultramarine blue of Mary's cloak. Or that hue, deeper than any found in life, that you get sometimes in Ilford transparencies. You know the ones? Lying in the backs of cupboards, underexposed, showing a scene on a beach from long ago where a child they say is us sits in a nappy and a sunhat and eats sand. If only it could always be like that. But it lasts a week, no more, and the pale blue sizzling fire of the scent lingers a while longer.'

'I like bluebells too. What was the question?'

He scooped out a fistful of dried flowers and placed them down on the window sill like Scrabble counters and formed the letters of a question.

I read it and said, 'I could have saved you all the trouble. He doesn't know the answer Himself. That's why He's been hiding all these years.'

'Go now, Louie, back to your people in Aberystwyth, they need you. There is nothing for you here. Take one of the chocolate bars I taped to the tree if you like. But they're not very good. They keep melting.'

'It's hard trying to create a heaven on earth.'

'Yes, isn't it?'

I signalled to Cadwaladr to make ready the boat. And as I turned to leave, Brainbocs's thin white arm shot out from under the rug and grabbed my wrist in a girlish grip. 'You know, Louie, if He had made a better fist of the universe, you and I . . . you and I would have been friends – drinking nectar together in a sun-dappled harbour-side bar, and there would be Myfanwys for everybody . . .'

'If He'd made a better job of it, there wouldn't even be an Aberystwyth.'

Brainbocs looked taken aback. 'Oh yes! There would, Louie, there would! . . . But not as we know it.'

He let go of my arm.

He was still sitting on the balcony as I sat in the boat and glided across the water in which was contained another sky. And I thought about his question. The simple question that seeps like fog under the door down the corridors of our heart. The one Cleopatra had asked every day even though the wishing well of her eyes had long ago divined the answer. That simple ancient question, spelled out in dried bluebells: Why?

The sun flashed on his cane, and a lone gull cried and the only other sound was the soft splash of the oars dipping into the liquid blue silver as two men in a boat rowed across the sky. One man who manned the oars and one who opened the Woolies bag and took out the present he would shortly give to his partner. A small gift, just a token, really, to help her find her way in a confusing world. Just an old grey cowboy hat. He took it out and placed a small footprint on the brim.

A NOTE ON THE AUTHOR

Malcolm Pryce was born in the UK and has lived and worked abroad since the early nineties. He has held down a variety of jobs including BMW assembly-line worker, hotel washer-up, aluminium salesman, deck hand on a yacht travelling through Polynesia, and advertising copywriter. He currently lives in Bangkok. His previous two books, *Aberystwyth Mon Amour* and *Last Tango in Aberystwyth*, are also published by Bloomsbury.

A NOTE ON THE TYPE

The text of the book is set in Fournier. Fournier is derived from the *romain du roi*, which was created towards the end of the seventeeth century for the exclusive use of the Imprimerie Royale from designs made by a committee of the Académie des Sciences. The original Fournier types were cut by the famous Paris founder Pierre Simon Fournier in about 1742. These types were some of the most influential designs of the eighteenth century, and are counted among the earliest examples of the 'transitional' style of typeface. This Monotype version dates from 1924. Fournier is a light, clear face whose distinctive features are capital letters that are quite tall and bold in relation to the lower-case letters, and *decorative italics, which show the influence of the calligraphy of Fournier's time.*